GIDEON

LILY MORTON

Text Copyright© Lily Morton 2019

Book cover design by Natasha Snow Designs

www.natashasnowdesigns.com

Professional beta reading and formatting by Leslie Copeland, editing by Courtney Bassett www.lescourtauthorservices.com

This book is a work of fiction. Names, characters, places and incidents are products of the author's imagination, or are used fictitiously.

References to real people, events, organizations, establishments or locations are intended to provide a sense of authenticity and are used fictitiously. Any resemblance to actual events, locations, organizations, or persons living or dead is entirely coincidental.

All rights reserved. No part of this book may be reproduced, scanned or distributed in any printed or electronic form without permission, except for the use of brief quotations in a book review. Please purchase only authorized editions

The author acknowledges the copyrighted or trademarked status and trademark owners of the following products mentioned in this work of fiction: Vans, Converse, Ralph Lauren, Ray Ban, Ladbrokes, Hallmark, The Star, The Sun, Mills & Boon, Dettol, National Enquirer, Medical Gazette, Top Man, SlimFast, Lucozade, Dyson, Land Rover, iPad, Superdrug, Debretts, MacBook

All songs, song titles and lyrics mentioned in the novel are the property of the respective songwriters and copyright holders.

Warning

This book contains material that is intended for a mature, adult audience. It contains graphic language, explicit sexual content and adult situations.

BLURB

Gideon Ramsay is so far in the closet he should be a talking faun.

A talented, mercurial, and often selfish man, Gideon has everything he should want in life. Fame, money, acting awards – he has it all. Everything but honesty. At the advice of his agent, Gideon has concealed his sexuality for years. But it's starting to get harder to hide, and his increasingly wild behaviour is threatening to destroy his career.

Then he's laid low by a serious illness and into his life comes Eli Jones. Eli is everything that Gideon can't understand. He's sunny tempered, friendly, and optimistic. Even worse, he's unaffected by grumpiness and sarcasm, which forms ninety percent of Gideon's body weight. And now Gideon is trapped with him without any recourse to the drugs and alcohol that have previously eased his way through awkward situations.

However, as Gideon gets to know the other man, he finds himself wildly attracted to his lazy smiles and warm, scruffy charm that seem to fill a hole inside Gideon that's been empty for a long time. Will he give in to this incomprehensible attraction when it could mean the end of everything that he's worked for?

From the bestselling author of the Mixed Messages series comes a story about a man who needs to realise that being true to yourself is really just a form of finding home.

This is the third book in the Finding Home series but it can be read as a standalone.

"I must learn to be content with being happier than I deserve."
Jane Austen
Pride and Prejudice

PROLOGUE

> You'd need a medium and a séance to bring my dick back to life tonight

Gideon

I sit in the back of the limo and blink to clear my eyesight. *Jesus, that last drink was strong.* I think I should probably be concerned, but instead I take a huge swig from the bottle of tequila in my hand. There's nothing like a hair of the dog that bit my eyes.

I look idly at the two men curled up in a corner of the backseat beside me, their mouths and hands all over each other. Normally, it'd be hot, but not much seems to excite me at the moment. I swallow hard as the car takes a sharp bend and vomit rises in the back of my throat. There can't be much left in me, as I evacuated the contents of my stomach all over a flowerbed a few hours ago before we went into the nightclub.

I frown. *Was it a few hours ago, or was it when we came out of the club?* I squint ahead, ignoring the throaty groans coming from the couple next to me. Then I shake my head. Who cares? I'll probably throw up again soon, so I might as well make it worth it. I nod and, taking another swig of the drink, I feel the alcohol burn a path down to my stomach.

It swirls uneasily in there, reminding me that I really ought to eat something. I haven't felt like eating since I got over a bad bout of flu a month ago. It's left me feeling like hollowed-out shit and shows no sign of getting better. The wardrobe mistress had pinched my waist last week and muttered curses as she took my costume in again.

The car slows to a stop, and when I peer blearily out of the window I can see we're at the hotel. "Oi," I say, nudging the man on top with my foot. "We're here."

He looks at me, his eyes heavy and his mouth swollen. "Shall we just fuck in here? I can't be bothered to go upstairs."

Ah, Christian, my current hook-up. He's a model who seems to have cornered the market in pouting and drinking. He's so laid-back he should be lying on the pavement, and he's magnificently lazy. He could also outdrink Peter O'Toole in his heyday. I remind myself that he's also a discreet fuck and only interested in how I spend my money on him. Just my type.

I shake my head. "Better not fuck in here. The bill for valeting this car is starting to approach the cost of Donald Trump's hairspray."

His companion snorts and I stare at him, wondering what his name is again. We'd picked him up in the club tonight. I shrug. *Who fucking cares?* I'll never see him again after tonight.

Christian slides off the other man's lap and straightens his shirt. "We'll see you in there. Yeah?"

I nod, tossing him the room key card.

"Why isn't he coming in with us?" the other man asks.

"Because there might be press about. The driver will take the car round the block and drop him off in a few minutes," Christian says patiently.

"Okay, we'll see you later," the man says brightly.

I nod. "Okay–" I come to a stop and both men stare at me. "Erm." I look at Christian for enlightenment but it's obviously hopeless as he hasn't got a clue. "Yes, in a bit, Eddie."

"That's not my fucking name," Eddie starts to say and Christian snorts.

"Do you honestly care if we know your name?"

He looks at the two of us slowly and grins. "Nope."

"Wait," I say as they go to open the door. I lever up and remove the plastic baggy from my back pocket, tossing it to Christian. "Take that and get it ready, will you?"

He smiles, his eyes lighting up as he pushes the coke into the pocket of his jeans. "Baby, of course I will."

They spill out of the car, laughing, and then blessed silence falls. I take another swig from the bottle as the privacy screen slowly lowers and the lined face of Russ appears. He's been my driver since I started in films, and I always insist in my contract on having him. My manager, Frankie, can't stand him, but I adore Russ. He's got me out of more trouble than I can remember over the years, and consequently appears to view me as some sort of problem child. I don't need a crystal ball to know he's going to give me some shit tonight.

"Round the block?" he intones in a gloomy voice.

I nod. "Yes, please."

The car moves off slowly. He examines my face in the mirror. "You okay, sir?"

I look up, surprised. "Of course," I say abruptly. Then I ask, "Why?"

He shrugs, returning his attention to the road. "You don't look so good, Mr Ramsay."

"Oh Russ, you old charmer, you," I drawl, slugging some more tequila. "What's with the 'sir' and 'Mr Ramsay' business anyway?"

He ignores the question. He's more passive-aggressive than Taylor Swift. "You haven't eaten properly for a few days now," he says instead in a concerned voice.

"I have eaten," I say crossly.

"Tequila and vodka aren't any of the major food groups."

I shrug. "I had a Pop-Tart this morning."

"You had that *yesterday* and very charmingly regurgitated it into a jasmine bush earlier on."

"I'm fine," I say dismissively.

"I surely hope you are," he says wryly. "Because you've got your hands full tonight."

I shake my head, thinking of the two men I'm about to get into bed with and looking down at my very disinterested cock. "Russ, you'd need a medium and a séance to bring my dick back to life tonight."

He laughs loudly and then sobers. "Maybe you should call it a night then. Go to bed on your own for a change, sir."

"Okay, Nanny McPhee. And maybe I'd be better with a box of tissues and a wi-fi connection." I sigh. "Actually, that sounds a lot quieter." I stare blearily at the back of his grey head. "I hope you also know that tagging the word 'sir' on the end of a sentence doesn't make it any less bossy."

"I am aware of that," he says tartly. He pauses before saying in a rush, "Why don't I get them out of your room for you? You can get an early night. And see a doctor in the morning," he adds sternly.

"I don't need a doctor," I say peevishly.

"Yes, you do, Gideon. I'm telling you now that you are not well."

"I'm fine." We pull up to the hotel and I wave him off as he goes to get out and open my door. "I think we're far past the point of ceremony, Russ, when you're lecturing me on my choice of bedmates."

"Choice isn't the right word," he mutters. "Conveyor belt is more like it."

I get out but stagger slightly and lean back in, resting my hand on the roof of the car for balance. "What the hell? Have you been speaking to Frankie?"

He makes a moue of disgust at the sound of my manager's name.

"Of course I haven't. I don't work for him. I just know he'd be right here if he knew what was going on."

"Nothing's going on."

"Okay, only a complete meltdown. Nothing to see here, folks." He glares at me. "Gid, you've been destroying yourself for a long time, but this last year you seem to have stepped up the effort. You've got a lot worse very quickly. Frankie hasn't spotted what you're doing to yourself yet, but either he or the press will. I hope for your sake that it's Frankie."

I wink at him. "I'm not doing it to myself. That's the whole point of the evening."

He sighs and shakes his head as I give him a half salute which goes slightly awry when I forget where to put my hand.

I give up and wave to him as I stumble blearily into the hotel. I blink. *Jesus Christ, it's fucking bright in here.* I feel the ever-present headache start to throb painfully and take another sip from the bottle as I wonder where I put the ibuprofen I had to buy earlier.

A member of staff approaches me. It's the man from reception who has made it subtly clear that he disapproves of me. "I'm so sorry, Mr Ramsay," he says officiously. "Would you mind if I took that bottle off you?"

"I would, actually," I say, hearing the slur in my voice. "I'm not big on sharing my things so you should get your own."

"It isn't our policy for guests to bring their own alcohol into the hotel."

"I'll give you three hundred pounds if you leave me alone," I say, digging in my pocket, and he hesitates.

Then he politely says, "Of course, sir," taking the bundle of cash I thrust into his hand. I'm pretty sure there's more than three hundred quid in there but I honestly can't be arsed to check. "Maybe you'd like to go to your room," he says smoothly.

I smile at him, taking another drink. "You sound just like a matron," I offer.

A smirk plays on his lips as he presses the lift button and it arrives as quietly as everyone and everything seems to move around here. The place is like heaven, but with chocolate on the pillows and bribable staff.

I slump back against the mirrored walls of the lift as the door closes. Three or four Gideons look back at me. Pale and sweaty with big circles under their eyes. I look closer. *Shit, I do look terrible.* Sweat rushes up my body and my stomach seems to turn over. I suck in air. *Fuck, I don't need to be sick in another bloody lift.*

Luckily, it arrives at my floor and I stumble out of it, knocking into the door as I leave and dropping the tequila bottle. The corridor seems to stretch ahead of me and move like something from *The Shining*. If I hear a tricycle coming, I'm getting the fuck out of here.

I fumble in my pocket, looking for the other key card. It seems to take a long time as my fingers appear to be three times their normal size, but eventually I find it.

"Honey, I'm home," I say as I come into the expensive suite. The only answer I get is a chorus of groans. I come round the corner and grin as I look at the couple writhing on the bed. I admire the long lines of their naked bodies against the pale gold of the sheets.

The other man in particular holds my attention. Fred? Ed? Whatever his fucking name is. He's slim and has an arse you could bounce pennies on. I smile slowly as my cock finally gets with the programme and plumps up. I suddenly have plans for that arse that don't involve coinage. His dark hair and tanned body contrasts beautifully with Christian's blond hair and pale skin. They look like a wet dream come to life.

The gorgeous image is slightly ruined by Christian rolling over and saying in a querulous voice, "Are you getting involved tonight, or have you actually died and no one has noticed yet?"

I shake my head at him. "Let's hope I haven't died or who on earth will pay the expensive hotel bill?" I say acerbically. He pouts and I relent because otherwise I won't get laid. "Just coming."

"No, that'll be Fred in a second."

"Hey!" the man says indignantly. "My name is Teddy."

"Of course it is," I say with a laugh as I strip my clothes off, staggering slightly as I do. However, the laugh catches in the back of my throat, and with a sense of trepidation I feel my chest heave and tighten and my breath hitch. *Shit! Not again.* These coughing jags have got worse and worse lately, and last night I'd struggled to even catch my breath. My vision had gone dark and I'd got a red-hot pain in my chest. It had frightened me, but then it had passed and I'd smoked a spliff to calm my nerves and never thought about it again. Until now.

I attempt to breathe slowly in through the mouth and out through the nose while my bed partners grow bored of waiting and turn back to each other, but it's no good and I start to cough again. It's a hacking cough that steals my breath and makes my eyes water, and I bend double for a second. In a break between the spasms I swallow hard and grimace at the foul taste in my mouth.

Spying the brandy left on the table, I stagger over to it to the soundtrack of breathy moans and grunts coming from the bed as they both completely ignore me hacking up a lung in the corner of the very expensive hotel suite in Italy.

I grab the brandy and take a big gulp, but a cough launches midsip, and I splutter and cough up most of it. The coke lying in neat rows on the table like a ploughed field scatters and blows all over the floor. I look down at the white powder sinking into the expensive oriental rug and then watch as the brown-gold liquid of the brandy runs in funnels down my naked body and I feel a wave of heat run through me. At first I relax and settle into the burn, enjoying the respite from the coughing, but then I get hotter and hotter until it feels like my whole body is glowing. *What the fuck is wrong with me?*

Covered in sweat, I spy a nearby armchair and collapse into it. The floor seems to be roiling under my feet like I'm walking on water, and I wonder if I've finally achieved sainthood. If I have, somebody hasn't been listening to my many critics. I hear myself start to laugh in the distance but then I start to cough again. And cough. And cough.

Christian sits upright to a protesting whine from Freddy or Eddie. "Gideon, you're really fucking spoiling my flow. Will you bloody shut up, for Christ's sake?"

"I'm *so* sorry," I wheeze, waving a hand. "I do apologise if my coughing up a lung is spoiling your penis's enjoyment of the evening. I'll try to do better and be quiet when I die."

He frowns at me and I take another swig of the brandy, but the heat suddenly goes as a cold icy wave runs over me, making the sweat dry up, and I watch as goose bumps break out on my arms.

My harsh breaths sound loud in the room. For a split second I almost seem to be echoing the action on the bed, but then reality kicks in with a reminder that actually I sound more like I'm giving a death rattle.

The thought that I could be dying runs through my head in a dreamy sort of way that strangely doesn't scare me. The flu really knocked me on the arse, but I didn't have time to be ill so I just carried on. I know I should have done as my brother Milo said and got a doctor at the time, but I was too busy shooting a bloody film to bother. I wonder whether the film will stand as my shining epitaph and try to be more bothered that it won't. The cast was terrible and the director a twat. My subsequent bad mood and wild behaviour has probably ensured that I won't be getting any glowing eulogies from that direction, either.

I start to cough again and a sharp pain runs through my chest while the rest of me starts to shake with the cold. *Shit, this is serious,* I think hazily. My next thought is woozy and predominantly seems to be full of concern that I didn't clear my browser history, and I hear myself laughing. Then there's nothing but the sound of my breaths sawing in and out of my chest as the room seems to warp around me.

I sway forwards as if gravity is pulling me, and the carpet seems to rush at my face as I fall into it. I just have time to wish profoundly that I wasn't naked and destined to be on the front page of *The Daily Star* before everything goes dark.

CHAPTER 1

Hallmark doesn't have anything to rhyme with 'you're behaving like a total wanker'

Gideon

I come awake slowly, becoming aware of beeping sounds and the low hum of voices. At first I wonder whether I've died, but when I inhale I smell the scent of antiseptic and relax. I'm fairly sure heaven won't smell of Dettol. I stir, trying to open my eyes, and someone's hand comes down on mine, the skin so hot it makes me aware of how cold I am and that my teeth are chattering.

"So c-cold," I mutter.

"It's okay," the voice says. "You're alright, Gid. I'm here."

I want to smile because that halting but warm voice belongs to my baby brother, Milo, but sleep beckons me again and I fall into its welcoming arms.

The next time I wake up it's easier. My eyes flutter open and I wince against the brightness of the light. "Fuck," I mutter, and a low chuckle sounds from somewhere near me.

"I see your vocabulary hasn't been improved by your brush with death."

"*Niall!*" Milo sounds horrified. "What the hell?"

My best friend and old hook-up chuckles. "Relax. I've read that people who have near-death experiences come out of it changed. I thought maybe his intellect would have improved and he'd be using fancy words."

I shake my head and force my eyes open again. "Oh, my God! That bloody light is burning my retinas. Close the fucking blinds." My voice sounds thick and unused.

Niall laughs. "No, don't worry. His intellect is still at base level, as is his temper. Yes sir, I'll get right on it for your majesty."

There's movement and then the room dims welcomingly.

I open my eyes fully to look at my companions and immediately frown. Milo looks worn at the edges, his clothes rumpled and his hair messy, while Niall has huge circles under his eyes. I notice Niall's hand on my brother's arm and want to roll my eyes. Since they got together and declared their love it's been like being on the set of a romance by Barbara Cartland.

"You both look fucking awful," I say hoarsely.

Niall laughs. "Oh my God, you came back with *compassion*. It's like Simon Cowell has morphed into Mother Theresa."

"I certainly didn't come back with any patience for your shitty sense of humour."

"Your throat sounds terrible," Milo observes worriedly. He pours me a glass of water and slides his arm around my shoulder to hold me up so he can put the straw to my mouth.

"I am perfectly capable of taking a drink on my own," I say acerbically. "I managed that skill when I was fairly young and it's held me in good stead ever since."

"Neither I nor *The Sun* are ever disputing your ability to drink,"

Milo says and I give in and open my mouth for the straw, sucking greedily at the water. It's ice cold and the best thing I've ever tasted, so I make a noise of protest when he withdraws the cup.

"No," he says gently. "You'll be sick, Gid."

Niall smiles at me and runs his hand softly through Milo's hair as if he's comforting him, and Milo visibly relaxes.

He immediately turns to me and rubs my arm in a worried fashion. "How do you feel?"

I breathe in and cough immediately. "Shit!" I splutter.

"Easy," Niall says, pressing a button and raising me up. The coughing eases slightly and I shoot him a grateful look. He presses another button on the wall and within seconds a nurse bustles in, her uniform almost crackling with efficiency. A red-faced consultant in a very expensive suit follows closely behind.

"Well, Mr Ramsay," he says in a very hearty tone. His English is heavily accented and has disapproval running heavily through it. "You gave everyone quite the scare."

"I'm sure they'll cope," I say coolly and he blinks.

"Still, we've been a very naughty boy."

"I'm not sure if you have," I offer offhandedly. "But then that's none of *my* business."

"Ha ha, your sense of humour is very English. But luckily we have a lot of experience of *that* type of humour here." He hums and laughs in a very unamused way. "Lots of tourists around here who think they're comedians." This doesn't sound very complimentary and he looks around and stiffens as if he expects Vic Reeves to pop out of the wardrobe any minute and punch him. I stare at him with my eyebrows raised and he fidgets. "Hmm. Let us have a look at you."

He and the nurse bustle around, listening to my chest and poking and prodding me. She takes down the clear bag at my side and I look down at my hand, noticing the needle in my hand at the same time that I feel the pain and tug as she removes it.

"What was that for?"

"Antibiotics and fluids. We've been giving you them intravenously and they seem to be working nicely," the consultant says. He steps back so the nurse can fasten my hospital gown back up. "You seem to be coming along nicely, Mr Ramsay," he says in a slightly disappointed voice.

"That's good, surely. Although not quite in keeping with the note of doom in your voice. You should really try a different bedside manner or you'll have patients queuing up to throw themselves out of the window."

"*Gideon*," Milo sighs, and the consultant shakes his head.

"You had a near miss, Mr Ramsay. We were very concerned for a while that you might not pull through. You've been neglecting yourself for a long time." He smiles at me in a very patronising manner. "We can't burn the candle at both ends without damaging ourselves."

"Well, you might not be able to, but I'm sure if I work hard enough at it I'll succeed. Our nanny always said that nothing worthwhile ever comes without hard work and dedication."

Milo sighs again and the consultant blinks, looking slightly discomposed. "I'm going to let you have a chat with your brother while I organise another X-ray of your chest."

He leaves and silence falls for a blissful minute.

"How could you be so bloody stupid, Gideon?" Milo hisses.

Okay, a blissful second, but it was nice while it lasted. I'm amused to see my shy brother fold his arms and glare at me. It's a bit like being told off by a gerbil.

"Oh, don't smile," he says ominously, and I wipe the smile away. He nods. "Better. You've had fucking pneumonia, you idiot."

"Have you ever considered a career in nursing, Milo?"

"I'd never fit my hair in that cap." I grin, but he turns serious. "I told you to go to the doctor. I actually said those words out loud, and what did you do?" I open my mouth but he shakes his head fiercely. "You decided to take care of yourself by smoking dope, snorting coke, drinking brandy, and having a threesome. What were you *thinking*?"

"That I wanted a fuck, a drink, and a spliff. And coke always cheers me up if none of that works."

"When *don't* you want all that?" he says sharply. "Well, this time it nearly killed you. They had to phone for an ambulance, and you were carted out of the hotel naked on a stretcher while Christian ran alongside you asking you if you'd paid the bill."

"Hmm," I say slowly. "Hardly a very good epitaph. I hope I said something memorable for posterity."

"You threw up in the foyer," Niall offers. "It was memorable enough for the hotel to ban you from staying there again." He pauses before offering cheerfully, "For posterity."

"Shit. Were there any press about?"

Milo shakes his head and sits back, looking disgusted. "*That's* what you're bothered about." I stare at him in consternation and nod. He huffs. "Well, luckily for you there were no press in the foyer at three in the morning. However, there are a lot of them downstairs at the moment writing feel-good stories about how you were so close to dying that they had to put you on a ventilator in intensive care."

His voice breaks a little and I feel heat in my face. "I'm sorry," I say in a small voice.

"What did you say?"

"Don't make me repeat myself," I say crossly. "I said it once. Don't ask for the moon."

"Oh my God, it's like William Shakespeare has been reborn," Niall says wryly, sitting back in his chair and propping his long legs up on my bed. "I must say there'd have been a lot less of the sonnets for poor students to analyse if you'd written them. Thou art more lovely than a rose. That's it. Finished. I'm not fucking repeating myself, you needy cretin."

I grin. "Pure poetry."

"Oh, you're smiling. How nice." Milo's voice has a sharp edge to it. "That certainly indicates that you're well enough for a little visit."

"From who?" I ask, worried now. "Mum and Dad aren't here, are they?"

"*No*," he scoffs. "They're on a safari for their wedding anniversary which you paid for. I rang them and told them you were alright.

Mum wanted to fly out and be with you but I persuaded her that you'd be cross."

"Bewildered, more like it. Surely if she ran true to form she'd have just rung up the matron from our old boarding school. Then she could mother me in proxy the way it's always been."

"Oh, don't say that." Milo sighs, and I can see the turmoil in his eyes.

The way our parents treated us so disparately drove a wedge between us as children that was strengthened by the ten-year age difference. I got packed off to boarding school when I was seven while Milo, who seemingly activated all of my mother's previously unused maternal instincts, got kept at home where she fussed over him twenty-four hours a day.

Once, I'd hated them for it when I'd hear of family trips I never went on, celebrations I wasn't part of. They never even came to get me when I had appendicitis. Just left me to the less than tender matron because Milo had a speech therapist appointment. Now, I don't feel anything apart from a distant affection for them. Something that I'm obligated to feel.

However, I love Milo. I never wanted to, and for many years I hated him for having the family life I'd always wanted. For the fact that my mother and father loved him even though they never managed it with me.

So, for a long time I distanced myself from him. Then he fell in love with Niall and it seemed to me that once again he'd taken everything away from me. Niall was my occasional hook-up, but more importantly he was my family, one of only two people I could be myself with. And it seemed like history was repeating itself all over again where Milo had everything, leaving me alone and on the outside. It seemed to reinforce all the lessons of my childhood over how unlovable I really must be and spurred me into behaving like that small child.

However, Milo still managed to edge under my barriers without me even realising. When he and I reconciled I made promises of closeness, but then I visited everyone at *Chi an Mor* and it just seemed to reinforce how isolated I was and how connected they all were, living and working on the estate and involved in each other's lives. They had their own jokes and stories, and I'd hovered on the outside trying to take part but feeling the sting of failure. There was a distance between us all that I couldn't bridge no matter how I tried. I didn't visit again but instead immersed myself in very bad behaviour. The same bad behaviour that has landed me in hospital.

Despite all this, Milo is probably the only person in this world apart from my two best friends who I love, and I therefore can't say anything more about our parents without upsetting him.

"So, who's visiting?" I ask instead.

"Frankie," he says with an evil smile, and I blanch at the thought of my manager.

"Fuck!"

"Yes, I thought you'd say that. He's even more worked up than normal because as well as your little PR present to him of a three-some with drugs and – even worse in Frankie's eyes – men, I then barred him from your hospital room and wouldn't let him see you."

"*You* did?"

Niall nods and shoots my brother an affectionate and proud look. "Yep. Told him to fuck off and said as he wasn't family he wasn't coming in. He's been cooling his heels in the waiting room and winding the nurses up ever since."

"I really don't know why you don't like him," I say to Milo, coughing and shifting as my ribs protest.

He instantly rises and plumps my pillows up. I slide back against them and he shakes his head.

"You don't know why I don't like him? Let's see. He's a terrible old fossil of a homophobe who took advantage of my brother's yearning for family when he persuaded him to leave school at seventeen to make him famous, and incidentally make Frankie a lot of money. Then he proceeded to remake you, telling you that people would never accept a gay actor and that the idea of you with a man would send the world into mourning."

"He's alright," I say slowly. "He's looked after me all these years. I need him."

"He's looked after himself more," my brother argues. "Look at his house and the car he drives. Look at the women who hang around him. You pay for all that."

"I pay him a wage."

"You pay him to tell you that an integral part of you is wrong and disgusting. He's told you it so often that I'm sure you half believe him. As a consequence we've had to watch you get wilder and wilder over the years and not give a shit about yourself."

"Do we need Frankie?" I say faintly. "You're doing a good enough job of character assassination without getting a member of paid staff to help."

"Shut up," he says sharply, and I subside obediently back against the pillow.

"Can I have some more water?" I ask meekly.

"You do it," he huffs at Niall. "I'll drown him in it if I get too close."

"Don't judge yourself too harshly. It's his personality," Niall assures him. "Most people embrace murder as a valid interaction with him after knowing him for just a few minutes."

"This is really lovely," I say faintly. "Aren't people in hospital supposed to get Lucozade and grapes and members of their families weeping on them, or is that just stereotyping? Ow!" My brother retracts his fingers from where he just pinched me. "What did you do that for?"

"Because I love you."

"Can't you buy me a card like normal people?"

"No, because Hallmark doesn't have anything to rhyme with 'you're behaving like a total wanker,'" he says firmly. Niall snorts and I glare at him as Milo carries on talking. "You need to clean up your act. No more drugs, no more hook-ups with random men and women."

"But what on earth will I do on set? *Knit?*"

"You're not going on set."

"*What?* I've got a film starting in a week."

"Gideon, you've had pneumonia. I don't think you know how serious that is."

"I thought only old people and young ladies in eighteenth century novels got that."

"Well, add thirty-nine-year-old dissolute actors and you'd be right." He shakes his head. "You can't work for a few months. We told the director and he's replacing you."

"Who is *we?*" My voice is icy and Niall shifts, ready and able to come to Milo's defence. My brother shakes his head at him and he subsides.

"Me as your next of kin, which believe me was needed as you nearly died, and Niall as my boyfriend and your best friend," he says defiantly.

"Frankie would never have gone along with that."

He smiles and it's slightly evil. "Frankie has no authority here."

I blink. "You've created a monster," I say accusingly to Niall, and he shrugs.

"He's very bossy now. It's extremely beneficial in the bedroom."

"Ugh!" I shake my head. "I don't want to know."

"Are you bothered about the film?" Milo asks, and that quickly his bossiness is gone, replaced by worry. I exchange a look that says everything with Niall. Love and tenderness towards the kind, gentle man that my brother is.

I consider myself and realise how really awful I feel. Weak, drained, old, and tired. So very weary. "No," I say finally, seeing Milo sag with relief. "It's alien to me not to want to work because it's all I have. I just don't think at the moment I could stand the idea of being on set. Even thinking about it is fucking exhausting."

"That's good," my brother says gently. "According to Frankie's wails, that means that you now have a six-month window in your diary for the first time since you were seventeen. That's plenty of time."

"For what?" I ask nervously.

"For us to get your life in order."

There's a rap on the door before I can argue and a nurse puts her head around the door. "Mr Grantham is waiting very anxiously out here." She grimaces slightly. "Any chance he could see Mr Ramsay?"

"He certainly can," Milo says sweetly and sits back in his chair. "Please tell him to come in. I'm sure Gideon will be ecstatic to have a conversation with him."

Niall and the nurse wince in unison.

"Could I have some morphine first?" I ask mournfully.

Frankie explodes into the room a few seconds later, and I take the time to look at the man who's been my agent since my career started. I met him after a school production of *Hamlet* in which I'd played the title role. He came up afterwards and introduced himself as a talent scout for a well-known agency.

He'd been full of praise and bright admiring eyes, and I'd lapped it up, knowing that there was no one in the audience who belonged to me apart from my best friends Niall and Silas. Everyone else had their families sitting in the seats they'd been allocated. I had no one because my mother and father were taking Milo to a pantomime. I'd felt almost embarrassed to have to give my tickets to other people and ended up telling a story of my parents being away for work. That excuse had been accepted unquestioningly as we were at boarding school.

This man who was then in his mid-twenties had been interesting and bohemian-looking, wearing ripped jeans and a *Sesame Street* T-shirt when all the parents were in their Sunday best. I'd been amused by his chain smoking despite the Head's pointed glances at the No Smoking sign, and I'd been intrigued by his honeyed words of praise and offers of more money than I could imagine. He'd been like the pied piper of cool and I'd happily followed him, abandoning my plans for a university career without a backward look.

He'd abided by his promises and when he announced his intention of leaving the agency to set up independently I'd followed him again, lending my name to the operation which I'm pretty sure is why he has so many A-list clients now.

I look at him now as he paces angrily over to me and it's like I'm seeing a stranger. Gone is the man with the overlong hair and penchant for wearing T-shirts with political slogans. Instead, Frankie now wears bespoke designer suits and shiny wingtip shoes. His wild hair is corralled into a short back and sides and slicked ruthlessly down. His expression has lost that laid-back charm that so appealed to me and become tense and angry-looking.

Still, I can't fault him for that. There's no trace of that starry-eyed boy in me anymore either. No sign of the lad who wanted to act more than anything. Now, I mostly make money and headlines for bad behaviour and the public as a whole love me, but I know they'd turn on me in seconds if they really knew me. I know this because Frankie has told me often enough.

"What the fuck, Gideon?" he growls, pushing his hand into his suit pocket and drawing attention to the big belly he now sports because of too many expense lunches. *Mostly my expense,* I think idly.

"Hello, Frankie," I say smoothly. "Thank you for your concern. Yes, I am fine, thank you. I'm sure I'll manage to pull back from my headlong rush towards death."

"So dramatic," Niall breathes. Milo huffs, glaring at Frankie as if he's imagining dissecting him.

Frankie waves a casual hand. "I knew you were alright," he scoffs. "Your brother was kind enough to pass on a few pieces of information." He throws Milo an acidic look, and I stir.

"My brother is my next of kin," I say coolly. "And unlike mostly everyone else, he was actually concerned about me. As such, he can do as he bloody well pleases. If I die he gets everything. I'd give it to him while I was alive if I thought he'd accept it."

"Oh, don't talk about that," Milo protests, looking upset and grabbing my hand. Niall kisses the top of his head and I watch as Frankie makes a moue of disgust at seeing two men behaving affectionately.

He looks up and flushes as he catches me watching him with a raised eyebrow. Obviously realising that he's misstepped, he changes the subject fluidly. "Lovely as that is, we need to talk, Gid. This is a complete disaster." He shakes his head. "I've done the best I can. The two blokes have been paid off and signed nondisclosures."

"W-Why," Milo stutters slightly and we all turn to look at him. I smile encouragingly and he carries on. "N-Nondisclosures imply that he was doing something wrong. He was just in a threesome, n-not running around dismembering hotel guests."

"I'm so glad I cancelled that portion of my evening," I say, and he grins at me suddenly before turning back to Frankie.

"He's not married. He's n-not with anyone. It might be scandalous to the general public but it's hardly a hanging offense. He's …" He pauses. "I was going to say that he's a responsible man, but I couldn't get the words out."

"Because of the stutter?" Frankie asks.

"No, because it would be an appalling lie," Milo says pertly, making Niall laugh.

Frankie turns back to me. "Lovely and idyllic as that all sounded, the reality is that Gideon lives in a world where his actions have repercussions because he's judged on everything he does."

"I hope you're not judging me on Christian," I say tiredly. "I'd hate for that to be held against me."

"Enough," Frankie barks. "You know the reality, Gideon. It's too late to come out as bisexual or gay or whatever the fuck you are this week. The fans will turn against you in a heartbeat because you'll be a liar to them. Someone who has consistently lied for years in order to make money and be famous." He shakes his head. "You'd be lucky to get a job doing panto in Margate after that. It'll be the end of your career."

"I think you're m-more concerned about your own c-career," Milo bursts out, the words emerging disjointed and halting but full of passion. "Stop forcing your homophobic b-bloody views on him. He needs to know that people will love him regardless of his sexuality."

"They won't." My voice is flat, and I suddenly feel like I'm a hundred years old. "They won't, Milo. Frankie's right."

Frankie shrugs, looking smug. "As I said," he says pointedly. "We need to spin this." He pauses. "I'll ring Jacinta. She can come out. We can get a few pictures of her nursing you, a few pap shots of you eating out and her looking at you lovingly."

"No," I say harshly, glaring at him with the last of my strength. I can feel weariness beating at my body, wanting to drag me under. "That's not going to happen," I say slowly. "She's straightened her act up now – got clean and she has a really nice boyfriend." I stare at him. "You leave her alone. I mean it, Frankie."

He subsides somewhat sulkily, which has become more obvious over the last year or so. Like he owns me and makes my decisions for me.

"Well, Gideon, we've got to do something. You need to stay out of trouble for the foreseeable future. The bloke from *The Sun* is sniffing around at the moment asking very leading questions." He glares at me. "I don't want to hear anything apart from the fact that you're an angel for the next few months. I want you to have a reputation that Bonnie Langford would have been proud of."

"Oh, you've no need to worry about that," Milo says somewhat smugly.

"Why?" I ask, worry stirring.

His smile widens. "I've booked you on a cruise."

Niall's laughter drowns out my, "What the fuck?"

CHAPTER 2

Is this heaven? Because if it is, I want my money back. It's a *terrible* place

---

Gideon

I stare at Milo in stupefaction. "I'm sorry. I think my illness must have affected my hearing. I'm sure you just said that you've booked me on a cruise?"

"I have," he says calmly, sitting back in his chair and glaring at me.

"Does pneumonia have the side effect of aging me by forty years? Why am I going on a fucking cruise?" I look at Niall. "What the hell is happening here?"

He shrugs and Milo leans forward. "You can't fly back to England. Your lung collapsed and there's no way that any airline will let you fly with that."

"So, I'll stay here."

He shakes his head. "No, you're coming home so we can look after you, and a cruise is the only way to get you back."

"I haven't actually got a home at the moment," I say. "I sold the Primrose Hill house a few months ago, and I don't think the new owners will be very happy if I turn up and sit on the sofa."

"And you didn't buy another place?"

I flush. "I forgot." Everyone's heads turn towards me and I squirm slightly. "What?" I finally bark. "I was too busy."

"Getting laid," Milo says pertly. He grimaces at me. "It doesn't matter because you're coming back to *Chi an Mor*."

I think of the lovely Elizabethan manor house on the coast of Cornwall that belongs to Silas. "Why?"

"Because you can recuperate there with us. Away from the press."

"Hang on," Frankie says crossly. "Gideon needs the press."

"Why?" Milo asks and Frankie bristles.

"Listen, Milo, you may be very skilled at touching up pictures, but you know fuck all about show business."

"Touching up pictures?" I mouth at Niall and he shakes his head, his eyes brimming with mirth. He's always loved shit like this.

"Well I t-took time away from making sure that the artist had c-crayoned within the lines to take up my position as Gideon's next of kin," Milo says. I always thought it was impossible to stutter and sound threatening at the same time, but I have to say he has it down pat. Frankie moves back a step.

"Look," he says, trying for a conciliatory tone. "We're both on the same side here, Milo." My brother looks unconvinced but Frankie ploughs on. "I just thought he'd be better staying with me. I've rented a lovely villa on Lake Garda." I wonder idly whether I've paid for that. Strike that. I know I have. He carries on talking. "I've even hired a nurse."

"What? I don't need a nurse," I say quickly.

He nods. "You do, mate. We need to get you fully fit and we don't need you in the fucking hospital with the press hanging around."

"You're right," Milo says evenly, and Frankie looks rather surprised.

"I am?"

He nods at Frankie. "He does need to get fit and a nurse is a brilliant idea."

"Am I here?" I demand. "Or is this heaven? Because if it is, I want my money back. It's a *terrible* place."

Frankie and Milo ignore me, locked in a staring contest which Frankie breaks when he turns to me and hands me a piece of paper. I look blearily at it and then hand it over to Milo. "I've hired you a good one, Gid. She's called Ellie Jones and she's got a fantastic reputation. She's worked with loads of celebrities and she's known for her discretion." He pauses. "Hopefully she's good-looking too. Then we could spin it that she's your new bird."

"*Bird,*" Milo says in a tone of disgust. "She's a qualified professional. Very qualified, looking at this." He squints. "Was your printer running out? Because some of this is blurred."

Frankie waves his hand in dismissal. "It doesn't matter. It's just boring details."

Milo hands him the paper. "Perfect. She can accompany Gid on his cruise." He turns to me. "It's the only way, Gid. You need to come home for me to look after you. This way you'll travel back slowly, get some sun, relax and not overstretch yourself." He smiles. "No wild living. Just sun, sea, and lots of good books."

"What the fuck?" Frankie roars and the room explodes into loud voices, one of whose is Milo's. I blink as I never knew he could reach that decibel level. Frankie gets in his face but before I can move Niall is there, shoving between them and saying something to Frankie in a very threatening tone.

I blink, feeling my eyes get heavy. I'm so tired. I contemplate ringing the bell for security to evict everyone, but it's too far away.

They're all shouting too loudly to pay attention to anything, which is why it's only me who hears the knock on the door.

It opens and a figure steps into the room. I eye the newcomer. He's very tall with wide shoulders and a lanky build, but it's his face that gains my attention. It's angular with sharp cheekbones and a very strong squared chin. His lips are full and his nose is wide with a spray of freckles. With that, his outfit of cargo shorts and a navy t-shirt, and the wavy dirty-blond hair that falls over his face and brushes his collar, he looks like a surfer who's lost his way to the beach.

He looks around the room in astonishment and then fixes his gaze on me. His eyes are a pretty olive green that are so clear they look like the bottom of a brook. "Hello, are you Mr Ramsay?" he finally says, and I blink at the Welsh lilt in his speech.

"Hello," I say, clearing my throat. "Are you a fan? Can I help you?"

As one, everyone turns to stare at him, and he blinks. "I think it might be the other way round. I'm Eli Jones, the nurse who's been hired to look after you."

Frankie's mouth drops open, and I start to laugh.

He stares at me as I laugh harder and harder, and Milo turns to Frankie triumphantly. "Boring details? Hah!"

Eli

The man on the bed continues to laugh and the whole room has the feeling of a nuthouse. I look at my prospective patient and blink. *Gideon Ramsay.* I know him. I flush slightly. I should do. I watched a film with him in it last night. It had been a retelling of King Arthur and Guinevere and he'd played Lancelot. The film had been amazing, but there'd been a lot of gossip about it. The actor playing Arthur had apparently been very annoyed by Gideon's scene stealing, to the extent that he insisted on changing scenes and bits of the script.

If that's true, it never worked, because Gideon was the definite star. His brooding and sad presence had stolen every scene, but it was the naked scene he'd done that had led to me jerking off. I flush at the thought. His body had been spectacular. Naturally slim with a wide hairless chest, long legs, and an arse you could balance a plate on.

Now, however, he looks diminished. All of that energy is gone and only a slight feverish amusement is keeping him awake, I'd guess. I eye the black hair tumbling around his patrician face with its sharp blade of a nose, thin lips, and high cheekbones. He looks like a priest. A hot one.

His laughter turns to coughing, and I race to his side, my thoughts vanishing in the rush to deal with my patient.

"Easy," I say, holding him up with one arm while I raise the bed and plump his pillows up so he's sitting upright. The coughing eases and I smile down at him. "Okay now?"

He blinks, and I notice the colour of his eyes. They're so light a blue they're almost grey, and I'd guess they normally look cold, but now they just look tired. I reach out for the glass of water and guide the straw to his mouth. He gulps heartily, his throat working as he swallows the liquid. I tear my eyes away from his Adam's apple and try to remember that I'm a health-care professional, not a bloody groupie. *What the fuck is wrong with me?*

I pull the straw away and lower him back against the pillow. "You okay?" I ask softly. He nods, his expression dazed, and I turn to face the others only to find them all staring at me.

I feel a flush on my cheeks. "Everything alright?" I ask tentatively.

The older fat man glares at me. "Who are you?"

I blink. "Eli Jones. I was told to report here. I'm the nurse for this gentleman, I believe."

"What the fuck?" he breathes and runs an agitated hand through his hair.

I feel uneasiness stir. *What the fuck is going on in here?* "Is there a problem?"

"Well, Eli," the big man says in a very hostile tone. "You could say there is a bloody problem, and you're it."

One of the other men stirs. Tall and slender with a mane of wavy hair, he reminds me of someone, and then I realise that he looks vaguely similar to the man lying in the bed. It's in the shape of his mouth and eyes and the long nose. Brother, I'd say.

"There's no problem," he says, his halting speech and indrawn breath telling me that he probably had a stammer at one point. He smiles and his whole face lights up. "No problem at all. I'm Milo, Gideon's brother." He reaches out to shake my hand, and his long fingers close around mine.

The fat man stirs. "Mind your own business, Milo."

"Oi." The tall white-blond man who's standing close to Milo glares at the fat man. "Watch your fucking mouth, Frankie."

Ah, Frankie, my employer. I gaze down at the patient as if seeking clarification, only to find him staring back at me. I smile hesitantly and he closes his eyes for a second, exhaustion running over his face.

I turn back to the crowd. "Are you Frankie?" I ask, smiling calmly at him. I offer my hand but he ignores it, so I shrug and return it to my side. When I look down, my patient is glaring. I blink but realise that it's not at me, but at Frankie, who hasn't noticed. "You asked me to come here to take charge of my patient."

"Well, now I'm telling you to fuck off," he says harshly. "You're no good to me."

"*Frankie!*" Milo exclaims. "What the hell? You have no right."

"I have every right," the big man roars. "I employed him. Now, I can fucking sack him."

Milo opens his mouth, but at that second the man in the bed stirs. "Actually, I employed him," he says coldly. "Seeing as I am *your* boss." He stares coolly at Frankie, who flushes. His voice is cold but the richness of it, the clear precision of his speech, is instantly recognisable as someone who records many audiobooks. It's a gorgeous voice, and I'm sure I remember reading that an actress said she'd got wet listening to him reading the telephone book at a party. I'm drawn back to the conversation as he continues talking icily. "I presume I am still your employer, Frankie. You haven't staged your coup yet, have you? My brain and free will are still my own?" Frankie nods. "Phew," Gideon says acerbically. "I don't mind admitting that's a huge relief. I thought I was in a cult for a second."

"What colour robes would you wear?" the white-blond man says and Gideon considers.

"I think blue. It makes my eyes pop and accentuates my all-round perfect appearance."

"Gideon," Frankie says imploringly. "Gid, I know what's best for you. Trust Frankie."

"I can't trust anyone who has started to refer to themselves in the third person," my boss says coolly. "It's far too reminiscent of Donald Trump." I hide my smile. He stares at Frankie coldly. "As I still have my own free will and control of my bank balance, I'm going to look at this as one of your good decisions, Frankie. You've hired me a nurse who appears to be very well qualified. And now I employ both of you because Eli is staying as my nurse. Are we clear?"

"Crystal," Frankie says sulkily.

Gideon closes his eyes, looking suddenly weary, and I spring into action. "Okay," I say cheerfully. I'm keeping my voice calm and even because of years of training, although my brain is teeming trying to work out what the dynamics in this room are. However, one thing is clear. The man in the bed is the boss, and I'm now working for him. "Okay," I repeat and look at Frankie. "My patient is tired," I say calmly. "Time for you to go."

"Who the fuck are you talking to?" he blusters. "What gives you the right to tell me what to do in here?"

"My nursing degree," I say cheerfully. "I didn't get it by eating Pot Noodle and watching *Neighbours*, you know." I wink at him. "Well, not all of it anyway." I point to the door. "You can come back when he's had a sleep. He'll be much happier then." I usher him to the door and open it for him. "But knock first," I say happily and shut the door on him as he mouths expletives.

Gideon

I watch open-mouthed as my new nurse shuts the door neatly in Frankie's stunned face.

"Oh my God," Milo breathes and Niall nods.

"Epic," he says happily.

Eli turns and looks at us hesitantly. "I hope I didn't overstep any boundaries."

"You'd have to find Frankie's boundaries first," I say tiredly, closing my eyes. "I think they're buried very deep under a mountain of hot air." I sink into the pillows he plumped up for me.

I must have blacked out for a second because, when I open my eyes, the three of them are talking quietly.

"So, is that o-o-okay?" Milo stutters slightly. "Is a cruise a bit out of the ordinary?"

My new nurse shakes his head, smiling sunnily at my brother. "Not at all, mate." The Welsh in his voice is clear now. He looks relaxed and laid-back, but I don't miss those clever eyes of his that are looking around the room, lighting on the medical equipment and glancing down at the clipboard in his hand which I'm pretty sure contains my medical notes.

I think about intervening and letting my presence be felt as they are, after all, talking about me as though I'm a child or a dog that he's been given custody of. However, the pillows are so soft around me and my body seems to sink into the mattress. It's as if by his entering the room he brought calm and order and comfort, but all with a sunny disposition. I frown.

"A cruise will be fine," he continues, putting the clipboard back on the bed with a snap. "It's a good idea, actually."

"And he'll be okay?" I wince at the note of worry in my brother's voice.

Eli smiles at him. "I'm sure he will. He needs to rest and not fret. Get some monitored exercise, lots of sleep and fresh air. The warm weather will help his lungs, and the fresh air at sea will be really beneficial."

"And you've done this sort of thing before?"

"All the time," he says reassuringly. "I've travelled all over the world to be with my patients. He'll be safe with me, I promise."

Milo relaxes visibly at the conviction in Eli's voice, but then looks a bit hesitant. "He's rather difficult," he finally says in a low voice, and Niall snorts softly.

"That's an understatement."

"Okay, he can be *very* difficult," Milo says in a rush. "He's arrogant, always convinced he's right, and hasn't had anyone telling him what to do apart from Frankie for years." Eli winces and Milo nods enthusiastically. "He's grumpy, moody and–"

"A couple more and I could meet Snow White," I say acidly. They all jump and I wave my hand. "Oh no, please do carry on talking about me like I'm the dog or senile. Why don't we mention the fact that I bite my nails and can't tolerate Pernod?"

Instead of reacting to my sarcasm, Milo nods earnestly. "He really can't. It's weird. Just a sniff of a bottle and he throws up."

My new nurse's mouth quirks and I huff irritably.

"Here's what's going to happen. Eli, can I call you Eli?" He opens his mouth and I rush on, noticing that mouth quirk again. "Never mind. The fact is that my brother is bound and determined that I embark on a cruise with a group of people whose average age is probably one hundred and four. As such, and regardless of my own wishes that obviously do not matter, I shall do as he wants. Now, Eli, although my brother is seemingly giving you the impression that you are in charge, it is very far from the truth. I am in fact your boss and as such you will do as I tell you. If I want to do something, I'll bloody well do it because the only person who tells me what to do, is me. Now, after that instruction, is there anything else you need to tell the newest member of my staff, Milo?"

Milo nods and turns to Eli. "Keep him away from coke and twinks," he says earnestly.

Eli blinks, and I shake my head. "Milo," I sigh. "For fuck's sake." I'm trying to work up a head of steam over the fact that Milo just outed me to my nurse, but I can't summon it today and the poor bloke looks so confused after everything that's just gone on, he probably didn't notice anyway.

Milo nods energetically at Eli and ignores me. "I'm so sorry for this. We will, of course, double what Frankie is paying you, and to be honest, even that amount of money won't cover dealing with him. Still, will you be okay with all of this?" He waves his hand in a dismissive fashion at me. I glare at him and expand that to include Niall who is now laughing.

Eli considers me and for a wild second I remember the way he held me up, the strength in his arms and his scent. He smells of coconut, bringing back memories of long days on sandy beaches under a hot sun. The clean, sweet scent seems to encapsulate the best of summer, and it suits him as he looks like he's just come in from surfing. I blink and push it to the back of my mind and settle for glaring at Eli now as well.

For some reason he looks vastly amused, which would make my anger flare if I weren't so tired. "No worries," he says cheerfully. "My great-grandmother thought her dog was in charge of the house. He ate at the table with her and I had to ask his permission to go in the kitchen."

"Oh my God," I say, but Milo nods gloomily.

"You might be wishing for that before this cruise finishes," he says in a very doom-laden tone of voice. "A dog at the table might be the least of your worries, knowing Gideon's tastes. It'd certainly have more table manners than some of Gideon's conquests."

CHAPTER 3

You're extremely pert for someone who's in my employ

One Week Later

Eli

I wheel my employer into the suite on the ship where we're going to be spending a lot of time and only just prevent my jaw dropping. *Fucking hell, it's huge.* I seem to spend my life in rich people's homes, but I've never stayed in a suite like this on a ship.

We're standing in an open-plan lounge and dining room. I have this same arrangement in my flat but it's very different, mainly because in my place you could stand in the middle of the room and touch the walls on either side. You definitely couldn't do that here unless you had arms like Stretch Armstrong.

The room is huge and full of light from the floor-to-ceiling windows which offer a stunning view of the ocean. On one side is a table big enough to seat ten people and on the other is a massive sectional sofa and some comfy-looking armchairs grouped around a flat-screen TV. It's decorated in white and silver, and expensive-looking pale rugs are dotted about on the light oak floorboards. I tap my foot on the floor. Definitely not laminate.

The butler who apparently comes with the suite hovers next to us. "Can I get you anything?" he says pleasantly. "Anything to eat and drink?"

"I'll have a large gin and tonic," Gideon says, but I shake my head.

"He'll have a peppermint tea." Gideon looks at me disbelievingly and I wink at him. "Good for your chest."

He shakes his head at his brother who has come to see him off. "Well, Milo, please make a note. By the end of this trip my chest will be fine but my head will have exploded in boredom."

The butler hesitates and Milo shakes his head at him. "He's an *actor*," he says sotto voice, pointing at Gideon who blinks.

"An actor with perfectly workable eardrums. Why are you talking about me as if I've got to be handled?"

"Because you do," Niall says cheerfully. "You need more careful handling than a box of crockery."

The butler smiles and moves out of the room, hopefully to obey my instructions and not my patient's. At the thought of him I look over and suppress a smile. He has moroseness down to an art, sitting slumped in the wheelchair with his arms folded.

It's been a week since I first met him, but, as if he was establishing who was boss, he let me know with barked commands and acerbity left, right, and centre. I've therefore spent the days shopping for stuff for him and coordinating with the hospital staff and the ship crew so we have a plan of action for everything.

"Well, here we are," I say cheerfully and, I admit, loudly. A tiny part of me is enjoying actually winding him up simply because it feels like the right thing to do, and I love the slight twist of humour on his impatient face that shows he actually enjoys a bit of backchatting.

"Oh, joy," he says sulkily. "Am I allowed out of this chair or will I have to stay in it for the duration of the voyage?"

"No, out you get," I say heartily, winking at Niall who has a half smile on his face. It appears he's Gideon's best friend and the boyfriend of Milo.

Gideon sneers at me and gets out of the wheelchair gingerly. He's wearing jeans, a navy short-sleeved t-shirt, and camel-coloured suede Vans. The clothes suit him but they're hanging on him and highlighting how thin he is. I watch him intently under the guise of taking his navy woollen hoody off him and hanging it in the coat cupboard by the door. He's pale and looks exhausted. His legs have a faint tremor and I shoot Milo a look of warning which he immediately understands.

"Gid, sit down," he says impatiently. "I hate it when you tower over me."

"I don't want to sit down," he says peevishly, while slumping onto the sofa with a thankful sigh that we all tactfully pretend not to hear. "Because then I'll go to sleep and I really don't want to leave such a precious day as this has been. One that will stay evergreen in my memory. The day when I was wheeled onto a ship like I was in a bath chair while people fifty years older than me sprang up the gangplank like fucking toddlers." He shoots Milo a glance. "It hasn't escaped my notice that every single person embarking today appeared to be seventy. What's going on?"

Milo fidgets. "Ooh," he says happily. "What a lovely view you have."

"Milo?"

He subsides onto the sofa. "It's a golden oldies cruise."

Gideon starts to laugh. "I could have sworn you just said that you'd booked me on an old aged pensioner's cruise."

"I did say that."

The laughter stops. "What the fuck?"

Milo holds up one hand rather imperiously. "No, I'm not listening to any more whinging. This was the only cruise ship docking that was going back to England. If we'd waited for the next one you'd have had to stay with Frankie." He looks around as if the man is going to appear in a puff of smoke. He needn't worry. The fat controller was talking to the captain last time I saw him. Milo continues talking. "I had to do some really fast talking to get you on this because there's an age limit to take the cruise." He pauses and laughs. "Well, fast talking for me anyway."

"Well, can I just say how glad I am that you worked so hard. What did you say to perform this magic trick?"

"Hmm." Milo mumbles something and Gideon's gaze sharpens.

"I'm sorry. What?"

"I said you were forty-five," he says in a rush.

"You said *what?*"

I can't help my grin of enjoyment, but luckily no one is watching me.

"I said you were forty-five and honestly, Gid, you look it at the moment."

"I do not," he hisses. "I'm thirty fucking nine. I'm not even forty yet, you cheeky twat. Go and tell someone that right now."

"How? Do you want me to get a loudspeaker and announce it outside the shops?" Milo asks peevishly.

"In my experience of cruises you'd catch more people outside the bar. It's like a mob at five in the evening," I offer and subside at Gideon's glare.

"You don't look good," Milo says primly. "Which is probably your style of life for the last few years showing in your face. So, I had to say you were forty-five." He pauses. "They'll know from your passport, but I don't think they were that bothered anyway. This was empty and I paid well over the normal price for it. You get a butler and everything," he finishes cheerily.

"Everything? What, like bingo and quoits?"

"Cruises with old people can be quite wild," I say, winking at him.

His mouth twists in distaste. "Please don't try and help. I need mind bleach now."

Niall laughs but it dies as Frankie comes in.

"Well, that's sorted, Gid," he announces. "I've told the captain who you are. Made sure he knows how you should be treated. He's under no illusions who he's dealing with now."

"Oh lovely," Gideon sighs. "I'll look forward to the staff spitting in my food for the duration of the voyage."

Frankie ignores him, wandering around the room and touching objects randomly. As the others lapse into a soft-voiced conversation he comes to my side.

"I don't know who you are," he mutters.

I smile cheerfully at him. "You do. It was on my CV."

"Hmm," he says in a low voice. "Well, Mr Jones, nurse extraordinaire, your job is to get him better. He's got a film in six months. We need him back up and earning again as soon as possible."

"Like a prize cow," I say, my smile dying. This is his manager. Doesn't he care? Can't he see how sick Gideon still is?

He eyes me in a disgusted fashion. "Don't be so bloody naïve. If he doesn't work, none of us get paid. Now, get him better and watch your fucking step." He leans closer. "You've signed a non-disclosure but I'm warning you as well. If any stories get sold about him I'll know who it is and I'll fucking ruin you." He looks me up and down with a sneer twisting his lips. "I know you're gay."

"How?" I say sharply. "Did you look into me?"

He shakes his head. "Don't be such a fucking Pollyanna. Of course I did. Eli Jones has student loans and a large overdraft because he was in hospital for an extended period of time. Not sure why that was, but I'll find out soon. He lives a very itinerant life travelling from one job to the next. Currently shares a shithole flat with two other men. He prefers one-night stands to relationships."

"Goodness, what a wicked person I sound," I say lightly, hopefully covering up my intense desire to punch him. *How dare he set someone to investigate me.*

He glares at me. "Gid's currently a little confused. He might find you attractive but it doesn't mean anything." I blink at the fact that while Frankie is lecturing me on keeping secrets he's just spilled that Gideon Ramsay might like men. I shoot an instinctive look at Gideon and feel a spiral of heat inside me that I quickly squash as Frankie carries on haranguing me. "He's been doing a little bit of experimenting lately before he settles down with Jacinta Foxton. Now, remember this, you fuck him and I will bury you so deep they'd need a digger to find you. I'll destroy your career." I stare at him and he smiles. "Just a little warning for you, Eli Jones. Remember what I said. A nurse sleeping with a celebrity. Gid might recover from it. Your career? Not a chance."

I want to laugh at the ridiculous threats, but I can't. There's a malice under the bellicose words that's almost frightening. This is not a man to be crossed. And he's not wrong. I would lose my job if I slept with a patient.

"Frankie." Gideon's sharp voice breaks into our conversation, and when I look up, he's slumped on the sofa. His colour is even more off but he's glaring at his manager. "What are you saying to Eli?"

"Nothing, Gid," Frankie says, his face wreathed in a big smile, no trace of the bully boy anywhere. "Just offering him some advice."

"I'll prepare for death, then, because what you know about the medical profession and nursing wouldn't even take up space on the back of a stamp."

Gideon raises one eyebrow at me in query and I make myself smile, but I know it's shakier than I'd like because his gaze sharpens.

"Time to go, Frankie," he says. "Otherwise you'll be stuck on the boat and we really can't have that."

Frankie laughs. "Not likely. The age range isn't even close to my chosen choice of partners." I make a moue of disgust at the thought. He claps a hand on Gideon's shoulder that makes him cough. I start forward but Gideon waves me back. "I'm going to meet the boat in Nice. I'll bring any paperwork with me then. Okay?" And then he's gone, leaving the room without even bothering to acknowledge Milo and Niall.

"I'll look forward to that visit more than a root canal, if it's possible," Gideon says acerbically, but his tone belies the weariness in his body. I shoot Milo and Niall a look and they get up.

"We're off," Milo says. He bends and hugs Gideon, and something twangs in my chest at the bewildered way that Gideon receives the embrace like he's never been hugged like that before. Yet these two men are brothers. Niall hugs him too, yet Gideon seems more relaxed in his embrace as if he's used to it. Curiouser and curiouser.

"Take care of yourself," Milo says. "Please use this time to really rest up. I worry so much about you."

"Don't," Gideon says testily. "It's ridiculous." But he kisses the hand that Milo puts on his face and his expression is soft. "I'll be fine," he says and looks at me imploringly.

"Of course he will," I say. "I'll look after him. He'll have so much clean living and fresh air that when you see him next he'll look twenty-five and be in the process of being turfed off an OAP cruise." The two men laugh and leave in a rush of hugs and goodbyes.

I close the door behind them and the suite becomes quiet. When I turn back I find Gideon has closed his eyes.

"Come on," I say briskly. "Come and climb into bed."

"What an offer," he says tartly. "You'll have to excuse me though, Eli. As the Bible says, the spirit is willing but the flesh is weak at the moment."

"Cheeky," I muse. I help him up and catch hold of his arm as he sways. "You okay?"

He nods. "Just felt dizzy. What the fuck is the matter with me? I've literally just got out of bed, sat in a car and then on a sofa, and I'm fucking knackered."

"Pneumonia," I say, guiding him into the bedroom. I inhale and get a whiff of his aftershave. It's a spicy vanilla smell. It even smells expensive, so it seems very him. "It'll be like this for a while. You have to give in and listen to your body, Mr Ramsay. It's trying to tell you what it needs to be done to get well again, and there's nothing better for an ill person than sleep. It mends most things."

I help him onto the wide bed which is full of pillows and dressed in expensive white Egyptian cotton sheets and a thick eiderdown embroidered in a white and grey pattern. I pull off his shoes and lift his legs up onto the bed before covering him with the eiderdown. He subsides with a sigh, his long black eyelashes fluttering on his thin cheeks. "I'll leave you, Mr Ramsay, but I'm only in the other room. Shout if you need anything."

I go to stand up but his eyes shoot open and he grabs my hand, so I still. "Gideon," he says, his voice slurring with tiredness. "You might as well call me Gideon. Mr Ramsay sounds like I'm up in court."

He's asleep before I can answer, but I stare down at him for a few seconds. Mr Ramsay might be a better option. Safer all round. But he's already Gideon in my head, so that's what it'll have to be.

Gideon

I come awake with a start to a room full of the shadows of encroaching twilight. I struggle to sit up, throwing the covers off me impatiently. Reaching for my watch, I shake my head. I've been asleep for four bloody hours.

Lowering my feet to the carpet, I sit up fully and wait a few seconds for the now customary dizziness to leave. Then I lever up and pad over to the window. The blinds are down but there's a switch to the right, and when I press it they swirl up and away smoothly with an expensive hum. I look out at my view and whistle. The windows are floor-to-ceiling across the whole wall, and consequently all I can see is a vast expanse of blue-grey water with violet clouds skidding across the pinkening sky.

I turn around and view my room for what's the first time, as when I came in all I could see was the huge bed beckoning. It's a lovely room decorated in white and grey, which might be boring if it weren't for the vibrant colours of the sea and sky. The central focus is the huge bed which is positioned so you have a panoramic view of the sea. The walls are lined with expensive grey wood wardrobes and a large white sofa is set in front of a TV.

I swallow, realising my throat is dry, and wander out of the suite looking for my wavy-haired nurse. I threw everything I had at him this week, demanding things left, right, and centre, and all I got for my pains was a sunny smile and a cheerful voice. They breed these Welsh people hardy. He's therefore won my grudging and very tentative approval. Let's face it, he won that when he turfed Frankie out of my hospital room and shut the door in his face.

I think of Frankie, and my smile dies. Something needs to be done about him. Over the last year or so I've noticed a definite change in him. He's grown more belligerent, and where before he made a token effort to listen to me, now he dismisses everything I say with a wave of his hand and carries on doing everything the way he wants. I've let it go on because he's always been there for me and I feel a sense of loyalty, but even that's faltering now. I wonder what I should do, but just the thought exhausts me, so I push it to one side to be dealt with at a later date.

The lounge area is deserted and I gaze around, finally spotting a messy blond head outside on what looks to be a deck. I get to the door and peer at him. He's sitting in a comfortable-looking wicker chair, staring out to sea.

He made noises about wearing a uniform at the beginning of the week, but I vetoed that straightaway. I'd have looked like an inmate from *One Flew Over the Cuckoo's Nest* if he'd been wheeling me around dressed in a uniform. Now he has on a faded navy sweatshirt over his usual outfit of a white t-shirt and khaki cargo shorts, and he's remarkable in that he's doing nothing except staring out to sea with a smile on his face. No phone, no tablet, nothing but him and the view.

It's so alien to me, who always has to be doing something, that I stare at him like he's in the zoo.

Something must alert him because he looks round and when he sees me, he jumps. "Sorry," I mumble, flushing at the thought that he's just caught me staring at him like a lovestruck schoolboy. "What are you doing?" I burst out.

He looks amused. "Looking out to sea."

"Why?"

He blinks. "Because it's very compelling. Always different."

"Is it?" I look at the sea but it's still exactly the same as the last time I saw it. "It's water," I say finally.

He laughs. "It's the sea. It's very different." He gestures at the chair. "Come and sit down. How are you feeling?"

I settle into the chair and relax instantly. It's as comfortable as it looks, full of scarlet cushions that are just the right size and shape to cradle me. I sigh happily and his lip quirks.

"Shall I leave you alone with the chair?"

I shake my head. "Is it too late to employ a comedian to accompany us? Tell me it's not too late."

He grins. It's a lovely smile. Wide and sunny and relaxed with a charm that's emphasized by the spray of freckles over that wide nose. It makes him look naughty somehow. I realise I'm staring again and clear my throat.

"Is this all ours?" I ask, looking around at the wooden deck which is filled with more wicker furniture, all with the same scarlet-coloured cushions. There's even a hot tub and a bed under an overhang draped with gossamer-thin curtains. "I sincerely hope that Milo hasn't arranged for us to share this with a happy band of passengers. I wouldn't put it past him," I say darkly.

"Nope, it's private. I had a chat with Peter, the butler, while you were asleep. This is totally private and all ours."

"A week ago I'd have been planning what debaucheries I could perform out here. Now, I'm just thinking how comfortable that day bed looks." I yawn suddenly. "I still feel tired," I say in amazement. "How is that possible?"

"It's completely normal. You've been very ill. The body doesn't bounce back after something like that." He purses his lips. "Plus, Mr Russo the consultant spoke to me in a very dark tone about the lifestyle you'd been leading."

To my amazement I flush. *Me*. I'm never embarrassed. Life and my patience are too short for me to bother with other people's opinions. "Yes, well." I clear my throat. "I'm thinking he got that information from the *National Enquirer* and not the *Medical Gazette*."

"I'll have you know that the *Medical Gazette* does a lot of celebrity exposures," he says primly, and I laugh suddenly. He amuses me when few people do. The coughing starts immediately, and he pats me on the shoulder gently while I cough. When I've finished, he reaches for a tissue from a box on a side table and hands it to me to mop my streaming eyes.

Standing up, he lopes into the lounge and I track his movements until he's back in front of me carting his med bag. Pulling out a stethoscope, he smiles at me. "I want to listen to your chest," he says. "And take your pulse, if that's okay?"

"Why? Are you bothered by something?" I ask, trying to summon up some worry.

He shakes his head. "I just want to keep a check."

I raise my t-shirt, realising for the first time how scrawny I look out here in the warm light, especially next to him with his taut body and golden skin. Then I shake my head. He's my fucking nurse, not a new conquest. He's also vaguely irritating with his sunny obliviousness to bad moods. Like he's made of mood Teflon.

He listens to my chest, his expression concentrated, and I try to take normal breaths and not wind up with the scent of coconut in my nostrils that seems to linger around him as if he's the personification of summer.

He steps back and starts to neatly coil the stethoscope. "All good," he says cheerfully. "Now, if you're okay on your own I'm going to pop

GIDEON 43

along and see the ship's doctor. He needs to go over the details of your illness and treatment so we're all on the same page."

"Of course I'm alright on my own," I say peevishly. "I'm thirty-nine, not three."

"Well, okay then, Methuselah. I'll order you a nice cup of honey tea." He steps back and checks himself before reaching over to one of the other chairs. Pulling a cream throw from the back, he wraps it around me.

"What the hell?" I say crossly. "I do not need a fucking blanket, and do you know why? Because my blood temperature still regulates itself and I actually have a circulation system."

"According to Mr Russo, the consultant, that's largely run by brandy."

I pause. "Fair enough," I say grudgingly. "But I'm taking this off as soon as you're gone."

He smiles at me and in the next second he's gone, leaving me to the solitude of the deck. *Which I'm perfectly fine with*, I tell myself robustly. *I'm used to being on my own.*

But am I? I pause to think. I suppose since I was a child I've thought of myself as alone, but I've always surrounded myself with so many people and activities and noise that I couldn't have been. *Funny*, I think lazily, and I inhale the scent of fabric softener on the throw. Made of the softest cream wool, it's a chunky hand-knitted piece of nonsense, but I inhale again and snuggle down into its folds, letting it settle around me and make pockets of warmth which is offset by the briny breeze that blows my hair back.

I'll just sit with it for a while, I tell myself. *And throw it off before he gets back and thinks he knows everything. Or, more than he already does.*

I settle back into my seat, looking up when the butler makes a soft-footed appearance. "Here you are, sir," he says comfortably. "A cup of tea with honey. Eli says it'll be good for your chest."

"Eli is not the font of knowledge," I say. I smile at him and for a second he looks slightly worried, so it must be more sharklike than I intended. I let some warmth through and he relaxes slightly. "Eli is not my boss," I tell him and he nods earnestly as he puts the tea down on the side table.

"No, of course not, sir. Not at all."

"Saying that twice doesn't mean you believe it," I grumble and take a sip of the tea. "Oh God, that's *lovely*," I say, surprised.

His mouth twitches. "I won't tell Eli, sir."

"That would be good." I pause. "In fact, tell him I tossed it over the side and had a brandy instead."

"Of course, sir," he says, picking up a trailing bit of the heavenly blanket and tucking me in. "I'll tell him you smoked a cigar and swung from the decking too."

My lips twitch. "I think we'll be fine, erm?"

"Peter, sir."

"Okay, Peter. I think we've reached an understanding."

He inclines his head and glides away, and I take another sip of the sweet tart drink, feeling my chest settle and the soreness in my throat which is caused by coughing easing slightly. Then I go back to staring out to sea. *What is it that fascinates him?*

The light is dimming now and the water reflects hundreds of tiny golden gleams as lighting starts to go on in the ship. Some seagulls hover on the wind nearby, calling raucously to each other as if they're squabbling.

A launch appears, bright orange with bunting flapping in the breeze. On board seems to be about five hundred old-aged pensioners, and their shouts of greeting to people on the boat are as sharp and high as the seagulls.

Sometime later the engines start suddenly with a deep throbbing and I startle, realising that I've been staring at the sea for – I check my watch – forty minutes. What the hell?

When I next look, there are some people on the quay waving furiously.

I hesitate, unsure of the etiquette of the situation, but in the end politeness compels me to raise my hand and wave faintly back.

As soon as they see me, they increase the velocity of their hand movements.

"Okay, Jesus," I say out loud. "Goodbye already." I wave back. "Go away," I mutter as they start to shout something. "My hand's getting tired."

"What is going on out here?" An amused Welsh voice sounds from the door and I jump.

"What the fuck? You should wear a bell," I say crossly.

"And I might if I was a cat, but I'm not, so maybe some people should learn to use their ears."

"You're extremely pert for someone who's in my employ," I observe.

He grins. "I can't help it. I'm Welsh. I'm born to repress your English tyranny."

I blink. "There's so much in that statement that's wrong."

He laughs and, looking down at the blanket wrapped around me, his smile widens. "You look very comfortable," he says demurely.

"And that is the only reason I'm wearing this blanket. Because I was too comfortable to remove it," I say firmly and he nods, mirth brimming in those deep olive-coloured eyes, his face lit by the last red streaks of sunset.

"Of course." He pauses as the ship starts to move. It's smoother than I'd imagined somehow. He stares at me. "Why were you waving at nobody and muttering under your breath? Is there some history of mental instability I should know about in my position as your carer?"

"I think the mental instability is proved by my presence on this cruise," I say sourly. I gesture at the dock. "No, I was waving at those people. They started off friendly but then they started getting a bit frenetic. Reminded me of when Niall met Geri Halliwell." He laughs and I smile reluctantly. "They just kept waving and shit. Very enthusiastic. Do you think the ship pays them to wave bon voyage to passengers?"

He looks over at the dock and blanches. "They're not waving

farewell to passengers. They *are* passengers," he says, squinting at them. "I think they've missed the ship."

"Why didn't they say something?" I sigh. "Are correct diction and volume something that we now have to train people in?" However, it's to empty air as he rushes off, muttering something about telling the staff.

I shake my head and snuggle back down under my blanket and go back to watching the sea slide past.

CHAPTER 4

If you're that keen to live so close to the edge I could always do a few wheelies

Eli

The next morning I knock on the door of Gideon's room and stick my head around it, inhaling the spicy vanilla scent that seems to permeate the room. "Rise and shine," I say cheerfully.

The figure on the bed buried under a mass of blankets stirs. "Fuck off," he grumbles and burrows under the pillow.

"Tsk tsk." I wander over to the window and press the button to raise the blinds. Light floods into the room and Gideon jerks like I've tasered him.

"What the fuck?" he says, sitting upright. The covers fall to his waist and I know I'm looking at a sight that people would pay to see in the flesh. Gideon Ramsay half naked, the white covers showing off the swarthy tones of his skin and his sleek chest. His grey eyes are blazing and his hair is sticking up as if he's stuck his finger in a light socket and kept it there for a few days. My lip twitches and he scowls.

"It's not funny."

"Maybe a little," I say cheerfully and wander over to the wardrobes and fling back the doors. I blink at the meagre contents. "You have no clothes."

He huffs and throws himself back on the bed, scrubbing his hands down his face. "I left them in the hotel."

"Do you want me to arrange to have them shipped?" I say instantly. I feel antsy this morning. Gideon isn't so ill that he needs me all the time. He was up in the night coughing and I made him a hot lemon drink and sat until his cough calmed, but I'm not on the brink of action all the time the way I've been with other clients. Gideon doesn't seem at the risk of dying from a drug overdose or old age, which are my usual parameters. He's just perennially grumpy. I smile as I look back at him.

He opens his eyes and shakes his head. "No. I'll just buy more." He shrugs. "It's what I normally do."

"You leave your clothes behind when you move hotels and buy more at your next stop?" At his nod I whistle incredulously. "That's a bit Marie Antoinette, isn't it? Only with stubble and a head," I finish hesitantly as he looks like he's brewing for a temper tantrum. To my astonishment he laughs.

"I suppose so. I never understood the cake business myself. I'd have suggested a cheese board."

I laugh. "They'd have rioted a lot sooner if you were in charge and gave them Boursin."

He grins. "That's an absolutely horrendous French accent. Okay, you have my attention. Why are you waking me up at this ungodly hour?"

"It's eight o'clock," I say. "Sun's been up for ages."

"Oh God, you're one of those disgusting people who loves the morning, aren't you?"

"Yep," I say unrepentantly. "And you're going to turn into one as well." He shoots me a disbelieving look and I nod confidently. "I've woken you up so we can have breakfast and then we're due on deck at nine."

"Are we walking the plank?" he asks hopefully.

"Only you would think that was an improvement on a luxury cruise," I say tartly. "No, we have to attend the safety lecture."

"Can't you go and take notes for me?"

"No. The captain requires all passengers." I look at his wardrobe again. "And then I think we'd better see what clothes shops there are on the ship because I'm pretty sure this isn't a clothing-optional cruise."

Gideon folds his arms, looking entertained. "They have those?"

I nod. "One of my patients went on one a couple of years ago."

He grins. "And did you?"

"*No*," I say, scandalised. "I'm a very relaxed person normally, but I can't be a nurse naked. How can I administer medicine with my penis swinging in the air? That would be terrible." He looks like he might argue but I shake my head. "It was a very stressful trip. My patient was ninety. I spent the entire time terrified he was going to have a heart attack."

He throws his head back and laughs merrily, and I look at him surreptitiously as I move to pick up his robe. He looks a different man when he laughs. All the discontent and moodiness vanishes and his whole face lights up with a huge smile.

I dismiss the thought and chuck his robe at him. "Come on. What do you want for breakfast? We'll eat in the suite this morning, but I think once you start to feel better we should eat at one of the restaurants."

"It's like being with Gillian McKeith, but bossier," he says.

I laugh. "Shower and meet me in the lounge. I'll listen to your chest then. I've got your medicine all set up."

An hour later I wheel him down the corridor, the expensive carpet muffling the sound of my footsteps but not his whinging.

"I am perfectly capable of walking to the deck."

"I don't think so," I say in a singsong voice. "The fact that you were swaying by the time you reached the door makes that a big old fib."

"That was just my muscles gearing up for exercise," he says glibly and I snort.

"Okay. You're the expert." I pause. "I'm sorry that I had to stop you fainting. If you're that keen to live so close to the edge I could always do a few wheelies."

"The only edge I want to be close to is the deck when I throw myself off this bloody cruise ship," he grumbles. He cranes his head to look at me. "You can do wheelies?"

I nod. "I'm a professional. I can do anything."

"Well, we'll let your natural arrogance light the way forward," he says somewhat snippily.

I wheel him into the waiting lift and hum happily as the door closes and it goes up.

He shoots me a glare. "Are you doing that on purpose?"

"What?"

He gestures. "Being all cheerful and stuff."

"It's my natural state of being," I say solemnly, enjoying the way he hides a smile.

I'm coming to know him a little. Gideon is bored. He's surrounded by people who do as he says. He needs clapback to keep him entertained. I've heard him being described in the press as a complete bastard, but I've had the real thing as patients in the past. Gideon isn't a bastard. He's clever and quick-witted and bored.

Once we're outside, I lift my face to the breeze and inhale. "What are you doing?" he asks curiously.

"I love mornings at sea. The sunshine and the sea wind. Makes everything fresh like the world's been through the washer overnight."

I flush slightly as I open my eyes and find him staring at me, but he nods. "That's a nice way to look at it," he says somewhat grudgingly.

I bite my lip and push him quickly towards the back of the small crowd that has gathered around the staff member a few feet away who is talking earnestly about lifeboats and lifejackets. I park the wheelchair and push the brake down next to an old lady in a wheelchair. She's staring at the steward doing the talk with a slightly jaundiced air while a young man who's obviously her nurse leans on the back of the wheelchair and gazes around.

When we come up next to them he shoots me a quick glance and then stands up straight. At first I think he's recognised Gideon and my heart sinks, but then I notice the way he's looking at me like I'm breakfast.

"Hello," he says breathily. "I haven't seen you before."

Gideon snorts, but when I look down, he's facing forward and my old baseball cap is hiding his distinctive features.

"We just got in last night," I mumble, and the steward doing the talk sighs loudly.

"For the benefit of those who have just joined us, I'll go through that bit again. In the very unlikely occasion of the ship running into trouble, these lifeboats here will be yours. You will assemble here ready for us to disembark in an orderly fashion."

The old people around us nod eagerly, apart from the lady next to Gideon who sighs loudly as if she's dying of boredom. Dressed in pink trousers and a bright pink and blue kaftan and with her white hair coiled in a bun, she looks flamboyantly expensive. Like a flamingo.

"But darling, that's just not true," she drawls in a cut-glass accent. "If we get in a lifeboat and the ship goes down, it's highly likely that the lifeboats will all be sucked down with it in the vortex that it creates."

Several old ladies shriek and the group's noise level rings with worry as everyone turns back to shout questions at the steward, who immediately looks rather hunted. Everyone apart from Gideon. I sigh as he looks in fascination at the old lady as if he's found his soulmate.

"What an interesting perspective," he says happily.

"It's the truth," she says, waving her arms about cavalierly. "It's just designed to keep the surface appearances of normality working. Underneath is just chaos and death." I stare at her open-mouthed as she rummages in her bag and produces a hip flask. "Drink, darling?" she says brightly.

Gideon opens his mouth but I lean forward into her vision. "No, he won't, thank you," I say politely. "He's on medication."

"I'm sure it won't hurt," Gideon says, eyeing the hip flask like it's made of gold.

"I'm sure it will," I say firmly. I grin at the old lady. "It was a nice gesture."

"Oh, you're Welsh," she says happily, her voice carrying in that way that very posh people have. "I had a Welsh man once. Divine man," she says thoughtfully. "But he had an absolutely humungous penis. Far too big. Like he got his own ration and another couple of people's too."

The sharp intake of breath from everyone around is drowned out by Gideon's laughter. "I need to discuss this further," he says happily and she grins.

They start to talk and her nurse nudges closer to me. "I'm Oliver," he says throatily. I smile and introduce myself. He's a very pretty man. Small and slender, with tanned skin and dark hair that's been brushed until it lies sleekly against his skull. However, there's something off-puttingly perfect looking about him compared to my own scruffiness. "She's quite batty," he says, looking over at his patient. "But not really any trouble." He looks at her hip flask. "Yet," he finishes somewhat doubtfully.

I laugh and he edges closer. "It's nice to see someone my own age on here. I thought the trip was going to be very boring." He shrugs, running his eyes over my crotch so thoroughly that I feel like cupping my groin to protect it. "We'll have to get together and have a drink sometime."

"Maybe," I say noncommittally. "It'll depend on my patient, of course."

"Of course," he echoes with no conviction at all. He looks idly at Gideon and then stands bolt upright as if he's been shocked. "That's Gideon Ramsay," he whispers.

"No, it isn't," I say immediately. He stares at me and I slump. "Okay, it is him. But you need to not mention that," I say firmly. "He needs peace and privacy."

"I think he'll be fine," he says, his eyes running avidly over Gideon. "Considering the age range of people on here, they won't know him unless he was in a film with Charlton Heston in his pre-NRA days."

"Hmm." I don't like the way that he's looking at Gideon, so I edge forward slightly, blocking his gaze in a protective manner. I wonder where that's coming from but dismiss it in favour of moving us away. Noticing that the steward has stopped talking, I disengage the brake on the wheelchair. "Well, we must be going," I say cheerfully. "We've got some stuff to do, haven't we, sir?"

"*Have* we?" Gideon sounds astonished but he catches my glare and subsides, though not before shooting me an incredulous look. "Sir? Well, Eli, that's very polite of you."

I shake my head. "We should be going," I murmur.

He obliges with a slightly suspicious manner, raising the lady's hand to his mouth to kiss and saying goodbye in a low voice.

As we move away he twists to look at me. "Is there a reason why we're leaving them like they've got the clap in a brothel?"

An older lady passing us gasps and I send her an apologetic look. "Sorry," I mutter. "He's not well."

She shoots him a look like she's expecting him to combust and scuttles off.

"The other nurse recognised you," I say as I wheel him through the crowds milling outside the shopping area.

"So? That happens all the time."

"I know it does – for you – but you need peace to get well."

He shoots me an inscrutable look. "That's very nice of you but there's no need, Eli. It's part of the business. There isn't much peace."

He faces forward and conversation lapses. I wonder if I've done wrong but dismiss it. I don't believe in looking for problems. If I've made a mistake, I'm sure he'll tell me. I wheel him determinedly towards an expensive-looking menswear shop that he points out like a very grumpy captain.

Two hours later I drop down onto the sofa in the suite and groan. "Jesus, that's two hours of my life that I won't get back."

He lowers himself onto the other side of the sectional. "I thought you'd have more stamina."

I open one eye. "For surfing, running, or dancing I have lots of stamina. Shopping, not at all."

"Yes, I got that with the constant sighing. It got so bad the sales assistant thought a window was open."

My lips twitch. "I just can't understand it," I admit, rolling onto one side and finding him looking at me.

"Shopping?" I nod and he smiles. "I like shopping. Particularly for clothes."

"I don't mind it, but I tend to get everything from Top Man."

Gideon makes a moue of disgust as if I've admitted shopping in a shithole.

I open my mouth to say something else but my phone buzzes. I look down at it and sigh. "My mum. Is it okay if I take this?"

He looks amazed. "Of course it is. You're not a prisoner of my whims." I raise my eyebrow and he grins. "Okay, you might be a bit." He waves his hand. "Go on and answer it. I'm going to ring for a drink and sit outside."

"No alcohol," I say, hesitating over my still-ringing phone.

"No, of course not. It's like sharing a suite with the Salvation Army."

I nod and, palming my phone, I move into my room and shut the door. "Hi, Mum," I say.

"Eli, how are you? Where are you?"

"Well, I'm currently onboard a cruise ship travelling around Italy and France and I'm fine. How's Dad?"

"He's busy. I haven't seen him in a couple of days. He's been sleeping at the hospital."

In any other marriage that might have been a cause for concern, but my parents are both surgeons and totally married to their jobs even though they love each other. I'd grown up knowing very firmly where I stood in the pecking order. First was patients, second was my mum and dad's relationship, third was appropriate schooling for me, fourth was the managing of their expectations of me, and finally fifth would be me. Maybe. At the end of the day. If there was a window of opportunity.

I don't want to sound bitter because I love my mum and dad. I had a very lovely childhood and wanted for nothing. But still, all our interactions were clouded by the weight of their expectations. Everything was about getting me into the best schools and socialising with the right people.

My strong desire to do the exact opposite of what they wanted every time bemused them, and needless to say when I left medical school and enrolled in a local nursing college it had come as a complete disappointment to them, to the extent that my dad refused to pay for my tuition fees any longer if I wasn't going to be a doctor.

But I'd been determined and had managed to work two jobs while attending nursing school. Even then he'd somehow seemed to view my actions as being purely an opportunity to thwart him and embarrass him in front of his high-achieving friends.

As if on cue, my mother says blithely, "Before I forget, I met Alan Fraser at a party the other night. His son Robert is in his second year of med school. He's hoping to specialise in orthopaedic surgery."

"Well, he'll never be short of patients," I say cheerfully while sighing inside.

I wander over to the window and peek out on my side view of the deck where I can see Gideon dressed in the khaki shorts and chambray short-sleeved shirt that he just bought. He's basking in the sunshine with a very expensive pair of Ray-Bans perched on the end of his long blade of a nose. He also appears to be looking at some papers which flap blindingly white in the sunshine. I make a mental note to whip them away if Frankie gave him some work. He's supposed to be having a complete rest.

My mother hesitates and I rub my nose, waiting for it. "You know, Alan said he could find you a place. He's on the board."

"Is that how Robert got in? Because I remember him in anatomy, and his complete ignorance of the human body might be a teeny problem if he's operating on someone's hip thinking it's their foot."

He couldn't find my prostate with a map and a torch either, but I keep that information to myself.

"Oh, Eli, don't take the mickey. Robert is a lovely young man. Very ambitious." *Unlike my son* is the unspoken narrative.

"Well, I wish him all the best," I say lightly. "I'm sure he'll turn out just like his father."

It definitely isn't a compliment, but my mother of course takes it as one. "I hope so. Alan is *so* proud of him."

Unlike my father, who hasn't spoken to me in six months and shows no sign of having any desire to break this run.

"Well, it was lovely to talk to you," I say brightly. "But I've got to go, Mum. My patient needs me."

"Oh really." She laughs dismissively. "What is it this time? Another celebrity recovering from an overdose or someone taking a fat cure?"

"Mum, they may not have the same needs as your patients, but they are still human beings."

She laughs. "I'll take your word for it. Now, what are you doing for your birthday? I know it's a few weeks away, but we could have a party for you at the club."

"I'll be working," I say quickly. Or cutting my toenails. Either seems more important than attending their tennis club.

"Okay, sweetie. I'll ring in a few days."

"Love you," I say, knowing she'll forget and suddenly call me in a few months when she remembers. It's been the constant theme of our interactions.

I end the call and walk outside, happier now that it's done.

It's hot outside, but the sea breeze is refreshing, and I note with satisfaction that Gideon has some colour on his thin cheeks. His skin looks the type to tan easily, but I still point at him. "Have you got cream on?" I say.

"Yes, Mother," he says irritably. "I've also moved my bowels and wiped my nose."

"Hope you washed your hands in between."

He snorts and shoots me a lightning-quick glance. "You okay?"

"Yes, why?" I ask, amazed.

He shrugs, looking slightly awkward. "You look a bit tense."

"I do?" I immediately want to check my reflection in a mirror because usually I cover everything up with a professional manner.

"Your shoulders are tight," he says dismissively. "I'm an actor. I read body language."

"I'm a nurse. I do it too. For instance, you have very much wanted to tell me to fuck off every time I've told you not to do something over the last two days."

"That is *not* reading body language. It's just listening to me because I very clearly have actually said fuck off."

"Silly me," I say, slinging myself down into the chair next to him and tilting my face up to the sun. "Can't keep a thought in my head for more than a second." I shoot a glance at the jug of clear liquid on the table next to him, which is frosty with condensation running down it. "Is that vodka?"

He laughs. "How very fortunate that this thought was the one that bucked the trend. No, it's fucking water, Mary Whitehouse, because Peter seems to be obeying all your orders now."

"As he should," I say comfortably. "Give in to my authority, Gideon. You know you want to."

He shakes his head, and the papers on his lap flap in the sea breeze as if the wind wants to snatch them away and only the firm grasp of his long thin fingers is stopping it. "That had better not be work," I observe.

He makes a moue of disgust. "Yes, I notice that the script Frankie sneaked to me is unaccountably missing from my room. It's a mystery."

"Not really," I say serenely. "I took it."

"It's like living with a fucking prison warder. Why?"

"Because you need to rest and recover and you can't do that if you're hyped up and focusing on work. In case you're wondering, I've also instructed Peter not to put through calls from Frankie. If he rings on your mobile I'd like you to pass him to me because he was told very explicitly by your doctor that he was to leave you alone."

"How explicit? Did he carve it on a cheque? Because that's the only thing Frankie pays attention to."

I shake my head. "What a pearl amongst men."

Gideon shrugs. "He is what I need, I suppose."

"Frankenstein's monster had more charm."

He laughs. "And definitely better taste in clothes."

I look at the papers. "So, if that's not work, what is it?"

"Your CV." He flutters the pages. "It's very informative."

For some strange reason I want to snatch it away from him, and my body actually tenses to do it. Why, I don't know, because this is my employer. He more than anyone should know what my CV says. Gideon's gaze sharpens, and I make myself relax. "Scandalous reading."

He grins wickedly. "I had to read it one-handed."

I shake my head and can't stop the laughter. Then I sober. "Well, I suppose you never actually got to interview me. Any questions?"

He looks at the pages and fans them out in his hand. "No," he says almost hesitantly. "It's very impressive, actually."

"You sound surprised." I laugh. "Rather like my parents who think all I do is wipe rich people's arses."

"Tell me you aren't going to be doing that for me?" he asks in a horrified voice.

"No, mate," I drawl. "Not unless you ask me nicely."

"That will never happen," he vows. He pauses. "Don't your

parents approve of your job?"

"They're surgeons."

"So? How does that impact? You're in the same profession."

"Not in the same pay bracket or with the same responsibility. It's like comparing a milkman with the owner of a big dairy company."

Gideon shrugs. "If the world were made up of surgeons we'd all just have a lot of stitches and probably far fewer internal organs."

I laugh and, to my amazement, I lean forward and talk honestly. "I was in medical school training to be a doctor when I decided that I wanted to be a nurse. They hate it with a passion. They think I'm wasting my talents and opportunities."

"If I'd abided by that way of thinking I'd be working on *Coronation Street*." I smile, and he carries on. "So, when you went to work for the Red Cross at twenty-three they weren't impressed?"

He sounds amazed, and something about that honest and abrupt reaction soothes a little of my rough spot over this. I shake my head. "Nope, because working with foreign people isn't as financially rewarding as private practice." I shrug. "I didn't care. That was what I'd dreamt of doing, and as soon as I qualified I was off. I had a couple of very adventurous years. My parents were horrified. Although my dad did like to brag about it at parties. I think he made me out to be a bit 'who dares, wins.'"

"Who dares gets shot, more like it," Gideon muses. I flinch and he looks startled. "Oh my God, were you?"

I nod. "It's not a totally safe job. It wasn't aimed at me, but I was administering medical aid to a man and I got in the way of the gunfire."

"Where were you shot?"

I fight back a grin. "Afghanistan."

He sighs in a long-suffering manner. "I mean where on your body were you shot, smart-arse?"

I gesture at my shoulder. "Clean through, luckily, but it destroyed complete movement and shattered the bone. I had to have a lot of physiotherapy."

"And then what?" He stares at me, his sunglasses down so I can see the cool grey of his eyes.

"And then I started this," I say lightly. "An ex of mine was doing it at the time and he got me a job. I never looked back. And put it this way, for excitement there isn't much that happens in this job that can rival being shot."

"I'll try and think of something to entertain you," he says solemnly. "How about if I maim someone?"

"Only if it's Frankie."

Gideon laughs but then sobers. "Do you miss it?"

I consider that. It seems weird to think of it now, like it happened to someone else a long time ago. "At first I did. I tried to go back, but I'd been out too long, and I think I'd have been a liability if anything happened. So, I settled for safety." I wonder if that comes across as ashamed, because sometimes that's how I feel.

"Did you have therapy?"

I nod. "Lots of it." I smile at him. "Don't worry. If gunfire breaks out on ship, I'll be okay."

"I think that might happen if they run out of scones. The older people this morning seemed inordinately concerned with getting back to the bakery." I laugh and he hesitates. "I'm sorry," he says. "I'm sorry that part of your life came to a stop."

"Just that part," I say, becoming caught in the troubled depths of his gaze. "I'd like to think there's other and better times ahead."

He doesn't mutter platitudes like everyone else would have done. He doesn't say he's sure I have better things ahead of me. Instead, he just nods and shrugs and goes back to looking out to sea. It's strangely refreshing and somehow more comforting than anything anyone else has said. Like fresh air blowing away the fugue of a party and making my brain clear again.

We sit in a contented silence until finally he huffs and hands me a tube of sun cream with an air of defeat.

"I *knew* you didn't have it on," I say delightedly.

"Shut up," he mutters.

CHAPTER 5

After breakfast I might push Eli overboard and then this afternoon I'm going to macramé myself a new nurse

---

A Few Days Later

Gideon

I hear his footsteps outside the bedroom door and grimace at the fact that my heart rate has just picked up. I hope he's not expecting to take my pulse because that could be embarrassing.

There's the customary soft tap on the door and then I hear his Welsh lilt. "Good morning. It's a lovely morning." He pauses. "Oh, you're awake already."

I'm sure I'm not imagining the note of disappointment in his voice. He appears to enjoy winding me up just as much as I enjoy him doing it. He crosses the room, and I shoot my gaze quickly down his body. He's dressed in three-quarter-length grey cuffed leggings with a white stripe down the sides and a white vest which shows off his golden skin and the bulge of his biceps. His hair has been pulled back into a stubby topknot that highlights those clear olive-coloured eyes and high cheekbones.

He looks over at me, and I immediately fold my arms. "I couldn't possibly sleep with the anticipation coursing through my body. What joys have you decided on today for my delectation, Eli? More line dancing or maybe some more of that lovely class in napkin decoration?"

He grins, going over to the blinds and raising them. "You can't tell me you didn't enjoy it."

"Eli, I have never folded a fucking napkin in my life and I never will. My dates don't get dinner. I fuck them and send them home."

He pauses in opening my wardrobe door, his brow creased in thought. "I'm sure there's a napkin fold that's been created with that message."

I shake my head. "So what's in store for the middle of the night?"

"It's six o'clock in the morning," he scoffs.

"The only way I see six o'clock in the morning is when I'm coming home to go to bed."

"Well, Mick Jagger, that wild way of life is over for the moment, so instead we've got wake-the-day meditation."

"Did you just compare me to a rock star who looks like a raisin on a pair of legs?" I blink. "Wake-the-day *meditation*," I say in a tone of absolute disgust. "What the fuck is that? Am I to be responsible for the sun coming up on this ship too?"

Eli tosses a bundle of clothes at me. "I'm sorry to interrupt your messianic leanings," he says, not at all apologetically. "Put those on and hurry up. We'll have breakfast afterwards."

I look down at the tight, grey marl, full-length leggings and black vest in dismay. "Surely there must be something else we can do?" I say, and I can hear the desperation in my voice. "My brother's the spiritual yoga person in our family."

He stops and looks at me curiously. "Is he? Is he any good?"

"Very," I say, hearing the pride in my voice. "He teaches a class in the village now."

"That's an accomplishment for him, I think."

I peer at him. "He had a stutter," I say. "You could probably hear a trace of it in the way he speaks now."

He nods. "It must have been nice having you as a brother."

I wince. "Not really," I mutter, feeling his interest sharpen, but he doesn't ask me any questions. His infuriating lack of pushing for answers always makes me want to knock him over the fucking head with them. "I was a terrible brother," I admit. "I was away at boarding school anyway, but when I was at home I was impatient with him and distant. I'm trying now, though," I finish earnestly. "I want a relationship with him."

"You must be doing something right," Eli says in a mellow voice. "He obviously loves you."

"That's family. You can't help that," I scoff. Nevertheless, I feel a relaxing in the tenseness that always surrounds me when I think of the mess I made of the relationship with my brother.

"Not always," he says, and there's a finality in his voice that makes me drop the conversation.

Even though it's early in the morning, there's still a bustle to the ship as staff hose down the outside decks and sort out the bars to the accompaniment of a multitude of languages spoken in bright, eager voices.

I follow Eli up the steps towards the top deck, trying not to stare at his arse in those leggings. It's actually impossible, as if my eyes are magnetized and he's got an iron backside. Nevertheless, I manage to wrench my gaze away from the magnet's pull and that's when I spot it.

"Is that a tattoo on your back?" I ask, looking at the grey lines I can see as his vest shifts.

He looks back, smiling slightly. "It might be. Why?"

"No reason," I immediately say, trying for an air of studied disinterest. By the quirk of his mouth I'm guessing I'm not hitting any acting strides today, so I give up. "I like tattoos," I say instead.

"It is a tattoo," he says. "It's a dragon, which is very stereotypical for a Welsh man. And also stupid because it fucking hurt having something that big over my back." He looks at me. "Have you got any?"

I shake my head. "Nope. It's not really good for an actor."

He comes to a stop, the breeze blowing strands of hair around his clear, unlined forehead. "But loads of actors have got them."

"Now they have. When I started in the business it wasn't encouraged."

He nods seriously. "I guess they were too concerned with introducing sound into films at that point."

For a beat I stare at him and then, to my amazement, laughter bubbles out and I give a disgusting snort. "Yes, damn those pesky talkies."

Eli grins at me happily before turning round and mounting the stairs in his characteristic long-legged strides. I've noticed that he never seems to rush anywhere, but somehow he seems to get to places quicker than anyone else. I follow a bit more slowly, and when I round the deck, I look around curiously.

The sky is a clear, pale blue and there's every sign that it's going to be a scorching-hot day. However, the breeze blowing across the deck has ensured that it's still cool at the moment. Set along the deck are padded mats in bright colours, and a group of people dressed in colourful yoga gear chat happily amongst themselves.

As Eli comes onto the deck, a slender dark-haired woman detaches herself from the group and comes over with a huge smile. "Eli, you came," she exclaims with as much enthusiasm as if Eli were her long-lost brother. "I'm *so* pleased."

My eyes narrow. *When did he meet this woman?*

He grins lazily at her, oblivious to the fact that she's currently eye-fucking him so hard I'll need a cigarette when she finally looks away. "I said I would," he says happily, the Welsh lilt very evident in his early-morning voice.

I shoot him a look of total incomprehension. As far as I know, he's been ensconced in the suite with me for the last few days, insisting that I sleep and relax. Yet every time we've left the cabin since then, people have hailed him left, right, and centre. How is this possible?

I come back to the conversation as Eli pats my arm. "This is Gideon."

I bite my lip because his tone of voice and gestures are currently suggesting that rather than being a famous actor, I am, in fact, a raggedy old sheepdog. She gives me a cursory glance and smiles before returning to eye-fucking my nurse.

I can actually feel my mouth drop open. *I'm not being conceited but... Oh, okay, I am being conceited but goddammit, there aren't many people that overlook me. I'm too famous.* I pause. *Or infamous.* I shrug. *Either fucking way, I'm bloody memorable. Apart from on this fucking ship where my nurse appears to be the headline act.*

I wonder whether I should be annoyed, but I'm far too amused to bother with that, so I stand, trying not to smile as she engages Eli in a very animated conversation while he shoots me occasional glances to check whether I'm okay or if I've died from boredom. Finally, when the group starts shifting about like sheep getting bored, she breaks away from the conversation and heads back to the front of the deck.

I turn to face Eli, leaning my elbows on the rail. "She seems very..." I pause, searching for words. "Very awake."

He starts to laugh. "It's usually better for the back and forth of conversation that both parties are conscious."

I shake my head. "I'm not sure about that. Sometimes I think it would be better for people if they were asleep when I spoke to them. Less chance of them taking offence."

He nods solemnly. "You might be right. Either that or dead." He dodges laughing as I elbow him and mouth "twat" at him.

After he's stopped laughing, I look at him. "She seems keen, though."

He shakes his head. "She's barking up the wrong tree with me."

There's a short pause as he looks at me and I feel my heart start to pound heavily. I swallow. "Why?"

"Because I'm gay," he says calmly. "Hope that isn't a problem."

I marvel at the coolness with which he says that. I wish I could be like him. "Why would it be a problem?" I finally say through a dry throat. Shit! He's gay, which makes him potentially available if it weren't for the small matter of my being his patient and me being, well, me.

"Well, your manager seems to have some rather homophobic views."

"Please don't paint me in the same colours as Frankie. He's only slightly left of Mussolini."

He looks at me and gestures with his hand and I stare at him for an overlong second, wondering for a mad moment whether he's guessed about me and is waiting for me to reciprocate with confession hour. Then he says, "After you," and I realise that the group is all on their mats and waiting for us to sit.

"Sorry," I say to everyone and scoot to the back where two mats are waiting as if they've got our names on them. I settle down and look over at Eli as he sits down on his own.

"What do we do?" I hiss.

He grins at me. "Can you sit cross-legged?"

"If I had a gun to my head."

He snorts. "Well, try pretending." He winks. "Try and act. If you can."

I shake my head, trying to ignore the piss-taking twat and not show him my grin, but I know he's spotted it. I stare ahead at the woman who introduces herself as Kim.

"Welcome everyone," she says in a tranquil voice which quite frankly strikes me as rather sinister. "We'll start with everyone getting comfortable. If you can sit cross-legged, great. If you can't, then come to a comfortable position that makes you happy."

I try not to think of the position that makes me most happy and purse my lips, but Eli shakes his head at me. "Smut," he mouths. I watch as he crosses his legs as easily as if he does it every second of the day.

It takes me a few longer seconds to get comfortable, and he's grinning by the time I've finished. "Shut up," I mutter. "I've just got very long legs."

"And a very intractable body," he observes. "I think there's a deep meaning in that."

I shake my head. "You've only been here five minutes and you already sound like Yogi Bear."

He wrinkles his forehead. "I'm not sure Yogi Bear actually did yoga."

"Ssh," I say reprovingly. "The plinky plonky music has started."

Some sort of music plays which is supposed to be relaxing, but instead just reminds me of the time in primary school when Niall was determined to learn the xylophone.

"Okay," Kim says happily. "Close your eyes, straighten your back, and raise the crown of your head so it salutes the sky."

I try to do as she asks, but now I'm imagining an enormous hand coming out of my head and waving at the clouds. It's rather disconcerting, and I sneak a peek at Eli only to find him looking serene and a mirror image to Kim's posture.

"Once you've done this, try to find a place where your body and mind come to stillness. A calm place within you."

Oh dear. I don't think I actually have one of those. I wonder if I'm faulty. Eli opens his eyes and I immediately assume an expression of serene contemplation. Anyone else would believe me. He just looks like he wants to laugh. I grimace at him and turn back to Kim.

"Take a deep breath in through your nose, filling your lungs as much as you can, and exhale through your mouth," she says. Everyone immediately makes a loud sound and I dismiss the idea of doing that in case it sets me off on the road to coughing up one of my lungs, which would not grant anyone any serenity at all.

Unfortunately, because of my inability to breathe through my nostrils and mouth, I seem to miss most of the point of the class as, for the next hour, Kim exhorts us to breathe.

"How are you doing?" Eli whispers.

"Well, I think I must be some sort of genius," I say modestly. "I must surely belong in the advanced class because I already know how to breathe."

He bites his lip before giving out a soft snort. "Just go along with it."

"I can't," I whisper. "She's asking me to breathe, so I can get to my special place."

"What's the problem with that?"

"Well, I don't think I can get to my special place by breathing. It usually takes buying someone a few rounds of drinks and getting a hotel room first."

He starts to laugh but smothers it quickly when Kim glares at him.

"She's not as serene as she appears," I warn him. "I bet she's hell on wheels if your chakras are out by even a millimetre."

He shakes his head. "I really don't think you should be allowed to talk about anything to do with spiritual serenity."

"I think you might be right," I say gloomily, putting my hand on my chest and the other hand on my stomach as she directs, resisting the opportunity to try and rub both at the same time like I'm at school again.

After another torturous few minutes of being exhorted to breathe through my nostrils, Kim stirs.

"Well done, everyone. Thank yourself for sitting down on your mat and starting the day properly."

"Starting the day properly?" I say in a low voice to Eli. "That's a bit judgemental. At the end of the day, I just sat and breathed. If I thanked myself every time I did that I'd never have time for doing anything I actually enjoyed."

"I think we might have hit upon the point of meditation for you," he says dryly, waving at Kim and saying thank you before moving towards the steps.

"Food," he says happily as we start down the stairs.

"I have an ominous feeling that this isn't going to go my way either," I say dourly.

"Probably," he says cheerfully, leading me along the deck and exchanging more happy greetings with complete strangers.

The restaurant he chooses isn't busy at this time in the morning, which is why I let him steer me to a table by the huge plate-glass window without too many protests while he goes to grab the food.

I look out of the window at the sea sparkling in the early morning sunshine. I'll never let him know, but I've discovered a peace in sitting and watching the world go by. The sea changes all the time just the way he said it did, and I find myself drifting in my thoughts for hours, sitting in a puddle of sunshine and quiet.

Today we're in port, as the ship mainly sails at night, and I watch a cluster of men on the dock gesturing at each other over stacked boxes. I run my finger over the table absently and look down at the card there. It's the same card that is pushed under our door every night, listing the day's events onboard. Eli always seizes it like it's got the winning lottery numbers printed on it somewhere. I marvel at the list. There are more activities on here than if they were in Tudor England catering for Henry the Eighth. I look a bit closer and grimace. And I wouldn't want to do any one of them. Fucking line dancing.

A tray is set down in front of me on the table, and I look up at him. "Why are we fetching our own food? This is a very expensive cruise, not the Welcome Break service station."

"Why are you using the word *we*? You didn't fetch anything."

I huff. "Point taken." I peer at the dishes. "So, what did you bring for me?" I can actually feel my nose wrinkle. "That looks like hamster food, which even in this service-station-like atmosphere I can't believe they'd serve. Which would make it ..." I pause and glare at him. "Muesli."

"That's right," he says cheerfully. "Muesli with Greek yoghurt and honey. It's a great way to start the day."

"Only if the alternative to starting the day is vomiting all over the table."

A lady who is just starting to sit down at the next table gives me a death glare and moves to another table with a great deal of dramatic posturing. Eli bites his lips as if repressing a smile. A smile or a grimace.

"You need to start eating healthily." He looks me up and down. "Or at all."

Is he saying I'm too thin? I sit up a bit straighter. I'm known for my fucking body, and he's looking at me like I'm one of the fucking Chuckle Brothers. "I didn't get this body without a lot of work," I say tartly. "It's the body of a Greek god."

"Well, give it back and settle into the body of a thirty-nine-year-old whose cholesterol needs sorting out," he says placidly, unaffected by my posturing, as usual.

I subside and drag the bowl towards me sulkily. Glaring at him, I raise a spoonful to my mouth. *Oh my God, it's fucking lovely.* The tartness of the yoghurt and the sweetness of the honey along with the muesli are gorgeous. Using all my acting talents, I keep my face expressionless and lower the spoon. "It's okay," I say grudgingly.

"That good, eh?" he says cheerfully.

I glare at him as I notice what he's eating. "That's fucking bacon and eggs."

"Yep," he says happily. "It's well lush too."

"Doesn't your nursing gene make it impossible to be so cruel to your patients? Surely it's against nature?"

"No, because nature also gave us patients like you," he says earnestly. "So, it balances the universe."

I can't stop my laughter, but it dies when I reach for my cup. "Is this fucking tea?" I hiss. "Where's my coffee?"

"It's over there where it can't harm your blood pressure. You drink far too much of the stuff. That's green tea. It's an antioxidant."

"I'm sure that's what they put in laundry detergent."

"And you would know that, how?" Eli asks, humming around his fork of food.

I stop my smile just in time. God, I love sparring with this man. I haven't had anyone interest me like this in – I pause to think – forever.

He pushes the event list towards me. "Pick something to do today."

"Can't we go ashore?" I say longingly, looking at the dock and thinking of being back on firm ground and not surrounded by people all the time. Maybe sitting in a pretty café and having a beer. That's if Nurse Ratched would let me within a mile of fucking alcohol.

"Nope," he says, popping the "p" quite obnoxiously. "Not yet. You're not back to full strength yet."

I look down at the list. "Jesus, what a mix," I say meditatively, taking a sip of tea and nearly spitting it out. "This is bloody disgusting."

"Drink it," Eli says serenely. "Or I'll make you join the crochet club this afternoon."

"If they'll teach me how to crochet an escape ladder, I'll go gladly." I look down at the list. "Ann Widdecombe and Terry Waite are both on this ship doing talks. What a strange mixture." I shake my head. "Poor sod. After a week on here he'll be wishing he were still tied to a radiator."

His snort of laughter is drowned out by a loud "hello."

We look up to find the old lady called Constance, who I met yesterday, and her nurse whose name I completely forget. He's wheeling her towards me with a put-upon air. I look at her and my mouth quirks. She's wearing red silk trousers with a green and gold shirt and her long white hair has been neatly plaited. She looks like a very expensive tropical bird. She also appears to be drinking a cocktail.

"When I'm her age I want to be just like her," I whisper to Eli.

"Behaviour-wise, I'd say you haven't got that far to go," he says placidly, smiling at the other nurse in a welcoming fashion that makes my eyes narrow.

"Gideon, darling," Constance flutes, waving her cocktail glass at me and narrowly avoiding spilling it. "Fancy seeing you up so early. I must say you're really spoiling my image of actors, sweetheart. I thought they were up all night having wild sex parties and proclaiming Donne."

"That's in a world not ruled by Eli Jones," I say smoothly. "His official title is Despoiler of Fun."

"I might have that put on my business cards," he says meditatively. "Besides, I think you'd be far too noisy proclaiming anything."

"I'll have you know that people pay a lot of money for me to read their work. I could do the telephone directory and they'd buy it."

"That's lovely, then," he says in a manner more suited to a nanny for a toddler than a nurse.

I open my mouth but shut it with a snap as Constance's nurse throws himself down in a chair at our table.

"Do join us," I say silkily, but he ignores me. Apparently, once you require a nurse, you automatically have the relevance of a Teletubby.

"Eli," he purrs, looking like he's thinking of gnawing my nurse's face off. "You look gorgeous."

"I do?" Eli looks down at his outfit then up at me.

"Don't look at me," I say sniffily. "I can't see your outfit for the impression of Napoleon that you're currently doing."

His lips twitch. "It's muesli, Gideon, not a political coup." He turns to the nurse. "Thank you, Oliver, that's a nice thing to say."

Ah, Oliver. That's his name. I study him while he simpers over my nurse. He's good-looking, I suppose, but if you ask me, his eyes are too close together and his hair is ridiculous.

"Darling, you look absolutely murderous," Constance proclaims, passing me her glass. I go to lift it, but Eli circumvents me by removing it from my hand and putting it on a nearby table. He pushes my tea towards me, and I turn to her.

"I prefer creatively murderous. It sounds more artistic."

"What are you doing today?" she asks, giving me a lopsided grin. I bet she was lethal as a young woman, because even now she has a raffish daredevil charm to her.

"Oh well, after breakfast I might push Eli overboard and then this afternoon I'm going to macramé myself a new nurse."

Eli snorts. "I hope it's not as bad as your napkin-arranging attempt. You'll end up with Jabba the Hutt."

"Who's probably more charming than you and who will more than likely let me have alcohol."

We grin at each other until Oliver clears his throat. "It's so nice to see a nurse get on with his patient so well," he observes.

It doesn't exactly sound like a compliment, and I watch as Eli's cheeks flush.

"I do get on with him," I say sharply, driven to stand up for him for some godforsaken reason. "He's not an imbecile like so many other people are."

Oliver looks like he's thinking hard, so I leave him to it, giving Eli a half smile of encouragement to ignore the catty twat.

He stares at me for a second with something working on his normally open, kind face. Then Oliver puts a hand on his arm and drags his attention away.

Constance moves into me. "What a little turd he is," she says. "Always on the lookout for trouble and the opportunity to bitch." She huffs. "And he can't pilot a wheelchair for love nor money. Richard Burton once rode past me on a bike while he was drunk, and he still had more balance and spatial awareness than my nurse."

I smile and stare at her as she shifts in her wheelchair. "You okay?"

She waves her hand casually. "Fine, fine. Just tweaked my back a bit last night doing the limbo."

I blink. "How did you manage that with a broken ankle?"

"Oh, I got a steward to hold the pole up. It's the spirit of the thing that's important, not the execution."

"Tell Eli that about my medication," I say sourly. "He's got more alarms going off in the suite than the headquarters at MI5." I smile at her. "How did you break your ankle anyway, if that's not too personal a question?"

She grins impishly. "I'd like to say something dashing, but unfortunately I tripped on the kerb in Tesco's."

"Eli, when's your time off?" Oliver's voice is loud and clear, and Constance and I look up.

"Time off?" Eli echoes.

Oliver laughs. "Yes, of course. Time off. When do you have it?"

I narrow my eyes. He hasn't had any, and I can't believe I've missed it.

"Whenever he likes," I say evenly. Eli sends me a surprised look, and I look awkwardly back. "You can take time whenever you fancy."

"I don't need to…" Eli starts to say but he's interrupted by Oliver.

"Excellent. Why don't we go out tomorrow? The ship will be in Cannes. I know a lovely beach there." He nudges Eli. "Naked," he says in a loud whisper.

"Oh, I don't know about that," Eli starts to say, looking slightly alarmed, but Oliver shakes his head.

"Of course you can," he says in a syrupy voice that has a steely tone to it. "Mr Ramsay will be fine and really we need time away from our patients or we lose our joie de vivre."

"I don't think you ever packed yours, darling," Constance says, but I look at Eli and something twists in my stomach.

Is that going to happen to Eli? I know myself, and I'm bloody hard work. I've had many people tell me over the years. I'm grumpy and irritable, and I don't suffer fools gladly. I'm also thirty-nine and a closeted actor. I look terrible at the moment, which was the only plus point to my character that I had.

He's good-looking, funny, kind, and brave, as I now know from his CV. Am I sapping the life from him? I thought he was enjoying himself with me sparring and snarking, but maybe I'm wrong. Maybe he's being kind to his patient and humouring me while he counts down the time until he gets paid and can leave.

I go hot and cold with the thought and can feel myself retreating like a tortoise into my shell. "Of course you must go," I say quickly, hearing the strain in my voice. So does Eli, from the look of it, because his eyes widen, and he looks suddenly flustered.

"I'm not sure about that, Mr Ramsay," he says with a quick look at Oliver who is staring at me like a cat with a mouse. "You might need me."

My phone beeps and I look down at it to bide myself some time. I read the message which is like a lifeline.

"No need to worry," I say heartily. "A friend is visiting tomorrow, so I won't be alone."

Eli's jaw firms slightly, and I watch a tic start up. Then he draws in a breath. "Well, if you're sure?"

"Of course," I say coolly. "I never say things I don't mean."

CHAPTER 6

First steps are always the hardest. Unless you're drinking gin and then all of them are pretty difficult

---

Gideon

    Well, it turns out that I do say things I don't mean. I don't want Eli to go out, and I definitely don't want him to go out with Oliver and have a good time. I'm not sure where that feeling is coming from. Maybe it's because he's *my* nurse, not Oliver's. I grimace at myself. Even in my head I sound like a five-year-old. Milo would shake his head in disgust, and Niall would laugh until he wet himself.

    I fidget in my chair on the deck. I'm supposed to be listening intently to my friend Jacinta's tales of a modelling job she's just done. What I'm actually doing is surreptitiously watching Eli move around the suite, gathering the stuff he needs for his date. He's dressed in bright orange shorts and a grey striped t-shirt that shouldn't go together but on him make him look like a model.

I watch as he stamps his feet into his old grey Vans and stuffs a pair of navy-spotted swim shorts into his backpack.

"I thought you wouldn't need them," I call out and instantly curse myself. I was being surreptitious. Jacinta's voice trails off.

He comes to the door. "Oliver can bugger off if he thinks I'm getting my tackle out on some random beach." He looks at the sky. "Particularly in this sun."

I toss him my tube of sun cream. He catches it and raises his eyebrow. "For protection," I mutter. "For your face," I add quickly. "Not your penis."

He pauses to consider. "I wonder what factor you'd need for that."

"Total sun block," I say grimly and he looks at me.

"You've gone nude, then?"

Jacinta immediately snorts. "Darling, when hasn't he?"

"Every day," I say glibly. "Usually before I go in the shower." I relent. "I have. I've done a lot of things that Frankie would have a coronary over, but I'm variable in my wildness. Depends on what day you caught me. Some days my career means a lot to me. Others I'd walk naked down the street if it meant I was myself." There was a lot more bitterness in my voice than I'd intended, and from the look on his face more than he was expecting. I smile quickly. "However, that is why I can say with experience that it's not wise to get sunburn on your cock."

Jacinta shudders. "And I can say the same thing for your tits. I couldn't wear a bra for a month."

I grin at her. "Sweetie, you don't need one anyway."

"Bitch." She chuckles.

I look up and find Eli staring at the two of us, his expression clouded. There's a knock at the main door of the suite, but he hesitates. "Will you be okay?" he says cautiously.

I nod quickly. "Of course I will. Jacinta's here for the whole afternoon with me. What trouble could we possibly get into?"

Jacinta snorts. "I think it's more appropriate to ask what trouble *can't* we get into."

Eli looks even more worried. "How do you feel?"

"I feel like a grown man who's telling my employee to take some time off," I say sharply, but as normal, it's like water off a duck's back as he makes a dismissive face.

"I'm sure that sounds very good, but it actually doesn't cover the reality that I'm in charge."

I grin unwillingly. "Let me have my illusions."

He waves a graceful hand. "Go ahead."

The knock comes again, and I watch his back as he paces to open the door. I can feel Jacinta's gaze on the side of my face like a fucking heat-seeking missile.

Oliver trails behind Eli as he comes back onto the deck. Dressed in tight red shorts, a white t-shirt, and expensive deck shoes, he looks bright and very good-looking. "Good morning," he says and then twitches as he undoubtedly recognises Jacinta. As a supermodel, she's well used to it and just smiles vaguely at him.

"How are we?" he asks brightly.

I open my mouth, but Eli forestalls me. "I'm not sure about this," he says slightly desperately. "I don't think I should leave Mr Ramsay alone all day. He's only just getting back on his feet."

I open my mouth, but this time it's Oliver's turn to speak over me. "I think we'll be alright without Eli for a while, won't we, Mr Ramsay?" he says in the same overloud voice that people talk to small babies with.

I raise my eyebrow. "I'll obviously try to contain my abject sorrow, but I'm sure I'll cope."

He pats me on the arm rather familiarly, and I see Eli repress a smirk. "Oh, we are a card aren't we, Mr Ramsay."

"What is this *we* business with everyone in the medical profession?" I ask in a bewildered voice. "I might be a card, whatever that means, but I'm quite sure you haven't joined me."

"Oh dear, I think Mr Ramsay needs a little sleep," he coos loudly as if I'm hard of hearing.

Eli bites his lip, laughter in his eyes as I brush Oliver's hand off my arm. "I don't need a sleep. I need a new pair of eardrums now. Why are you talking to me at that decibel level?" He starts to say something but I shake my head and look at Eli. "Go on," I say quickly. "Get off and have a nice day. Don't forget you have to be back at the ship by ..." I falter.

"Six thirty," he says, his eyes twinkling before he shakes his head. "And you were doing so well with your adulting."

I smile at him, hearing Jacinta suck in her breath for some bloody reason. "Fuck off."

Oliver stares at us, and Eli shifts, looking suddenly awkward in the face of his unhidden curiosity. He squints at me. "Remember, though, no alcohol," he says quickly.

I shake my head. "What the hell? I might as well enter the church."

Jacinta immediately bursts into laughter. "Gid, you'd burst into flames if you even entered a church, and black really isn't your colour." She pauses. "Although red is. You could be a cardinal. Do they still have them? How about lime green? Who wears that?"

"It's the church, not the catwalk in Paris Fashion Week," I mutter.

Eli looks earnestly at me. "I need you to promise, or I'm not going anywhere."

I stare at him. "Okay," I say slowly. "I promise I will not drink alcohol."

Anyone else with any knowledge of how often I break my word would hesitate, but strangely he doesn't. Instead, his expression clears of worry, and I know instantly that I've fucked myself because I don't want to break that look of trust.

He slings his backpack over his shoulder and looks at Oliver rather doubtfully.

"Go on then. Have some fun," I say heartily as if I'm fifty years older than him.

He nods. "Okay, I'm going. But I'll have my mobile with me all the time. I'll text you when it's time to take your pills. I want you to promise me that you will take care, and if you feel even the slightest bit poorly you will ring me."

"Okay," I say slowly. "I promise."

He nods awkwardly, gives Jacinta a faint smile and, with a wave of his hand he's gone, Oliver padding at his side and leaving me with a silence that is positively vibrating with Jacinta's need to talk.

"No," I say quickly and she scoffs instantly.

"Fucking hell, when has that tone of voice *ever* worked on me, Gideon Ramsay?"

"Never," I say dolefully. "Why couldn't I have taken up with a stupid person?"

"That's your tragedy," she says kindly.

I snort and look at one of my best friends in the world and arguably one of only two people who knows me. She sits curled in her chair, the sun shining on her blonde hair coiled at her neck. Dressed in a pale green, short sundress, she looks slender and tanned. But more importantly, she looks healthy.

"You're glowing," I say, and she flushes.

"Don't be ridiculous."

I nod. "You are, sweetheart. You look so well."

"I feel well," she says earnestly. "I haven't touched a drink or any drugs for ten months."

"Well done," I say passionately. "You still going to meetings?"

She nods. "Every week, no matter where I am." She looks at me. "Thank you."

I shift uncomfortably. "I don't know what you mean."

"Yes, you do," she says steadily. "You got me into that treatment centre by the scruff of my neck, and you were with me every step of the way."

"Only because I didn't have anything better to do," I say quickly.

She smiles at me lovingly. "Okay, sweetie. You're the heartless wanker who looked after me at the lowest point of my life better than my own family ever did."

I shudder at the thought of when I'd found her in a hotel room in Spain. She'd been thin to the point of emaciation and strung out with track marks over her thin arms and her complexion grey and pallid. I'd kicked out the two men she was in bed with and stuffed her in a shower while she shouted obscenities at me. Once she was clean I'd dressed her and driven her to a clinic I'd heard good things about. I'd stayed in a hotel nearby for two months after she made me promise not to leave her. I'd lost out on a film role and been fined a humungous amount of money for backing out of another film. I'd also cornered the nickname Reluctant Ramsay from the press, and Frankie had raged for weeks.

I'd ignored him and stayed out there, visiting every day once I was allowed. Then when she was discharged, I rented a villa for another month, the two of us taking long walks, swimming and talking. It had felt like the most intimate time I'd ever spent with her despite the years of us fucking each other and many other people. I'd got to know her, and unfortunately she'd got to know me even better, which is why I know she's not going to accept any bullshit.

"Where's Alex?" I say quickly in the hope of diverting her.

She smiles at the thought of the tall, gentle professor she met when she knocked him off his bike in London. Steady, kind, and loving, he's her perfect foil, and I couldn't have picked anyone better for her.

"He's giving us time to talk. He's having lunch."

"He's not jealous?"

She smiles serenely. "Not at all. He knows there's nothing to be worried about."

"Does he know?" I hesitate, thinking of the messy ropes of our friendship, the times I tried to fuck her and couldn't get it up, the threesomes we'd had so that I could fuck another man using Jacinta as cover.

She immediately shakes her head. "Never," she says. "I will never tell anyone that, Gid. That's our secret."

"We have so many."

"Not anymore," she says, standing up and flopping into my lap. "I have a feeling that all the things we kept secret for so long are rising to the surface."

"Like pond scum," I say grimly, thinking of the dark murk that my career has encased me in.

"Don't say that," she says softly, coiling her arms around my neck and gifting me with the scent of the Dune perfume that she's always worn.

"I'm sorry," I say quietly.

"What for?"

"For everything. For the way I used you as some sort of beard." I hesitate. "Are you sure that didn't contribute to the drug use?"

"Oh, get over yourself," she scoffs. "Not everything is about you."

"I'm sorry," I say piously. "I have to say that I think you're very wrong with that statement."

She laughs and hugs me. "Gid, you never used me. You were my rock. The one person who knew me and loved me anyway. Unconditional love is what I got from you, and I loved every minute with you. We were like twins."

"Only if it was in the Roman Empire," I mutter, but I smile, remembering the times we kicked out the other man and lay in bed sharing a pillow and room service, laughing and talking and plotting our next escapade. I feel a pang of loss that this won't happen again. I love that she's clean and happy, but I've lost the one person I could be myself with after Niall left.

She laughs. "Okay, I'll give you that." As if sensing my lost feelings, she strokes my face. "Gid, you're my family and I love you utterly. No matter what happens, I will always love you." She sighs.

"I just want you to admit that you're loveable and that you deserve happiness rather than living like this."

"Living like what?"

"On the edge of disaster. You're like a fucking boat that's slipped its mooring. You're so lost, love, and you nearly fucking died."

"You've been listening to Niall too much."

She smirks. "When he can stop talking about his boy toy."

"Ugh, that's my brother."

She laughs. "It's actually not the Roman Empire. It's the Borgias."

"Didn't that end in poison and death?" I say lightly, but her face falls.

"Don't mention death," she says fiercely. "I nearly lost you."

"You'll never lose me," I say softly.

"*Promise.*" She stares at me. "Promise me the way you promised that gorgeous nurse. I know you when you mean something."

I shake my head. "I thought for a moment you'd dropped it."

She scoffs. "Love, you know better." She nudges me. "He's *so* gorgeous."

I sigh. "He's also young, and he has his shit together. When did we *ever* pick people like that?"

"I think we probably should have."

I shrug. "Maybe, but this won't go anywhere. Yes, he's pretty, but he doesn't think of me as anything other than his patient."

She purses her lips. "I'm really not sure of the veracity of that statement."

"Darling, your vocabulary has improved since you stopped stuffing things up your nose."

She cackles. "It's Alex. He even punctuates his texts. He's a terrible influence." She nudges me. "Go on, have a go. Make a pass."

"What a terrible expression." I push her fingers away from my ribcage. "He wouldn't be interested in a middle-aged closeted actor anyway. I'm so old I'm practically Methuselah in the gay world. If I went to a club they'd be fetching my pipe and slippers."

She stares at me open-mouthed. "Who is this person talking?" she says in a tone of wonder. "Is it the same Gideon Ramsay who once replied to my request for an opinion on my outfit with the words, 'Who cares, sweetie? They're only going to be looking at me.'"

I laugh. "I wasn't wrong. Stop being jelly." The humour dies, and I sigh. "Anyway, he's far too happy and a nice person for me. Ouch!" I wriggle away from her sharp elbow in my ribs. "What was that for?"

"For constantly devaluing yourself. You've paid Frankie to do that for long enough."

"Not that again. You've been listening to Milo."

"I don't need to listen to anyone. Gid, he's poison. I know you look on him as some sort of father figure."

"Well, that's fucked up. The first useless one was given to me without a choice, and now you're saying I actually chose the second one."

"He chose you. He plucked you out because he saw how brilliant you were and how lonely. And then he spent years binding you to him, making you think you're wrong and the only person who can help you is him." She curls her lip in disgust. "He's a cunt."

"Let's not do this." I sigh. "He's right. I'll just carry on the way I am. I'm happy."

"Are you?"

I look out, seeing the sunbeams dance on the sea. "At the moment," I say slowly. "I take what moments I can get, to be honest."

"One day you're going to learn how to actually expect happiness as your given right because you'll own everything you are. And you're fucking epic, Gid. You don't see it, but I know it, and the day you're true to yourself, I'll know my best friend is finally happy."

I swallow hard, abruptly sick of this pointless conversation. "Speaking of family, where is Daisy? Where is your incredibly perfect sister?"

She smiles evilly. "She was coming with us, but she missed the tender. I made sure to wave at her from the boat."

"I would have thought that she'd be walking on water by now."

She laughs loudly. "Can you imagine her as Jesus? She'd never have fed the five thousand all that bread. *Way* too many carbs."

I laugh. "She'd have given them SlimFast and water biscuits."

She chuckles and curls into me, her weight familiar and warm as we talk. But part of me is listening for the phone and wondering what Eli's doing.

It's late afternoon by the time she and Alex leave the boat, and the sun is slanting low, gilding us in its soft glaze. I accept her hug, relishing the fact that her body seems supple and healthy again and not a bag of bones. "Keep going with it," I whisper. "Promise me, Jac."

She pulls back. "I promise." She leans closer. "And promise to shag your nurse, Gid. It'll do you the world of good."

I burst into laughter. "He's not Lucozade. And how come my comment was heartfelt and sentimental and yours was just crass?"

"You make me uncomfortable when you're nice."

"Oh, lovely." I stand back and Alex throws his arm over her shoulder. "Take care of her," I say and he smiles, holding out his hand to shake.

"I will," he says, his deep voice warm and serene. "I promise."

The engine starts on the tender and Jacinta looks around. "Isn't this the last boat? You're sailing in half an hour. Where's your nurse?"

I purse my lips, worry forming. "I don't know." I shrug. "I'm sure he's getting a water taxi. Don't worry."

We exchange kisses and hugs, and I linger on the deck to wave until they're out of sight. I stare out to the dock anxiously, but there's no sign of anyone on the other side, no messy blond head.

I turn to a crew member. "My nurse went ashore today and isn't back yet. What should we do?"

The man frowns. "Oh dear. Have you tried him on his phone?"

I hold up a finger, and he waits while I dial Eli's number. The phone clicks straight onto his answering service. I ring off and look at the man. "No answer."

He gives me an apologetic smile. "I'm afraid we can't wait for him. The ship must sail at its given time. That can't be broken." He pats my arm. "Please don't worry. It's happened many times. He'll just have to make his way to the next port of call, and he can board in the normal way. He's actually lucky because we're mooring in Nice which is only a few hours down the coast. He might even be able to get to us before we moor."

I nod my thanks and scan the water anxiously, but there's no sign of him. I feel worry churn in my stomach. What if something has happened to them? What if they've had an accident and he's lying in hospital? What can I do?

My phone has stayed silent all afternoon. The time to take my pills came and went with no phone call. I'd remembered and taken them, but this is so out of character for him. I ring his phone again and leave a message on his voicemail. "This is Gideon," I say abruptly, wincing at the fact that my tone sounds harsh. "I'm concerned as to where you are. If you're not here by six thirty the ship will sail. You need to make your way to Nice and wait for the boat so you can board there."

I make my way back to my cabin, thinking that he'll probably call. But he doesn't. Six thirty comes and goes, and the ship backs out of the port with the sun slanting low over the horizon. Night falls and, lit by a huge harvest moon, I stand on my deck and stare out over the sea that's roiling slowly and inkily under the bright moonlight.

What the fuck is he playing at? He acted all concerned earlier on. Please could I not drink. He wanted me to ring him if I felt ill. I snort. I'd be dead if I was reliant on that phone call. He hadn't even bothered to ring about my medicine, regardless of the fact that he seems to think I'm incapable of looking after myself and need him to do everything.

I wonder if he got a room with Oliver and they overslept. I imagine them sleeping unconcerned and entangled together, all young, taut flesh and golden skin, and anger stirs.

Fuck him. I don't need him. I don't need anyone. I've proved that all my life. Some nurse isn't going to disrupt that, no matter how close I feel to him.

"Back away," I say out loud. "He isn't worth the trouble."

The words float out onto the breeze, and they sound full of conviction, but nevertheless half an hour later finds me walking the length of the boat looking for Constance to see if she's heard anything from her nurse.

I look in the restaurant full of old people talking really loudly, and then the bars. She isn't in the gym, or the shops or the library. I poke my head around the spa to no avail, and she isn't part of the group dancing on one of the decks. I don't even bother checking the running track that Eli makes me walk round every day while he talks incessantly. She doesn't strike me as a jogger, even without a broken foot.

Finally, I round the steps to the top deck and find her kicking back in a comfy lounger staring out to sea.

"Here you are," I pant, and she smiles at me.

"Gideon, you're very red in the face, darling. Been banging that nurse of yours?"

"Oh my God," I hiss, falling into the chair beside her. "Keep your voice down."

"Sweetie, there's nobody here. Not many of them can manage the stairs, and even if they were all up here, the squealing from their hearing aids would drown out my words."

"Are you not the same age?" I ask, accepting the water she pours me from the jug on the table. I promptly choke. "Fucking hell, that's neat vodka."

She smiles prettily. "Much better for you than boring old water."

"You should really run the NHS. I'd certainly do as you say."

"I'd be no good there. Far too many rules."

I put the glass carefully down on the table. She eyes me. "Going teetotal?"

"No." I hesitate. "Just not drinking at the moment. Eli's like Betty Ford, but stricter."

"Ah, your nurse. Has he disappeared into the same black hole that my personality desert of a companion has fallen into?"

"You've not heard from them either?" I ask, anger taken over by concern again.

She shakes her head. "No. He'll turn up, especially if he wants his wages."

"You don't seem very concerned."

"Darling, he's a grown man and not a particularly nice one. I'm not in charge of him. Besides, you appear to have cornered the market in worry. Relax, Gideon, Eli will be fine."

"I'm not bothered," I say quickly, reaching out for the glass and sitting back before I can snag it. Dammit, I made a promise to him, and regardless of what promises he breaks, I won't do the same.

She shoots me a sceptical look which is warranted because I couldn't act my way out of a paper bag at the moment. Then she sits back and pats my knee. "I'm sure they're fine, Gideon. The ship will dock soon and they'll be waiting for it. You'll see."

"Hmm." I stare out to sea. It's dark, but there's a silvery carpet from the moon making it look like a magic path.

"He's a very nice boy," she says suddenly.

"Who?" I ask startled. "Eli?"

"No, William Shatner. Of course I meant Eli."

"Oh well, I'm sure he is," I bluster only to be cut short when she taps on my knee.

"Don't bother denying it, darling. I know attraction when I see it." She shoots me a warm smile. "You don't need to hide from me."

I stare back at her, all the customary easy denials hovering on my lips. They've tripped off my tongue so easily over the years. *No, he's just a friend. Jacinta is my girlfriend.* And suddenly I'm sick of it. I'm sick of lying and hiding and just for once, out at sea with the wind in my face, I want to be honest and true to me.

"I'm gay," I say loudly and clearly. "I've said for years to the public that I'm straight and to the people I was in bed with that I'm bisexual, but I'm not. I'm gay."

She smiles at me placidly. "Lovely, darling. I like cock too. We have so much in common."

My laughter catches me by surprise, and she grins impishly at me. "I like you when you're honest," she muses. "You look a lot younger somehow."

"Not as young as my nurse," I say grimly, honesty continuing to trip off my tongue.

"What utter claptrap," she says firmly. "Age has nothing to do with anything. My third husband was thirty years older than me and he had more fun in his little finger than the fourth husband, who was thirty-five and a completely boring bastard."

"You've led a wilder life than me," I say wryly.

"I sincerely doubt *that*. You've got a very uncontained look about you. Like a wild horse with no owner." She stares out to sea. "He might be younger, but he's interested," she murmurs. "It's written all over his face."

I laugh suddenly and harshly. "Not quite interested enough to return from his date with your nurse, who I may add is far prettier and younger than me."

"Pish," she says crossly. "He's a little prick. There's no way your Eli would be interested in him. His eyes fairly eat you up."

"Sounds painful," I mutter, feeling my heart patter and race at the thought of him being interested in me. I squelch that immediately. She's just being kind. Eli is not interested in me and never would be. Today has proved that.

Silence falls and then she reaches out and grabs my hand, her fingers long and slender, the skin soft as silk. "Well done for telling me, darling," she says softly. "First steps are always the hardest." She pauses. "Unless you're drinking gin and then all of them are pretty difficult."

I burst into laughter, enjoying the respite from the heavy atmosphere, and she joins me.

"It must feel like you've been boxed in all these years," she muses. "What a terrible feeling."

"I can't describe it."

"No need. I once got boxed in at the Cheddar Gorge."

"Sounds painful."

She roars with laughter. "Some twat deliberately parked right up beside me so I couldn't get out when I wanted to go. It was infuriating. Made my skin itch. Made me want to be naughty."

She's describing how I've felt for years. "What did you do?"

"Oh darling, I put a brick through his window."

I start to laugh. "That's a bit more than naughty."

She shrugs. "I know, and the nice young policeman said exactly the same. For a few hours." After a few seconds she stirs. "Fancy a joint?" she says casually, reaching into her Birkin bag and pulling out an old battered cigarette tin.

"What?" I gape at her.

She shrugs. "It's medicinal, darling. For my arthritis."

"You haven't got arthritis."

"Sweetie, I'm seventy. At some point I'm sure to have it."

I start to laugh as she sparks up the blunt, inhaling lustily and holding it out to me.

"I shouldn't," I say. "Eli will kill me." She looks at me unblinkingly and I square my shoulders. "I was always terrible with peer pressure," I say sadly and grab the joint.

For a second I hesitate, but then I remember who I am. I'm my own boss. There is no one to care for me apart from my brother and two close friends, and they've all got their own lives to lead. The only person who I thought was concerned is paid to do that, and it's blatantly obvious that the concern is surface deep because when he went off the clock he displayed his complete lack of interest by missing the boat and not checking in. *I'm on my own* I remind myself. *And I'm absolutely and utterly fine with that.*

"Fuck him," I say and take a long drag of the joint.

After all, he never banned dope is my last coherent thought.

CHAPTER 7

What do you remember about last night?

Eli

I fidget about on the dock, stepping from one foot to another and feeling the nervous energy thrumming through me.

"What the hell is wrong with you?" Oliver says peevishly, leaning against a post as if he hasn't got a care in the world.

"The same thing that I'd think would be wrong with you," I snap. "The fact that we missed the boat and neither of us have checked in with our patients. Fuck knows what's happened."

"Oh relax, for Christ's sake. Nothing will have happened more disastrous than Mrs Pritchard finally disappearing up her own arse, and Gideon dying from eternal grumpiness."

"You're joking."

"No. Fucking hell, I fancied the pants off the man for years. I can't tell you how disappointed I've been to find out that he's a bigger mood hoover than a Dyson."

I shake my head. "I value my job," I say and stare as he laughs.

"You mean you value your patient." He grins at me nastily. "I'm not saying I blame you. If he'd landed as my patient, the ker-ching signs would have gone off straightaway. I'd have bent over quicker than someone having a prostate check." He looks at me eagerly. "You know you can tell me. Is he gay? Bisexual? There have been rumours flitting around for years that he swings both ways."

"I have no idea what you're talking about," I say sturdily and unrepentantly dishonestly, because I've seen the glances Gideon's sneaked at me. I heard what his manager said. Jesus, I haven't been able to get that out of my head.

I think back to this morning and seeing Jacinta on his lap. It had made my stomach feel funny, and I'd been desperate enough to get out of the suite and not be around them that I'd accepted this date and the ensuing debacle. It was only at the last moment that I'd looked beyond their stunning beauty and seen the way they sat together so comfortably. It had been like they were brother and sister.

Oliver's whistle stirs me from my thoughts. "Are you sure you're not going to hit that?"

I stare at him. "He's my patient. Do you remember nursing college and that teeny insignificant thing called the Code?"

"Pah, that's more of a guideline."

"It's a pretty serious guideline if you can lose your job over it."

"Listen, Eli, I've known many private nurses, and well over half of them have fucked a patient at some point." I shake my head and he glares at me. "I have to say that you're another letdown. You've been shitty company all day."

"I can't imagine why. First I had to refuse your kind offer of a hotel room that rents by the hour, then accept with a smile the fact that you dropped my phone in the sea, and finally manage not to throttle you when we missed the tender because you were flirting with that waiter. It's been the absolute best date I've ever been on."

"I can't wait to get on that boat," he says fretfully.

"You and me both," I mutter, but for completely different reasons. I heft my rucksack as the bright orange tender boat comes towards us laden with happy tourists who are ready for an evening on the town.

Twenty minutes later I leave Oliver without a backward glance and race back to the suite. "Gideon," I call out hesitantly but I'm greeted with silence, the suite lit only by the murky shadows of moonlight. The doors are open, letting in the distant sound of music on the air and the lapping of the waves, but apart from that the suite echoes with silence.

Nevertheless, I check all the rooms before coming up short in the lounge again. "Where are you?" I mutter, feeling urgency tremble in me. I'm probably going to get fired as soon as I see him, but at least I'll know he's okay. I clench my fists. What if he had a coughing fit and fell and hit his head? I shake out my hands. What the fuck is wrong with me? I'm always concerned about my patients, but that's my nursing head, and I am always calm. This feels far more personal and my hands tremble slightly. Something about this grumpy man just means more.

"Eli," comes a voice from the door and for a split second I feel relief, but it isn't him and I sag slightly.

"Hi, Peter," I say, scrubbing my hand over my neck and feeling the gritty salt in my hair. "Sorry about going AWOL."

"What happened?"

"Missed the tender."

"I tried to ring you. Mr Ramsay was very worried."

"Was he?" My question sounds plaintive, and he smiles kindly.

"Of course he was. Mr Ramsay thinks very highly of you."

"I doubt that's a true statement right at this precise moment," I say wryly. "I'm probably going to get the sack. I couldn't ring because my phone's buggered. It fell in the sea."

"Would you like me to ring around and get you a replacement?"

"You can do that?"

He smiles slightly. "Mr Jones, I'm the butler for the first-class suites. I can do anything."

A small smile tugs free. "You sound drunk on power."

"Better than the cooking brandy," he says smartly. He pauses. "Are you looking for Mr Ramsay?"

"Is he okay?"

"Of course," he says quickly, and my shoulders sag. "He went to find Mrs Pritchard, one of the other passengers. He thought she might have had word of you."

"Shit," I say despairingly. "What a bloody awful day."

"Well, I'll inform the captain that you're on board safely."

"Thank you," I say gratefully. I pause. "I don't suppose you have any idea of where they are?"

He smiles. "It came to my notice while I was having an evening walk that Mrs Pritchard likes the top deck." He winks. "Not so many people about."

I stare at him. What is he winking about? I sigh heavily. Whatever it is probably doesn't mean good things. It also more than likely means that Gideon is in the thick of it.

I leave the suite, exchanging smiles and greetings and fighting the tide of people heading to the restaurants to eat. My stomach rumbles. I haven't eaten anything since first thing this morning. The whole day has been spent quelling the urge to strangle Oliver, and it didn't improve my appetite. Now that I'm on ship and I know that Gideon hasn't been taken to the med centre, I'm starving. I amend my thoughts. Not been taken to the med centre *yet*.

I jog along the running track that curves around the ship, offering a beautiful view of Nice glittering like a carpet of jewels in the night, and then mount the steps to the upper deck quickly, feeling my breath sawing in my throat. Shit, he's going to send me away. I stop dead and shake my head. I mean shit, I'm going to get the sack. It's because …

I pause on the stairs as I hear the laughter coming from above me.

I frown. Gideon's not prone to fits of laughter but he's had one a couple of times, usually in response to sarcasm. It's a shame because it's a lovely laugh, low and almost dirty-sounding but very contagious. I narrow my eyes. *Has he picked up anyone downstairs?* I think of the redheaded nurse who's adopted a sultry sway every time she's walked past us. Or the dark-haired ship steward who practically trips over his tongue every time he speaks to Gideon, to the extent that Gideon had asked me if he had a problem with his speech.

Another voice speaks, and I relax because it's Constance.

I round the steps and stop in amazement before coughing as the heavy dope cloud engulfs me. "What the fuck?" I say louder than I intended, and they both swing slowly round to face me. For a second there's total silence and then they both break into peals of laughter, holding on to each other. "Oh lovely," I sigh. I glare at the pair of them. "Who brought the dope on the ship?" I finally say resignedly, prompting another flood of laughter.

When they pause with tears in their eyes, I hold out my hand for the blunt and Gideon meekly puts it in my hand. "Thank you," I say sternly and promptly throw it over the side of the ship. Constance makes a sound of protest and I turn back, bracing my hands behind me on the railing. "This is terrible behaviour," I say and they hang their heads like recalcitrant children. My lip twitches but thankfully they can't see it. "You're here on this ship to get better. For shame." I shake my head at Gideon. "Smoking dope is most definitely not on your health care and recovery plan."

"Well, I think it should be," he says sulkily, making an effort to rally his authority but listing sideways into his partner in crime who is staring dreamily at the moon. "I'm sure I'd have got better a lot sooner."

"Well, it isn't and it also doesn't specify missing meals. Have either of you eaten this evening?" They shake their head in an exaggerated fashion and I make a shooing gesture with my hands. "Come on. We'll walk you back to your cabin, Constance, and then Gideon and I are going to order something for you to eat."

"I am hungry," he says eagerly.

"I'm sure you are," I say. "That's called the munchies."

I shake my head as that sends them into another fit of laughter.

Getting them back to the suite is a feat of ingenuity and that's not even counting the stoned old lady on crutches. I imagine it's a bit like being a sheepdog herding its charges. One of them veers off in one direction while the other tries to go the other way. They have the attention span of either toddlers or amoebas, branching off to ooh and aah over the glittering contents of the jeweller's window where Constance announces in her very loud voice that her third husband bought her a labia ring when she'd been good.

"Okay," I say slowly and gratefully once we pole up outside Constance's suite. "Wait here," I instruct Gideon. "I'm just going to make sure that Oliver knows what she's been up to so he can keep an eye on her."

"If your boyfriend can drag his eyes off you," he says fretfully and then his expression brightens. "That fire extinguisher is so *red!*" he exclaims.

"Yes," I say slowly. "So red, and so not going to be touched under any circumstances at all, Gideon Ramsay." He slumps back against the wall, looking like a sulky child, and I grin at him. "Wait here, trouble," I say affectionately.

Oliver is predictably sullen, but he rallies enough to practise being insincere with his charge, and I leave them to it. When I get outside, I stop dead. *Shit! Where's he gone?* For a second panic engulfs me, but then I see someone's foot poking round the corner and the faint tuneless humming of "Let's Dance" by David Bowie.

Grinning, I make my way to him and stand over him. He's lying on the floor outside our suite staring at the ceiling. "I can see the stars," he says dreamily.

I look up. "They're not stars, they're spotlights in the ceiling."

He waves his hand. "They are stars," he says crossly. "I can quite clearly see that they're twinkling at me."

"Well, of course they are," I say soothingly.

He stares up at me. "You're so gorgeous," he mutters in a low voice and my heart starts to pound heavily. "I want you, but I won't do anything. Do you know why?" he whispers loudly.

"Why?" I say softly, feeling the mood shift and change.

"Because I can't." He raises his finger to his mouth. "Shush!" he admonishes me rather loudly. "It's a secret. I'm gay, but you can't tell anyone."

I feel my whole body clench in shock as all my thoughts and half-formed suspicions are confirmed. My cock twitches instantly, but I ignore it.

"Gideon," I say softly.

He shakes his head. "Ouch! Someone hit me."

I smile helplessly. "No one hit you. You did it yourself by banging your head on the floor."

"Well, that was a bloody stupid thing to do," he says fretfully. He stares at me. "Don't tell anyone," he whispers. "No one would understand. I'd never act again. My fans would never forgive me. I can't be gay."

"I don't think you have a choice in the matter," I say softly, then earnestly assure him, "I won't tell anyone."

I feel so sad. I don't know why he thinks that, but I suppose I can't blame him. There's a lot of homophobia about, and he would more than likely lose some jobs. My concern is more for what this is doing to him. What must it be like to live your life being told that one of the most inherent parts of yourself is wrong? It must be soul-destroying. Is this why he's so wild and unmoored and grumpy?

"You can trust me, Mr Ramsay," I say, feeling the urgent need to tack the mister part on so it reminds us both where this soft mood could land us. In dangerous waters.

"I'm not Mr Ramsay to you," he says crossly. "I'm Gideon to you. I hate you being formal with me." He tugs on his jumper crossly. "I'm very hot," he says peevishly. "Why is the heating on?"

I bend over and help him pull his jumper off, and he emerges from the folds blinking like a tiny stoned mole. My mouth twitches, but any semblance of a smile vanishes as he looks at me, his eyes deep and dark.

"You're not for me," he says slowly. "Go back to your boyfriend."

"I haven't got one," I say sharply. "Not that that improves our situation at all." My head is still reeling as thoughts teem and churn. *He's gay. He's closeted. He's gay. That means I could have him. He's my patient. He's gay too.*

Dismissing them with difficulty, I crouch, extending my hand down to help him up. He grabs my hand and tries to get up but he displaces his weight, and I feel myself falling onto him. I try to throw my weight to the side, but I can't, and I'm heavy enough to warrant the startled "*oof*" he makes when I land on him.

For a second we stay still. Then he starts to giggle and it's so infectious that I join in, right up until he threads his hand in my hair and I tip my chin up to look at him.

"So pretty," he says almost wonderingly, and for a long second that seems to stretch out like hot toffee we stare at each other. I can feel every inch of his long, hard body under me as I lie between his thighs, including what feels like a very lucky eight inches pressing against my hip. He's hard. I inhale sharply, getting a gust of his spicy vanilla scent, and our gazes tangle and slip together.

I don't know who moves, but in the next second our lips meet and my head reels. His lips are full and slightly dry. I can smell pot on his breath, but that's my last thought because then our groins press together and we groan in synchrony.

His lips part, and I lose my head. Reason screams at me that this is a terrible idea and we're in a bloody corridor, but I throw it away completely. Instead, I kiss him back, forcing his lips open and tangling my tongue with his. He seems to melt back into the carpet in surrender and I follow him, chasing his mouth and taking it again as he gives a throaty groan. Every cell in my body is beseeching me to grind on him, to strip him and put my cock inside him, because his surrender tells me everything.

I card my hands through the soft waves of his hair, holding his skull gently and directing his face so I can get as deep into his mouth as I can. I want to meld into him so totally that you couldn't tell where he ends and I begin.

Fuck knows what would have happened, but at that moment the speaker above us crackles and reason returns to clear away the lust just enough for me to realise what I'm fucking doing. I move back, and it's so very hard to do – like I'm pulling away from the brink – and my cock throbs painfully. Gideon tries to grab me, but I pull free and sit back on my haunches, panting and staring at him.

As my thoughts clear, I look around frantically and sag with relief to find no one taking photos of us. We've been lucky that there are no witnesses to the supposedly straight famous actor rolling around on the carpet in the corridor with his male nurse. I wince at the thought of the shitstorm that would create.

I scrub my hands down my face, smelling vanilla on my fingers where they dug into his skin. "Fuck!" I say. "What the fuck am I thinking? You're my bloody patient."

He stares up at me, his expression dazed and blind for a second. Then he sits up, pushing me off him. "Nice of you to remember."

I sigh. "I'm so sorry," I say earnestly. "Oliver dropped my phone in the sea, and we missed the boat."

I stop because he's patently not listening to me again. He gets to his feet, swaying and clinging to the wall for a second. "Is it stormy?" he says vaguely. "Why is the ship moving about like this? Can't they get a competent captain?" I shake my head at his lord of the manor impression. "I'm *so* hungry," he says very loudly and plaintively. "I want something to eat now."

I get to my feet. "Okay," I say softly. "We'll talk about this in the morning." I pause. "If you remember."

He reels into the suite, and I follow him. *Do I hope he remembers it or not?* I can't make my mind up.

Gideon

I wake up the next morning coughing, and my chest feels sore enough for me to remember doing the same in the middle of the night. I cough and cough, feeling my breath catch and my eyes stream. I try to suck in some air but I can't get enough, and my head swims as I start to panic. *Fuck!*

The door bangs open, and Eli dashes in. He takes one look at me bent double and clutching at my chest, and he immediately grabs the portable oxygen tank that has sat redundantly in my room since the beginning of the cruise. Well, I hope it feels better now that it's needed.

"Easy," he says, his voice warm and steady, and immediately I feel calmer, the panic that fizzed inside me like lemonade, dissipating under his control of the situation. He straps the mask onto my face and props two pillows behind me, settling me back against them. "Deep breaths," he says, his hand on my wrist feeling my pulse. His face has that inward look he gets when he does anything like this.

I breathe in slowly, feeling the tight grip on my chest gradually ease. When it's gone and I can breathe steadily, I go to take the mask off, but his hand stops me. I swallow hard because it's warm and firm, the fingers long and spread over mine.

He looks at me and hesitates. I open my eyes, trying to make myself look pitiful, but it doesn't work, and I sag slightly as his face takes on a stern look that really shouldn't make my cock as interested as it is.

"What were you thinking?" he bursts out. "You've had pneumonia, for God's sake. Your lung collapsed. You were in intensive care. This trip home was supposed to be about rest and relaxation."

I lift the mask up. "Dope is very relaxing. It's a medical fact."

He snaps the mask back on, and I swear he pings the elastic far harder than he should. "Gideon, you use the words 'medical facts' the way that some people quote the Bible. At no point in any medical research has anyone added the words, 'And after they've had a collapsed lung, the patient should definitely roll a really nice fat doobie and try to eat his body weight in pizza.'"

I purse my lips and raise the mask. "Someone should commission that study." I take one look at his cross face and realise it won't be me doing that. I'm about to continue being flippant when I take note of the dark circles under his eyes. He's got to be as tired as me, since he was in here with me most of the night rubbing my back and talking me down from panic.

Regret fills me suddenly, and it's such an alien emotion that it takes me a few minutes to realise what it is. I speak before I can second-guess myself. "I'm sorry," I say honestly. "I'm sorry you've had to deal with this."

"Gideon, it's my job. But it would be much easier if my patient wasn't so hell-bent on self-destruction."

"I didn't drink, though," I say quickly, unable to bear the disappointment in his voice.

He shakes his head. "Well done," he says smartly, but his fingers when he removes the mask are gentle and his expression is softer, so I know he's forgiven me. He takes my pulse again. "I'm sorry about yesterday," he says suddenly, his eyes fixed on my wrist and his expression troubled. He looks up at me, his eyes like the depth of a clear brook. "My phone fell in the sea and Oliver missed the boat."

"Did you have a good time?" I hold my breath waiting for his answer.

He shakes his head. "Not after I refused his offer of a hotel room that rented by the hour. It sort of soured the afternoon."

"What a charmer," I breathe. "How on earth did you resist that offer?" I can feel relief settle in me at the note of aggravation in his voice, and I can't help the note of happiness in my voice.

"I'm still sorry,"

"Doesn't matter," I say loftily. "I didn't miss you."

"Really?" he asks, and I smile.

"Maybe a little bit." He fidgets and I stare at him. "You okay?"

"What do you remember about last night?"

I rack my brains but can't come up with anything much apart from the strong desire to never smoke dope again, and also to not think too hard as it's making a headache sing between my brows. "Was I bad?" I ask tentatively. "That dope must have been really strong shit, because all I can remember is looking at the moon and then you snatching it off me and jettisoning it. That's it for me as far as the evening went."

"I didn't snatch it off you," he protests. "I simply confiscated it and chucked it over the side." I raise my eyebrow but he hesitates and something complicated crosses his usually open face.

"Eli?" I ask, but he shakes his head and stands up.

"Come on, time to get up. Have a shower and then meet me in the lounge. We're going to have a slow walk around the running track so you can get some fresh air and then a nice healthy breakfast."

"You know you say it like you've got a fun time planned," I say darkly. "But I'm here to tell you that it doesn't work." I bite my lip. "No yoga?"

He shudders. "You'd totally spoil their chakras with all that coughing."

"Old people are very unforgiving," I muse, and he smiles but it's slightly half-hearted and I frown after him as he leaves the room. I lie still for a second, enjoying the sight of the sea glistening in the early morning sunshine, but then the lingering dope headache and sour taste in my mouth shoves me out of bed and into the bathroom.

I potter about, cleaning my teeth and starting the shower. I'd always thought cruise ships had poky bathrooms, but this has a full-size walk-in shower and even a whirlpool bath. I step under the spray with a hiss of appreciation. The water is hot and I duck my head, feeling the steam twine around me and ease my chest. It seems to cleanse away all the cobwebs from my head which is probably why I stiffen in shock as I soap myself up. *What the fuck?*

I stare ahead for a second and then, without stopping to switch the shower off or even rinse the soap off me, I grab a towel and wind it round my waist. I march through the suite, but I can't see any sign of him in the lounge or out on the deck. His bedroom door is wide open, so I race towards it.

When I clear the door, he looks up. He's sitting in the armchair looking out of the window, his face lined with thoughts. He jumps up as I barge into the room.

"Gideon?" he says quickly. "What is it? What's the matter?"

"You kissed me," I blurt out, my voice loud in the quiet of the room. "I mean, we kissed each other."

"Oh my God," he says, digging his fingers into his eyes. When he brings his hands down, he looks apologetic. "I'm so sorry, Mr Ramsay." I glare at him and he stumbles over his words. "I mean Gideon. I'm so sorry. You can have my resignation immediately."

"I don't want your bloody resignation," I say harshly. "Why the fuck would I want that?"

"Because I'm your nurse. I've crossed so many guidelines I think I'm one paragraph short of a manual on how not to lose your job spectacularly."

I shake my head impatiently. "Eli, I am a thirty-nine-year-old man who has largely recovered from pneumonia aside from dope-related incidents. I have all my faculties and manage to walk, talk, and down the pills the doctor gave me. I am not Elizabeth Barrett Browning and you're not exactly taking advantage." I swallow. "I also seem to remember telling you a few secrets."

"They're still secrets," he says immediately, his honest face looking impassioned. "They always will be with me." Almost as if it's against his knowledge, he drifts closer. My heart picks up speed, thundering against my ribcage. "You remember, then?"

"I remember," I say hoarsely. I raise my hands tentatively and touch his hips. It's a gentle touch, my fingertips barely skimming him, but he shudders. Our eyes meet and refuse to let go in the pregnant silence. In the next second, we fly at each other.

Our mouths meet and teeth clash, and then we're eating at each other's mouths furiously as if all of the attraction has exploded like a comet. I rub my tongue against his and moan deep in my chest when he begins to suck on my tongue lazily, sending pulses of need that seem to echo the beat of the blood in my dick. I groan as he suddenly pushes me back against the wall, letting his body weight fall into me.

I feel cool air as my towel succumbs to gravity and I grab his hips and pull him closer. His cock is hard and rubs deliciously against mine. He takes my mouth again, sucking on my tongue as his hand comes down between us, and I cry out as his hard palm encircles my cock. He moves his hand up and down, collecting the pre-come gathering at the head, and I tear my lips away, panting furiously. He moans low and follows my mouth almost drunkenly, only to jerk as the front door of the suite bangs open.

A male voice shouts, "Gideon, where are you?"

I close my eyes despairingly as his hand falls away. "It's fucking Frankie," I whisper. "Shit!"

CHAPTER 8

My life ran a lot easier when the only person who mattered in the world was me

Gideon

Eli springs away from me like I've confessed that I've got Ebola. Actually, he'd have probably stuck around a bit longer if I did have that and would most definitely have got his nurse bag out. My hands flail in midair, as if grasping for what I'd been holding only moments before, and I shift awkwardly.

"Gideon," comes the shout again, and Eli looks at me imploringly. For a second I consider doing what I'd have done a few weeks ago which is leave him to it, but this time I hesitate.

"*Fuck!*" I mutter as I grab my towel and wind it round my waist. "Go in the bathroom and come out in five minutes."

"What are you going to do?"

"I'm going to sneak out of the balcony doors like this is some sort of farce and be on the deck when he looks out." He hesitates.

"*What?*" I ask impatiently and he shakes his head.

"Nothing."

Then he's gone and I sidle out onto the deck where the wind catches my towel and flaps it threateningly about. I roll my eyes. *Could I be any more ridiculous?* At this point I've got to doubt it. And it's all for him. What the fuck is happening to me? My life ran a lot easier when the only person who mattered in the world was me.

I hear footsteps and fling myself quickly into the chair, tucking the towel around my cock and balls so I don't expose myself to Frankie. The thought makes me shudder and doesn't leave me much to expose as they're currently trying to tuck themselves back into my body at the thought.

A second later he appears in the doorway. "Gideon," he says heartily. "Didn't you hear me shout?"

"No," I say calmly, reclining in my seat as if I'm on the throne of England.

He looks at me and hesitates. "What are you doing out here?"

"Sitting down," I say serenely. "What does it look like?"

"In a towel?"

"Is there a dress etiquette I wasn't aware of for sitting on my private deck?" I ask in an astonished voice. "How I wish someone would give me this rule book that seems to follow me around in life, spoiling my fun."

He looks dubiously at me. "You're covered in soap suds, Gideon."

"I'm conditioning my skin." It's only years of training that makes that statement a fact rather than floundering. It's only years of him being in Hollywood that makes him accept it.

"Oh, okay," he finally says. He looks around and sidles closer. "Maybe don't sit around like that in front of your nurse, though."

"Why?" I ask coldly, and he falters slightly before he unfortunately recovers.

"Well, he'll get ideas."

"Because he's gay? Goodness me, I think you've put your finger on the problem because all gay men are obviously just waiting to pounce on the nearest display of flesh. It's not as if they have jobs and mortgages and relationships to bother about."

He shrugs awkwardly. "That's been my experience."

"Really?"

"No need to sound so disbelieving, Gideon," he says, sounding faintly stung that I don't believe him. "I have got a mirror, you know."

"Then you should learn to use it," I say smoothly. "Because it would have to be a very masochistic gay man that made a pass at a terrible homophobe like you."

"*Gideon*." He sounds incredibly affronted. "I do a lot of work for the LGBT community."

"Only if you class that as helping them back into the closet and locking the door."

"Is this about Christian?"

I sigh and rub my eyes, suddenly sick of this conversation. I hate that he treats me like a stupid five-year-old and dismisses everything I say. And I detest the bitchy sniping I sink into because of the dislike that has slowly been simmering inside me for someone who could have been everything to me, but who instead hates what I am. "No, it's not about Christian," I say tiredly, looking out to sea. "I'm just sick of this subterfuge, Frankie. Of never being honest. I'm gay, not Jack the Ripper."

He snorts. "Might have been easier to spin that."

I swing my gaze back to him. "No, it wouldn't. Have you actually heard yourself lately?"

"I've heard myself telling you time and time again that you'll fuck your career up. Do you know what I've got in my hands?" I shake my head. "It's an offer to star in Hal Finchley's next film."

"Really?" I try for an appreciative voice but I know I'm wide of the mark. Hal is famous for high-grossing superhero movies, but the thought of appearing as yet another boring, clichéd lead makes me feel like Frankie's covering me in a straitjacket.

He nods. "No auditioning. A straight offer." He glares at me. "And that's what it is, Gideon. It's a straight offer. One whiff of where your interests really lie and they'll snatch this away quicker than the baton in a relay race."

"They're not allowed to do that."

He scoffs. "Don't be naïve. Of course they can. They'll just do it another way without mentioning your sexuality. They'll make some excuse about artistic differences. But the end result is the same. You'll be off the film and your career will be done. You'll be lucky to get a part in *Midsomer Murders*."

I sigh, feeling suddenly unutterably weary. "Then maybe I don't want this career anymore that depends on me lying every day. Maybe I want my family and friends to really know me."

He throws himself into the chair next to me. "You don't mean that," he says urgently. "You're just feeling the after effects of the illness, Gid. You're an amazing actor, and I know all you want to do is act. Why don't you let me deal with all this and you just do what you love best, and keep your head down at the same time. Maybe next year the climate will be better."

I shake my head. "Is your middle name Mephistopheles?"

He looks at me, puzzled. "No, it's Simon. You know that."

I sigh. "I'm just saying that it's the same deal you offered me when I was seventeen and the same spiel you've given me every year since. It will *never* be time to be myself. That's got to be put off like a root canal appointment while I smile and take the money." I eye him. "Or rather you take the money."

He flinches. It's a very slight movement but I catch it and something roils in my stomach. A dim suspicion that's been at the back of my mind for a year now. It's only vanished from my head when I've pushed it out with drink and drugs. "I hope you're not taking money for putting things in front of me," I say quietly. "I always told you, Frankie, that it would be the end if you did that. I can't trust you when you're acting like you've got a horse in the game instead of looking after my interests. I can't abide dishonesty."

"Then maybe you should take a look in the mirror yourself," he says sharply, losing his hold on his temper slightly. "Because you've practised it every day since you were seventeen, and I may have made you a good offer, but I didn't force you into that closet, Gideon. You walked in, mate, and locked the door after you. So don't you fucking lay everything at my doorstep."

I stare at him, making a faint smile appear on my face to wind him up. Frankie has always had a temper. In my young days he'd cow me by screaming in my face and manhandling me. He stopped that when I got older, but for some reason I still stuck with him. Maybe it's because he knows me and if he wanted to, he could make my life very difficult with well-placed leaks to the press. Maybe it's because he's the only authority figure I've ever allowed in my life and I hate to admit that I'm wrong. Whatever it is, I can sense that it's finally coming to an end, though.

He grips the arms of his chair. "Don't smirk at me," he says hotly. "I'm all you've got, Gideon fucking Ramsay." He laughs. It's cold, with no humour. "The great Gideon Ramsay. If your family and friends even knew you, who can say if they'd like you, anyway? Let's face it, mate, you've got no relationship with your fucking brother. I've got a closer one with my tailor." He shakes his head. "None of those men you try to hang around with care about you. They've got their own lives, and you don't figure in them. For once listen to me and face the truth. You knew it when you went down there and tried to be part of their little group. They shoved you out quicker than if you'd been a magpie in someone else's nest."

I can't help the flinch, and he puffs up even further, opening his mouth, but we're interrupted by a footfall at the door and Eli appears. He's quite pale, the freckles standing out on his face, but he has a very resolute look.

"Eli?" I say questioningly.

"I'd like you to leave, Mr Grantham," Eli says steadily.

"What the fuck?"

"You heard." Eli's politeness is frigid. "You're upsetting my patient, and I can't allow that. The consultant warned you." He holds out his hands for the papers that Frankie is holding. "You can leave them with me or take them away with you, but the one thing that is absolutely certain is that I'm not going to allow you to give them to Gideon." He throws his hands out towards the door like a tall, blond butler. "After you," he says coldly. "You can make an appointment to see Gideon when he's feeling better."

Frankie stands up slowly. "Gideon, is it?" he says, moving towards Eli like a fat, suited shark. "Well, enjoy him while you can, because he'll toss you to one side just like all the others. There are no exceptions to that because his career is his one great love. And when he does throw you out, I'll have the nondisclosure and kiss-off cash sum ready." He looks him up and down. "I guarantee you'll accept it," he says coolly. "Gideon, I'll speak to you when you're in a better mood."

Then he's gone, leaving us in a pool of silence that Eli abruptly breaks. "How can you listen to that wanker?" he says loudly, waving his arms in agitation. "He's a total tosser, and you let him do it to you. Why?"

I settle back in my chair, contrarily enjoying the signs of him losing his cool. I shrug finally. "It's always been that way. He doesn't do it that often."

"But the way he spoke to you. You're Gideon Ramsay. You've got a sharper tongue on you than a fucking saw. Why do you allow it?"

I sigh, considering telling him to mind his own fucking business. The sharp words are actually on the edge of my tongue. But I look at him standing there ready to defend me, and I can't say any of the hurtful things I'd normally manage without blinking. "I let it go on because it was easier, and in the beginning it was just me and him," I say slowly. "I was his baby client and he went to town for me and looked after me. I guess I hadn't had anyone do that before. It was always just me on my own, really. No one ever seemed that interested in me. So, to have this powerful man convinced I was the next best thing to sliced bread and to tell me so was very flattering." I stare out to the port of Nice that is shimmering in a heat haze despite how early it is. "I don't know when it got worse, but it's hard to break ties when they're that strong."

"He wants you to lie," he says stubbornly, and I'm suddenly stung.

"Look at you," I say coldly. "You're just a baby. What would you know about lying? Everyone in my world does it. It's more common than blow. People smile and laugh and flatter you and it's all lies. Every single word."

"Then maybe you should leave that world," he says staunchly, his fists clenched and forehead furrowed. His blond, wavy hair lifts in the breeze, showing different colours of ash and platinum, butter and sand.

"And do what?"

"Live," he says passionately. "Because the way I hear it, you were cruising down a path fairly quickly that would have landed you dead. Isn't it better to be alive and doing something different rather than dead and cold?"

"Well, I'm one of those things at the moment," I say lightly, aiming to disperse this drama. "This towel isn't covering much."

His eyes betray him, and I catch the quick glance he sends down my body, the way his pupils dilate and the sudden deep breath he takes. I can see the rejection forming on his lips and suddenly I want to be somewhere else.

"Let's go out," I say and he jerks, looking at me in disbelief.

"*Now?*"

"Yes, now. Why not?" I stand up. "I can't change reality, Eli, so let's do something fun to fill the time."

"I somehow think that's a well-used expression," he says darkly.

"Of course it is. Along with 'of course I'll swallow' and 'I'll ring you.'" An unwilling smile tugs at his lips. "Come on," I urge. "We're in Nice. It's so beautiful, and it's only early morning. We've got all day. Let's hire a car and go out and see the place."

"Together?"

I nod briskly, ignoring my sweaty palms. "Of course. I can't promise that I'll throw your phone in the sea and book a room that rents by the hour, but I'm sure you'll make the best of it."

He hesitates but I can see I've won. "And you'll do exactly what I say?" he says slowly.

Ignoring the flare of heat at those words, I nod. "Of course." I raise my fingers and sketch a cross. "Cross my heart, hope to die."

"Oh please, not that again," he scoffs. He capitulates. "Okay. But I'm taking my med bag. There is to be no drug-taking, drinking, or casual sex whatsoever."

"Goodness, it's like going on a date with one of the Jonas brothers."

He stills. "Is it a date?"

I stare at him, silence falling that's only filled with the noise of the wind and sea. "Do you want it to be?" He looks at me for too long a moment, and I make myself shrug. "Of course it's not. It'll be a completely non-date where I will make no passes whatsoever and won't even attempt to rein in my natural grouchiness."

He smiles sadly. "That I can do."

CHAPTER 9

You and I both know that I don't actually need you at all, unless we count perennial nagging, in which case you're irreplaceable

---

Eli

I crane my neck out of the window as we approach Antibes. Our driver steers into the car park of a marina where seemingly hundreds of boats are moored, some of them huge yachts.

"That's a *lot* of boats," I say.

Gideon looks past me out of the window. "I think it's one of the largest marinas in Europe. You'll often see super yachts mooring here." He sniffs in a huffy manner, and I grin at him.

"Not tempted to buy one? You wouldn't need a big one with the size of your wardrobe."

He laughs and shakes his head as we get out of the car. "I've holidayed on one before. I've never seen such a poky cabin. And you're stuck in it for the entire trip. If I was paying that amount of money, I could buy a hotel and sleep in a different room every night."

"I think that might be a rich person's problem," I murmur, starting to stroll along the path that runs beside the water and feeling him come next to me. "You could fit my entire flat on the deck of that yacht over there."

"At least in your flat you're not stuck out at sea with arseholes."

"I'm not sure. Once when it snowed we were stuck in there for a week. By the third day it was a bit like *Lord of the Flies*."

He laughs. "Frankie said that you have flatmates."

I shoot a glance at him. "Was he reading it in the report from the private detective he set on me?"

He flushes and looks awkward. "I'm afraid that Frankie is rather overzealous, but then I've given him plenty of reasons over the years to never hire someone who might be talkative to the press." He stops and grabs my arm. "I know you're not like that."

"How do you know?"

For a second it's silent, the only noise the musical jingling from the rigging of the boats and the lonely cries of the seagulls. Then Gideon shrugs. "I think we've come to know each other very well during this trip."

"I know," I say softly because it's true.

You can't avoid getting to know someone when you're in close quarters with them, but I've never had such long and intimate conversations with anyone in my life before him, and that includes past lovers.

Each night we've sat on the deck, lit by fairy lights and with our hair blown about by the wind, and we've talked for hours, moving from politics to religion to TV shows and music that we like. I've cherished the time because he engages me and makes me laugh more than anyone I've ever met. His mind is so quick and his humour dry, and I think I could sit forever with him listening to that wonderful voice of his.

We walk in silence for a bit, enjoying the morning sun on our faces and exchanging random observations about the boats. Or if you're him, random sarcastic observations.

"There are a lot of people walking about," I finally muse.

"It's a walking town. A lot of the streets are pedestrianized and there's a lot to be seen, like artist walks. You can rent bikes and go high above the town and see the old villas. They're gorgeous."

"But we're not doing that," I say, looking at him sternly. "It'd be far too much for you at the moment."

"Oh, how dreadful that we're not hiking in the heat. What a terrible tragedy. What *will* we do?" he says acerbically. Then he nudges me. "I know. Let's go and sit in a bar and drink absinthe."

"Let's not," I say and grin at his put-upon sigh. It really doesn't work with me and he knows it. "We'll have a gentle stroll," I say. "With plenty of breaks."

"Okay, you're the boss."

"You know it," I say in a delighted voice.

We grin at each other a little bit too long, and the silence draws out as we stare at each other. I swallow hard and he echoes me, raising a hand and tugging at his shirt collar. "We'll go into the old centre," he finally says, his voice hoarse, and I turn and follow him obediently.

The old town is a maze of narrow cobblestoned streets lined with pretty shops and cafes with their brightly coloured awnings that send shady rectangles onto the hot pavements. "This is so pretty," I marvel. "I'm sure I've seen this before, though."

"You might have seen it in paintings. Loads of artists have stayed here over the years. Picasso stayed here for a while at the Chateau Grimaldi with his lover Francoise Gilot who was his muse. They seemed to have been very happy here. He painted a lot and left the paintings to the owner. It's a museum now." He pauses. "I like to think of that. The two lovers coming here to a sleepy little seaside town and living in this golden creative bubble."

He flushes slightly and I stare at him. It's becoming very apparent to me that Gideon Ramsay of the sharp tongue and jaded view of life, is actually secretly a romantic. The thought charms me but I say nothing and walk happily along beside him as he cuts his way through narrow streets, obviously knowing where he's going.

The town is fairly quiet at the moment as it's still early, but the streets are coming to life in the way that seaside towns do. Shop owners open their doors and call to each other, speaking in voluble French as the multicoloured bunting flutters in the sea breeze.

"You've been here before, haven't you?" I ask him as he cuts down a side street and then another.

He nods. "Many times. The Canvis gala is held here every year."

"There's posh, then," I muse and he grins.

"And fucking boring. The last few times I came, I ended up ditching the party after I'd donated and wandered the town instead. There's a lot of history here."

"You ditched the Canvis party?" I ask, amused because it's a huge annual charity event attended by loads of celebrities. Some of my old patients would have given their teeth to attend it.

He looks awkward. "I can't see the point of spending all that money on food and drink and clothes. Donate all of that to the cause instead. Ask me for the money and I'll happily give it without having to wear a dinner jacket and talk to people I don't want to know."

"You've just downgraded the event of the year to a children's party."

"At least children get jelly and ice cream," he says sulkily.

We pass through a bustling market where the air is sharp with the scent of fresh cheeses and meats. Gideon buys us a paper bag full of peaches and I bite into mine, feeling the juices run sweet down my throat. I watch him as he gives the vendor the money, exchanging some remark in quick French at which the vendor laughs.

"You fit here," I say, finishing my peach and licking my fingers. He looks handsome and urbane in navy shorts and Vans and a short-sleeved navy shirt that's open at the neck to show his tanned chest. His distinctive features are shaded by sunglasses and a straw Panama hat. I've seen appreciative glances thrown at him, but it's not to do with who he is because that's not obvious. It's more him. He stands out even when he's not trying.

"Do I?" He looks puzzled. "I don't think I've ever fitted in anywhere." He immediately looks profoundly uncomfortable, as I've found he tends to do when he's admitted anything personal.

I take pity on him and pull him into a bakery. "I'm still starving," I say. "Shall we get something?"

"When aren't you hungry?" he muses. "You're like a bottomless pit."

It's true, but I do have an ulterior motive. He's still too thin and genuinely doesn't spare much thought to food beyond a need to fuel. I've found, though, that if I say I'm hungry he's too well-mannered to let me eat alone.

"I need more than peaches," I say in a sad voice and he immediately capitulates, digging in his pockets.

"Of course. Let me get some change."

I grab his arm, and we both still as a charge runs between us. I breathe in, hopefully unobtrusively. "No, it's my treat."

He hesitates before gracefully complying, and I order us both an almond croissant to take away as well as a couple of milky coffees.

"I don't take sugar," Gideon says, wrinkling his nose.

"You do until you've fattened up a bit."

"Lovely. That'll get me lots of jobs."

"Are you worried by your weight?" I ask, astonished.

He shakes his head immediately. "No, that's the last thing I'm bothered about. I usually do an intensive gym course for a month or so before a film, but apart from that I can usually eat what I want and not gain weight."

We leave the bakery and meander past colourful shop windows. Flowers are everywhere, glowing in terracotta pots and hanging from the walls, making the air heavy with the scent of flowers and the sea. He throws out observations, and it intrigues me to see the workings of his mind and watch those clever eyes of his.

For a supposed hellraiser, he notices the smallest, most charming things.

I don't know how to do this. I'm so attracted to him that it makes my stomach hurt, but it's more than that. I just want to be with him. Just talking and wandering like this makes me as happy as I've ever been. I've never felt like this about another man before, and it's so fucking typical that it's the one man I can't have.

We finally make our way to a beach, and as if by mutual accord we settle down on a bench to eat our croissants. He finishes first, tossing the last of the pastry to a waiting bird who sits with his head cocked to one side appraising us curiously. I look at Gideon's long, slender fingers and imagine them round my cock and immediately launch into speech.

"Can I ask you something?"

He smiles and looks at me. "I'm sure you will."

"What was home like?" He stills and I look at him. "You said you never fit in anywhere. Was that the same for home?" I stop. "I'm so sorry," I burst out. "That was bloody rude."

I just want to know everything about him and the time is seeping away for me to find it out.

"No, it doesn't matter," he says quickly. "I don't mind telling you stuff." He pauses, looking out to sea, and I turn in the same direction, hoping to relax him as it's horrible to talk with someone making an X-ray of your face.

"I'm not sure my home was what everyone else had," he finally says slowly. "I went to boarding school when I was seven."

"That's early," I murmur, and Gideon shrugs.

"Not really. Not for the people my parents knew. It's about average." He pauses. "I didn't want to go. I'd have loved to stay at home. I wanted to be with my mother, but she was very busy with charity commitments, so it wasn't to be."

"Did it get better when Milo came to the school too?"

He stares ahead, sitting very still. "Milo didn't go to boarding school. My mother wanted him at home and my father does as my mother wants."

A silence falls as I grapple with what he just said. "And she didn't have you come back too?"

His long, thin fingers tighten on his coffee cup. "No," he finally says slowly and wearily. "She didn't. I was older anyway by then, but I stayed where I was."

"I'm sorry." My stomach feels like it's full of snakes, writhing and making me feel sick at how rejected he must have felt.

Incredibly, he laughs. "It was slightly awkward sometimes because I had friends who were boarding because their parents lived abroad. Mine only lived about ten miles away from the school. I used to pretend that my mother was a mountain climber and my father a mountain guide. I told some incredibly elaborate stories about their daring adventures when I was ten, but they were slightly spoilt when my mother and father actually came to a swimming gala. She had a panic attack because of the height of the stands, and he made a fuss when he got tomato sauce on his jacket."

I can't smile, and he looks confused for a second before he shrugs and gives me a thin smile. "No need to be sorry. It is as it is. Milo had an accident when he was five which left him with a stutter. That took up the last of my mother's attention. There wasn't anything left after that and really, she did me a favour."

"How?" I whisper.

He grins. "It was very freeing not having to worry about parents' evening, for a start. I could behave as badly as I wanted and school put up with it because of the fees, and my parents didn't want to know." He grimaces. "I was a bit of a monster."

"*No*," I say lightly. "I can't believe it."

He smiles, and it's more natural this time. "I had friends, so I was okay."

"Are Niall and Silas your family, then?" I say, remembering the name of the other boy from Gideon's stories.

He shrugs. "I suppose so," he says in an unsure voice.

"Did you enjoy school?"

"Not really." He sighs. "I didn't feel at home there either, you see. I'm a bit of a nomad. Not at home anywhere."

"I think nomads are at home everywhere," I say softly, and he shrugs again.

"I'm a renegade nomad. I'm obviously a trendsetter. What can I say?" Then he brightens. "Everything changed when Frankie came along." He shoots me a look. "I know you don't have a high opinion of him." I snort and he smiles. "I know you don't have a single good opinion of him at all, but he was good to me. He discovered me when I was at school, and everything I am is because of him."

"I think everything you are is because of you," I say steadily. "Your talent. Your personality. You."

"Don't say that," he drawls. "Now I've got no one to blame."

I look at him askance and then, incredibly, we burst into laughter, leaning into each other. We rest against each other, and his hand touches mine for a brief, precious second. Then he pulls back and looks down the promenade.

"Let's get a hotel room," he says.

I start. *"What?"*

He gives me his half smile which has a wicked twist to it. Out of all his smiles, I like this one best because it's like he's showing a hidden side to me. "I'm sorry to disappoint you, but not for any nefarious reasons," he says. "The beach at the Belle Rives in Juan-les-Pins is the best around, but you have to be a resident to go on it. I feel like sleeping in the sun while you will probably want to do something appallingly energetic."

"There's posh, then," I say wonderingly. "Does it rent by the hour? Because I just can't stop in anything less."

"I'll endeavour to descend to your standards. Although it's probably better if I just fall."

"Sarcastic," I say happily and nudge him.

. . .

Gideon

The Belle Rives is as gorgeous as ever. It's my favourite hotel to stay in around here because of the art deco interior and the association with F. Scott Fitzgerald, who stayed here with his wife and child when it was a private house. Usually, I'll steer straight upstairs to the Fitzgerald piano bar, which serves bloody lovely cocktails. That's probably the reason why I can't remember what the hotel rooms actually look like.

However, it's different being here with Eli. We sit outside on the terrace which I don't think I've ever sat on before, usually being far too hungover to eat in the sun. We eat delicious sea bass and talk and laugh. I find myself noticing small details so that I can point them out to him. Like the way the bougainvillea that grows up the walls makes the yellow stones of the hotel glow. And how the huge pots of lavender fill the air with a heavy and quintessentially French scent.

Once we've eaten, we stroll down to the beach where we spend the afternoon lounging on comfortable sunbeds and ordering cold drinks which are sadly non-alcoholic because of my martinet of a nurse.

Later on, I lie in the late afternoon sun as Eli tries his hand at water skiing. I watch him surreptitiously, admiring the long lines of his body and the way his red and navy patterned board shorts hang from his narrow hips.

I'm not the only one to notice him. With his body tanned a golden brown, that riot of wavy blond hair that's turned nearly white in the sun, and the lazy full wattage of his smile, he's beautiful. I'm the only one who has to hide my attraction, however, because this is a celebrity hangout and the paparazzi are never far away. The thought leaves a bitter taste in my mouth.

Finally, he comes back and flings himself onto the sunbed next to me. His body rests against mine for a brief, precious second, and I feel the coolness of his skin as water droplets seem to rain down on my body and sizzle. He lies back happily, and the next few hours pass the way they always do, with him in a contented sprawl as we sit chatting and laughing and occasionally falling into a comfortable silence. I've never met anyone like him before. His mind is so quick and agile and his humour so warm. Every moment with him feels easy and right.

However, the afternoon slides into the evening with an awful finality, marking the time we have left before we separate as hours rather than days. I feel a desperate urge to grab him and demand that we go somewhere else, anywhere we can be together, because I don't want to be without him. But I say nothing and we lie in a loud silence.

Finally, I sit up on the lounger looking out to where the sun is setting, a salt-scented breeze blowing my hair back. It's that time of evening where everything seems to be touched in gold. The beach is practically empty now as the guests head into the hotel to dress for dinner. Beach attendants wander back and forth, picking up rubbish and preparing for the following day. "We'll need to meet the car soon or we'll miss the boat," I say reluctantly.

Eli comes to sit next to me on my sunbed, and for a second I can feel the heat of his body, but then he moves so there's a careful and decorous gap between us. I breathe in almost desperately and relax slightly when I smell the familiar scent of coconut.

Silence falls for a long moment and then I sigh and stir. "This isn't one-sided, is it?" He looks at me and I gesture between us. "This thing. This attraction. I'm not the only one who feels it."

He looks torn, and I'm just about to take the statement back so he's not uncomfortable, when his expression turns resolute. "You're not the only one." I sag a little in relief, but he carries on, talking quickly. "But it can't be anything while I'm your nurse. It's against everything I stand for. It would be totally wrong, and I would worry that I was taking advantage of you."

"Makes me sound like the heroine in *Poldark*."

He smiles, but it fades quickly. "I've been looking after you for a while, and we've got close. It's very common for the patient to mix up feelings of gratitude for something else."

"I think I'd have had to have felt gratitude for something in my life in the first place." I shrug. "I'm not terribly good at being grateful. Makes my skin itch."

He shakes his head reprovingly, but his mouth twitches, and I take that for slight encouragement. I'm coming to realise that I would take anything from him.

"I'm thirty-nine years old," I say slowly. "I'm not bedridden, and you and I both know that I don't actually need you at all, unless we count perennial nagging, in which case you're irreplaceable." He snorts, and I conceal my smile. "I'm grumpy, as stubborn as a donkey, and resistant to all forms of authority. It doesn't make me a candidate for romantic dreams."

He nods, but he looks torn. "I just need to protect you," he says almost staunchly, and I feel something warm in my stomach at the earnestness in his words. I don't think anyone has ever said that to me before, let alone wanted to do it. I've had impassioned words of longing poured into my ears, declarations of infatuation, but nothing like these simple words which are all the more touching for being plain.

I consider his earnest, open face, the freckles on his nose which have multiplied in the hot sun, and the wavy mess of his hair, and I feel something tug in my chest. Something I've never felt before. A desire to make things better and easier for him because I don't want him to feel conflicted or sad.

"If we're not going to be anything else, then why don't we be friends?" I say slowly. "I know there's probably a codicil somewhere that prevents that, but surely it would be okay?" I hate the faint note of begging in my voice but I can't do anything about it.

He stares at me for a long second. "I can do friends," he says slowly. "While I'm in your employ I'll be friends with you."

"And when you're not?" I ask, holding my breath.

He bites his lip. "Then we'll take it as it comes, but friends is a good start."

I settle back on my lounger. "I'm not sure whether either option is much good for you, Eli," I say softly. "I'm not good for much, I'm afraid. I haven't got many friends and the ones I've had I've treated spectacularly badly."

"I can't say I've seen much evidence of that."

"Google me. In fact, just read *The Sun*. They'll tell you everything you need to know, as they have a very unhealthy obsession with me." He laughs and I sigh. "Maybe you're different. All I can say is that I'll try because I want to be friends with you."

It's only the partial truth, because I want a lot more. Unfortunately, I can't name what that is. All I know is that I feel a yearning and a pull towards him. It's so strong I can feel it like invisible strands of silk tethering me to him even while we sit unmoving and staring out to sea as the sun sinks into a fiery ball on the horizon.

∽

The next day, I stand on the deck, leaning against the railing and looking at the grey mass of Southampton coming into view. Footsteps sound behind me, but I would know it was Eli even if he walked silently. He only has to enter a room and it's like my senses are tuned into his wavelength.

I remain staring out to sea and he leans on the rail next to me. I shoot him a quick glance. He looks smart for a change, wearing a black short-sleeved shirt, stone-coloured shorts, and black Vans. His hair has even been tamed, and for some reason he doesn't look right. I've grown used to seeing a slightly scruffy Eli who is relaxed and barefoot, and I have a sudden urge to mess his hair up. I resist it, because he looks resolute and a bit sad. I force my gaze back to the view.

"Where are you going when we land?" I say softly.

He shifts his stance against the railing. "I've got a couple of jobs that'll keep me in Dubai for four months. The first job starts in two days. I'll go home, do some laundry, and pack again."

"*Dubai*," I burst out. I turn to face him, unable to stop, and he looks at me, his eyebrows raised. "That's so far," I finish quite spectacularly lamely.

He smiles almost sadly, and it doesn't suit that wide-open, freckled face. It's wrong, as if he's put a mask on. "It needs to be far," he says grimly.

Too far to meet, I think, and wonder if that's his reason. "Four months?" I say softly.

He shrugs. "I need you to have some time to think. Some space to work out what's going to happen between us."

"I don't need space," I start to say demandingly and stop. If this were me a few months ago, I'd have shouted and demanded and behaved so badly that I'd have got what I wanted. Now, I just stand with the words dying away into the wind that whips between us, and I swallow the rest because they would upset him, and for some reason I can't have that.

I nod. "I'll do as you want," I say softly. I hesitate and then the words flood out in almost a begging tone. "Will you write to me?"

I flush because I have never, *ever* begged anyone to do anything or be anything for me. Not since the grisly morning when I was seven and I cried and clung to my mother and begged her to let me stay at home with her and my father. She'd pulled my arms away, and my father had summoned my new house master to help. As he'd held my arms and talked cheerfully, I'd watched them drive down the winding drive away from me, and I'd sworn right then that I'd never ask anyone for anything personal ever again. However, that obviously doesn't ring true with this man, and I brace myself for his refusal but it doesn't come. Why I thought it would is beyond me. He doesn't do anything I expect.

Instead, he smiles. "That would be nice." He turns to face me. "I'll give you my email address." I nod and his expression clouds. "But only once a week, Gideon. You need the rest of the time to be by yourself without me influencing you."

"I don't know where you get the idea that you're some sort of

Derren Brown," I say loftily, and I'm gratified when he smiles and the shadow in his eyes lifts.

"I'll miss ..." he starts to say impetuously but then shuts himself down. "I've enjoyed very much being with you," he finishes very formally. "It's been an experience that I won't forget."

"Like appendicitis?"

He grins. "Not nearly as painful." He pauses. "Well, not quite."

I shove him and he laughs, but I retract my hand quickly. He can say all he wants. I know my own mind for once, and the clouds of confusion and rage that have been my constant companions for years have swept back, leaving me in an uneasy sort of clarity. I have to let him do this, to separate us, because he needs to do it. I know if I stepped into him, his control would snap, and I could have what I want, but he would blame himself and some of that sunny sheen to him would be tarnished and damaged, and I can't have that.

"Four months?" I say, holding out my hand.

He bites his lips but takes it, the zing in my palm somewhat familiar by now. "And if you've changed your mind, you'll tell me straightaway," he says quickly. "No hard feelings. I will totally understand."

"And the same for you," I say.

He smiles almost helplessly. "It's a deal."

Our hands separate and we turn to see the land drawing close, but my hand tingles as if he's still holding it. I wonder if that will be enough to tide me over for the next few months.

CHAPTER 10

Until now you've just bobbed along on life's stream like an oblivious and very grumpy cork

Gideon

It's twilight when we pull up the long drive leading up to *Chi an Mor*. The great Elizabethan manor house glows in the last rays of sunlight like it's been lit by a spotlight.

I stir in the back seat. "Where am I staying?" I ask.

Milo glances back at me and smiles. "Oz and Silas have got a cottage on the estate. It's lovely and private, so they thought it would be perfect for you."

Niall looks at me in the rear-view mirror. "The house is still open to the public, so that's no good for you. It would be like staying in a goldfish bowl."

I wonder with a pang why they haven't suggested me staying with them. Then I remember that I used to sleep with Niall. That's probably a step too far even for Emily Post.

As if sensing my thoughts, Milo reaches back and squeezes my leg. "We're at the main house at the moment because we're having the patio done at the house and the hammering is driving me crazy."

That twang eases, and I smile at my baby brother. He looks well. He's lightly tanned, and his hair is a crazy mess due to Niall's habit of having the windows open in the car even while doing ninety miles an hour down the motorway. It had made conversation impossible, but I'd been glad of that, as it gave me the opportunity to stare out of the window and think of my last glimpse of Eli.

He'd greeted Niall and Milo pleasantly and accepted their hugs of thanks for looking after me. Then he'd turned to me, hoisting his bag onto his shoulder.

"Well, this is it," he'd said in a low voice.

"For now," I'd reminded him, and he'd smiled.

"We'll see." For a second he'd hesitated and then had stuck out his hand. "It's been an honour to look after you," he'd said steadily.

I'd stared at him, accepting his handshake and trying to memorize the rough grasp. "A sentence which has never been said before."

"There's a first time for everything," he'd said levelly and then, touching his fingers to his forehead in a mock salute, he'd turned and moved back through the crowd. I'd watched as a tall, dark-haired young man came out of the throng to grab him in a hug and then they were gone, swallowed in the mass of people as if he'd never been in my life. My fist had clenched in my pocket around the strip of card with his details as if it were made of gold.

Niall takes a side turn, dragging me from my thoughts. We follow a winding, almost overgrown, path with trees hanging over it until we emerge from the trees, and he pulls up outside a small cottage.

Built of a honey-coloured stone, it looks Georgian in origin, with sashed windows that have been painted a grey green, and wisteria climbing the stones, the purple looking almost psychedelic in this light. Trees surround it and the air is full of the chattering song of the birds as they prepare to bed down for the night.

I climb out of the Land Rover and stretch, feeling my muscles pop. "It's lovely," I say, and Milo comes up next to me, taking my arm companionably.

"It's pretty inside. Silas and Oz have had it done up so they can rent it out. You're their guinea pig."

"What would his guinea pig name have been?" Niall asks, hoisting my bags.

"I can do that," I protest, but he shakes his head.

"I think Flossie," he says happily.

I glare at him. "Why?"

He shrugs. "It suits you."

"I'd have preferred something a bit more butch."

Milo laughs. "You won't like mine, then." He snorts loudly. "I'd have called you Princess Sparkles. You'd have been my beloved guinea pig who met a sad end when he escaped his cage and got in the gin bottle."

Niall starts to laugh, and I groan. "I know that's sticking. I just know it."

"Don't be so touchy, Princess Sparkles," Niall says, making Milo laugh harder.

I shake my head and hold out my hand for the intricate iron key. I fit it into the front door and push it open.

I find myself in a small hallway. A crooked-looking staircase climbs up and away, and to my right is a small lounge. It has an open fireplace with a basket of logs next to it, giving out a woody sap smell. Floor-to-ceiling bookcases that run on either side are stuffed with paperbacks. A small sofa and armchair upholstered in a lavender-coloured cotton and an oak coffee table are the only other furniture.

I walk through to a small kitchen at the back. The cupboards are painted a rich cream and it has an old wooden worktop that glows with age. In one corner is a small round pine table and two chairs. I move over to the back door and look out onto a wild-looking garden with a huge oak tree shading it. At the bottom of the garden is an old stone wall, and, over it, I get a glimpse of fields undulating in shades of green like a fertile magic carpet. I turn as Milo walks in.

"Niall's putting your bags upstairs," he says, touching the basket that's sitting on the countertop. "Oz had this made up for you. There's coffee, tea, biscuits, and everything you need initially. Fresh milk and bread will be delivered to you every morning." He winks at me. "No vodka, though."

I shrug awkwardly. "I'm not drinking at the moment. I promised Eli."

I break off, but his gaze sharpens. "Oh, you promised Eli. That's lovely," he says innocently. I glare at him, and he smiles. "You look good, Gid," he says, coming near and examining me with the same focus I've seen him apply to a three-hundred-year-old painting. "You looked terrible last time I saw you. Now you look ..."

He hesitates, and I stare at him. "What?"

"New," he finishes somewhat uncertainly. "You look new."

"No, still the same shop-soiled thirty-nine-year-old body," I say flippantly, and he shakes his head.

"No, I don't think so." He hesitates. "I was going to keep your phone and laptop. But I don't think I will now."

"Why?"

"Because I think you'll do what's best for you this time without being forced into it."

I shrug. "I won't be rushing to get in touch with anyone," I confess, sitting down on a chair at the table.

He settles down opposite me, his expression lively and interested. "Why?"

I shrug awkwardly. "I just don't want to at the moment. I like being away from everyone. My head isn't so cluttered."

He looks as pleased as if I've just declared that Hogwarts is real.

"So, what will you do?" He gestures to the living room. "Silas and Oz have filled the bookshelves, so there's plenty to read. And Oz found an old record player in the attic at the big house along with a box of old records. They might be fun to have a listen to."

"That sounds good," I say and huff. "It sounds good now. I don't think I'd have been so receptive a few months ago."

"Let's focus on the now," he says steadily, his eyes clear and filled with unspoken messages. "Forget about the past for a while."

"Thank you," I say, impulsively reaching out and squeezing his hand. "I love you."

He looks startled, and his eyes glisten. "I love you too, Gid."

Niall comes to the door, his eyes softening with approval as he looks at the two of us. He seems to have made it his mission for us to get over all the awkwardness and be family. It's funny but somehow it doesn't seem so impossible anymore.

"Alright, Sparkles?" he says, and Milo laughs.

I grin and sit back. "I think I'd like to take cooking lessons," I say consideringly, and Niall chokes.

"Pardon?"

"Cooking lessons."

"For meth?" he asks hesitantly.

Milo huffs indignantly. "It's not *Breaking Bad*, Niall."

I laugh. "No. I think I'd like to learn how to cook, read some books, and just relax."

Niall stares at me for a long second before dismissing the retort that is quite obviously dying to come out. "How about asking Maggie, the cook up at the house? She loves teaching people how to do things."

"Ooh, yes," Milo says enthusiastically. "Her cooking is wonderful, Gid." He grins. "This is going to be brilliant. I'm *so* glad you're here."

I sit back. "I think I'm going to like it here," I say contemplatively.

. . .

Eli

My best friend, Jesse, hugs me and steps back. "Fucking hell, you look good," he exclaims loudly, ignoring the glare of a middle-aged lady next to us.

I smile an apology at her and drag him away. "Where's the car?"

"'Wow, Jesse, how lovely to see you. Thank you so much for driving all this way only to turn round and drive back again.' No really, Eli, you know how I live to get stuck behind fifteen caravans and a tractor for four hours."

I look apologetically at my best friend. Tall and slender, he has shiny mink-brown hair with a quiff that often threatens to collapse all over his high-boned face. "I'm sorry," I say immediately. "Thank you so much for doing all this driving. I could have caught the train, though. Are you too tired to drive?"

"Dreadfully," he says soulfully and then grins. "Not really. I picked up a job in Newquay yesterday, so I stayed overnight."

"What was it this time?"

"New boyfriend for a promotion party to honour the bloke's ex."

I blink. Jesse works for an agency that deals mainly with LGBT clients, supplying people for all sorts of needs. In his time, he's posed as an admirer to make an ex jealous, landscaped a garden for clients, walked dogs, and he once even babysat some goldfish while their owner was away. But we still call him an escort, and Charlie, our other friend, calls him Vivian from *Pretty Woman*. He's a very beautiful man who, when he wants to, can be very charming, which accounts for his success rate. However, he's also quick-tempered and funny and my best friend since primary school.

"How did it go?" I ask, taking my jacket off and throwing it over the back seat as we get in the car.

"Interesting." He purses his mouth. "It was going pretty well, if I do say so myself. I was quick-witted, attentive, and all-round perfect. The food was lovely and the cake was a masterpiece."

"So, what happened?"

He shrugs. "The ex threw the cake at me, stormed to the toilet, and my client followed him in order to have very loud bathroom sex while we all waited in an awkward sort of silence in the dining room."

I burst out laughing. "What did you do?"

"I love the way that my pain is yours," he says wryly. "You'll really have to stop being so empathetic."

"Bugger that. What happened?"

He huffs. "I pretended to be devastated for at least an hour. Then I pulled one of the junior partners."

I shake my head. "You are truly a tart with a heart of gold."

He laughs. "Thank you very much. Can I have that inscribed on a cup?"

"I'll even do it in italics. So what's next for you?"

He shrugs. "Who knows. Zeb will tell me when we get back."

As if united, we both sigh wistfully. Zeb is his boss. Suave and absolutely gorgeous, he's also entirely oblivious to the stunning men and women he employs, having a very firm rule about not shitting where he works.

Jesse slides a look at me. "So, how was it? This was a surprise pickup. We expected you back a couple of weeks ago."

"I did Maria a favour," I say, thinking of my boss at the agency. "She needed someone quickly, and I was in the city, so I said yes."

"Another oldies cruise. Was it really boring?"

"No," I say slowly and sigh without meaning to, thinking of that last sight of Gideon. He'd looked sad, awkward, and cross all in one go. It's not an easy thing to accomplish. "Not boring at all," I finish softly.

He darts a swift and sharp look at me. "You alright? You sound a bit funny."

"Just tired," I say quickly.

"So, who was the celeb this time?"

"You know I can't tell you."

"I know you *won't* tell me," he corrects me. "And for the record, I absolutely hate your discretion."

"Duly noted," I say solemnly. "I'll try harder next time."

"Just give me an age range. Was he or she nearly dead?"

I shake my head. "For fuck's sake. No, he wasn't. He's in his late thirties." I smile. "And very grumpy."

"Oh my *God*," he says slowly. "What have you done, Eli?"

"What do you mean?"

"You fucked a patient."

"I did *not*," I say crossly. "Never. You know I wouldn't."

"So what's with all that?"

He gestures at my face, and I frown. "All what? I haven't said anything."

"You didn't have to. It was the way you said it and that sad, longing face."

"It's like being friends with Uri Geller."

"Can I just say how relieved I am that he's using the power of his mind to sort out Brexit for us all." He laughs and then sobers quickly. "You sounded all soft and fond when you spoke about your patient."

I sigh and rub my hands down my face and then stare out of the window, struggling to find the words to describe the time I've spent with Gideon. Jesse's endlessly patient, so he waits for me. "I wanted to so badly," I say finally. "For the first time ever, I wanted to fuck a patient."

"And?"

"Don't you have anything to say to that?"

I'm definitely expecting something because Jesse is religious in not sleeping with his clients. He lives by that maxim.

"I'm wondering what he's like to make you practically forget everything you've always sworn by."

"He's just lovely." I sigh. "I can't describe him properly. He's sarcastic, funny, grumpy, and the most lonely person I've ever met."

"And did he want you back?"

I nod. "He did," I say sadly.

"Sounds like your perfect match, then."

"What?"

He smiles. "Eli, you like looking after people. It's why you're as good at your job as you are. Combined with his other attributes, which you've always said you look for, he sounds perfect." He pauses. "Apart from the grumpiness. I've never heard you express a penchant for that before."

"It's a new thing for me," I say wryly and then sigh. "I can't do anything."

"Of course not," he says calmly. "It would be totally wrong."

"I know."

"But you're not his nurse now and you won't be his nurse again. There's also hopefully plenty of time to pass between you both leaving the ship and dying."

I jerk. "What the fuck? You should be a motivational speaker."

"I'll leave that to Charlie Sunshine." We smile at the thought of our other flatmate, Charlie, who is happiness personified and perennially cheerful.

"So, what are you intending to do?" He sneaks a look at me and pushes the hair back from his face. "I hope you're not thinking of doing something self-sacrificing and quite frankly fucking stupid."

"No," I sigh. "I'm going to give it a few months and then see. That'll give him the chance to work out that there are much better options around for him than a broke nurse."

"Fucking hell, Eli. Do you want me to bake a cake for your pity party?" I snort and he punches me lightly on the arm. "That's better. Now listen to Jesse. You go away and give him space, but if he still wants you after that, you are to fucking go to him. Bugger everyone else's opinion. You're an amazing person and a bloody good best mate. He couldn't do any better than you. Fuck the bills. You got those by being brave and working for the Red Cross, not placing bets at Ladbrokes."

"Thank you," I say softly, grabbing his hand and squeezing it. "You always make me feel better."

"I make everyone feel better," he says somewhat dolefully. "It's in my job description."

"But not your life description," I say sharply. "You need to remember that."

Jesse is a born people pleaser with an absolute shit ability to pick men. His exes have all been horrible.

"No," he says slowly and not entirely convinced. "No, I suppose not."

A companionable silence falls, and I grab my laptop from my rucksack.

"What are you doing?" he asks.

"Emailing him. I promised him we'd be friends and keep in touch that way."

"That's more like it," he says approvingly. "Keep it clean, though. No dick pics, young man."

His laughter as I pinch him rings around the car as I start typing.

Gideon

I wake up the next morning, unsure where I am for a second. Then I feel the weight of the sheets and blankets on me and see the sandblasted beams in the low ceiling and remember that I'm in the cottage. I relax back against the pillows. I fell asleep with the window open last night, and instead of the noise of the sea I'd heard the steady beat of rain on the roof and smelt the sweet scent of rain on dry earth. I look out the window. The sky is a merry cornflower blue now and the air filled with the sound of birdsong.

I stretch and hear the beep of my phone. For a second I hesitate. I don't want Frankie or my job in this place, as if they'll somehow contaminate this peace. Then I realise it was my email notification and hope seizes me, making my fingers shake as I grab at my phone, almost dropping it before I check my email and see one from Eli.

To: Gideon Ramsay

From: Eli Jones

I hope you got to your brother's home safely.

I wanted to give you some tips for your health. I'm smiling as I type this because I can tell that you're already rolling your eyes. However, you only left me a few hours ago and my contract doesn't finish until tomorrow, so I still feel quite able to be your nurse and tell you what to do.

As such, I'd like you to remember that drinking to excess isn't good for you. Neither are drugs, random twinks, and keeping the same hours as Keith Richards.

Now, going to bed early, eating regular meals, and leading a monastic lifestyle – they're all *fantastic* for your health.

That's my spiel as your nurse done. Now for my tips as your new friend. Please make time for your brother and let him in. I promise you won't be disappointed. I know this from just a few days of watching the two of you together. He wants to get to know you and, speaking as someone who's done that over the last couple of weeks, I have to say that it's worth doing.

Go for plenty of walks, not just for your health, but because it gives you space to think. You really need to do this because it seems to me that up until now you've just bobbed along on life's stream like an oblivious and very grumpy cork. Take control of your life, and if it means that you won't ever let Frankie talk to you again the way he did on the ship, then your friend will be very happy.

I'd like to see you take up some hobbies too that don't end up with you being stoned, drunk, or passed out. I know those activities filled most of your timetable before, but trust me, there is life outside a hotel room.

Well, that was your introduction to life as my friend. I

hope it wasn't too bossy. Who am I kidding? It was totally bossy and totally needed.

I fall back against my pillow with a smile on my face. Right at this moment it's like he's with me, his Welsh lilt sounding warm and sunshiny in the room as he bosses me around with a smile. I miss him fiercely already. It just feels wrong to not have him here. I feel awkward around my brother and friends, and it strikes me that I've never felt that with Eli. When I'm with him I feel whole, as stupid as that sounds. I'm me, and I'm not constantly looking for the door to escape.

I shake my head. Time to shower and dress. However, the smile lasts even through my shower in the tiny bathroom where you'd be hard-pressed to wash a Borrower without inadvertently squashing them. When I'm finally dressed in grey shorts and a blue T-shirt, I bound downstairs, feeling my stomach rumble. I'm starving.

The knock on the front door startles me but I pad over and open it, finding myself staring at a dark-haired man with a sharp-looking face and very blue eyes who has a small dark-haired toddler on his hip. She has a mass of silky curls held back by a pink bow.

"Can I help you?" I say slowly.

"Thanks, mate" he says in a voice heavily tinged with an Irish accent, and to my amazement he hands me the child and saunters past me.

The child and I look at each other appraisingly. I expect her to cry, but instead she gabbles something and bops me in the face with a tiny fist.

"Ouch!" I say and the stranger turns.

"Cora, we don't do that to strangers, lovey." He looks at me appraisingly. "Unless they're Gideon Ramsay come to cause trouble, my love." He runs his fingers over the wooden mantle and stares at me unblinkingly.

I feel my lips tugging into a smile, and I settle the little girl onto my hip comfortably and with the ease of practice, relishing the surprise he can't quite hide. I'm well used to small children. I was ten when Milo was born, and I've worked with many children in my career. "You must be Oz," I say, walking through to the kitchen and hearing his footsteps following me. "I didn't meet you on my last visit here because you were visiting your mum. I've heard a lot about you, though." I pause. "Although the words never quite managed to conjure up what a smart mouth you've got."

He snorts almost reluctantly. "All the better to lecture you with, Mr Ramsay. I think when you descended on us before, you stayed at Niall's house and caused a wee bit of trouble."

His voice is light but there's an undercurrent of warning there. I try hard to be outraged, but I can't summon up even a tiny bit. This man is my brother's best friend, and he's looking out for him. How could I be annoyed?

I switch the kettle on and turn back to him, shifting his daughter on my hip. This must be Cora, Silas's daughter. I feel a sudden sense of shame that I've never seen her before. This is my oldest friend's child, and I wouldn't know her if I passed her on the stairs. I never meant to stay away despite the invitations that Silas sent me. It just seemed like I was an outsider here the same way I was at home, where everyone seemed to belong to each other and no one to me. That feeling gets very old, very quickly.

I look at the little girl and she gives me a toothy smile, reaching for my face. I grab her fingers and kiss them soundly, making a smacking sound that makes her chuckle delightedly. I look up and Oz is watching me closely, surprise and something else running across that clever mobile face.

"Let's get this over with," I say wryly, handing him his daughter as the kettle boils. "I love to start my day with a lecture. Either that or a big old punch in the face." He laughs, and I look at him. "I'm not here to make trouble. I know you're here to warn me."

He sits down at the table, letting his daughter down to the floor and watching as she toddles around the room, looking at the place appraisingly as if sizing it up for trouble. "That *is* why I came," he says slowly. "You caused a lot of trouble last time you were here."

"And Milo is your best friend, and you want the best for him and Niall, and you don't need me butting in."

"You know, a lecture and a warning is much more satisfactory if the recipient doesn't take over warning himself."

I laugh suddenly, a harsh bark, and for a second we look at each other before he grins, his face lighting up.

"You don't need to warn me," I say steadily. "I love my brother, and I'm ashamed of the way I behaved before."

"Would you do it again if you had a do-over?"

"Probably," I say honestly. "Which might make me a bad person, but at least I'm a predictable one."

"I don't think you're predictable at all," he says, his eyes bright in the sunshine. "But I like honest people."

"How about grumpy ones, because I can say with certainty that no matter how many epiphanies I have in life, that facet of my personality will never change."

He laughs suddenly. "Fuck, that's good to hear. There are far too many Suzy Sunshines on this estate. I like a bit of vinegar with my chips."

"I'm sorry we haven't met," I say. "We would have met before if I'd got my act together."

He shrugs. "Then or now doesn't matter. It happens when we're ready." He smiles at me. "You know Silas is absolutely fucking cuckoo about this place. Swears it works a magic of its own."

"Oh God," I sigh, getting up to pour tea. "I had enough lectures about that when we were teenagers to last a lifetime. I'd rather do algebra than listen to him talk about his magic house. Once, I got off a train and stranded myself in Wakefield when he started talking about it. I can still see his face as I waved him off."

He laughs, looking at me appreciatively, and for a second it seems like we're rival armies who've come to a rapprochement that might end up in a permanent ceasefire. "Some of it makes sense, though," he says meditatively. "*Chi an Mor* does seem to attract people who need to find a home for a while or permanently."

"Please don't say that," I say wryly. "I came for a break, not to grow a beard down to my ankles and talk in a Cornish accent."

"At least your feet would be warm."

Cora grins at us from her place on the floor by a cupboard where she's occupied in removing some paper plates, and the sunshine fills the room as we settle down for a chat.

Eli

I let myself into my room. The air conditioning is on and the room is thankfully cool, which makes a difference from the heat. I thought I knew what heat was, having worked in Australia in the summer, but it's got nothing on Dubai. Not for the first time, I yearn for the sunny cabin on the ship with the doors open, letting in the sound of the sea and a breeze that would billow the curtains. For a second I look at my balcony as if expecting to see a tall, dark-haired man with blue grey eyes and a sharp blade of a nose. I blink and the vison passes, but I hurry over to the table where I left my laptop charging.

This job is easy, caring for a middle-aged lady who had appendicitis and is rather frail. She's friendly and funny and very appreciative, and it seems strange to say that I'd have loved a difficult client this time. Someone who'd have shouted and demanded. Someone who would have taken my mind off Gideon and how hard it was to walk away from him that day in Southampton.

I shake my head. "I did the right thing," I say out loud. And the thing is, I know I did. It would have been abhorrent for me to have taken advantage of that situation. Gideon was vulnerable in far more ways than could be explained by the pneumonia. He was grumpy, demanding, impossible to deal with, and the most fascinating person I've ever met. He was also generous in a manner suggesting he was trying to hide it, soft-hearted, and astonishingly kind. I knew all that by the end of the trip, but what I didn't know was how I'd end up feeling like my arm had been cut off when I left him.

A thousand times a day I turn to tell him something, and I find myself thinking about him at random times. Worrying whether he's taking care of himself, hoping he's not drinking or taking drugs again. Wishing he would find a healthy, safe path for himself and be the person he is underneath the bad-boy reputation that will take him nowhere but an early death.

It's not just worry though. I want to tell him about the little black and white cat that comes to sit on my balcony in the late afternoon sunshine, and how her slightly disdainful air reminds me of him. I want to tell him about my dessert tonight of baklava, the crunchy texture of the pastry and sweet honey on my tongue, and how the strong coffee served in tiny cups is sharp and almost shocking. Somehow sharing those details with him makes them more real and wonderful.

"I did the right thing," I say again and smile when I open my laptop and see a red number over my email icon. *Gideon.* I open the email, and for a second I try to slow my reading so I can savour the words that are so like his way of speaking it's as if he's in my room, his face alight with sardonic amusement. But I can't restrain myself and I gallop through it.

To: Eli Jones

From: Gideon Ramsay

You would love this house. It's tiny and already there are certain parts of it that are my favourites. Like the old armchair that nestles in a corner of the room by the floor-to-ceiling bookshelves so I only have to reach over and pluck a book out.

I'm reading like I haven't done in years. I used to read

voraciously as a child, but I grew out of it when I started acting. There was always something or someone to do and a great deal of trouble to get into. Now, at night I sit in the chair and read rather than drinking the night away. So far I've read most of Ruth Rendell's backlist, and I'm now working my way through the works of PD James.

There's no drink apart from tea at my side. I'm even drinking that disgusting green-tea shit that you made me drink on board. Is it worrying that I find myself liking it?

There's a TV, but I haven't watched it since I got here. Instead, I've been listening to music. There's a record player on a shelf, as well as a stack of records. There doesn't seem to be a record in there from the current century, but it seems appropriate for the sort of life I'm living at the moment. It's actually like becoming a pensioner ahead of time, only without the sciatica, joint pain, and casual rudeness.

It's actually the first time in my life that I've been alone for such a long time. Usually, I'm surrounded by people and noise. It's one of the reasons why I tend to do films back to back and stay in hotels, because the silence has always seemed so full of noise.

I wondered at first whether I'd end up going mad and talking to myself. Although thinking about it, it's usually the only time that I hear any sense spoken. However, I seem to have brought a little bit of you back with me. Thankfully, it's not the opinionated part. Just the bit that can sit quietly. Maybe we've swapped personas, and while I'm behaving like an old man, you're hitting the town like Robert Shaw on payday.

Every morning I have fresh bread and milk delivered by a Mrs Granger who makes the cakes in the tea shop here. She brings her granddaughter Molly with her sometimes, and they will come in and put the bread and milk away while Molly chatters to me as she does handstands and regales me with the minute details of her life, her voice as high and fluting as the blackbird who comes for the bread crumbs in the garden.

I've taken your advice. I'm actually wincing as I type that. Last night I went up to the big house to have dinner with my brother and friends. We ate chicken baked in a tray with chorizo and tomatoes and peppers. They washed it down with a rich red wine and I drank water. And we all mocked Oz for splitting his jeans on a house tour. Apparently he had to wrap a tea towel round his waist because he'd gone commando.

It was a nice dinner but a bit awkward at first, like meeting people for the first time. As I've been pissed the last few times I've seen them, I suppose I *was* meeting strangers. A few months ago I'd have probably given up and gone out and got drunk. Instead, I stuck it out, and it got easier.

Later on, I walked back to the cottage along the gravelled paths. The air was heavy with the scent of hawthorn and my way was lit by a huge yellow moon as bats flitted above me. It was a beautiful night and all I could think of was how much better everything would have been if you'd been there beside me.

When I've finished reading it for the third time I sit back and smile. I can almost see the small cottage and the low-ceilinged rooms, and already my room seems brighter and clearer. It's as if he's sent me some mellow Cornish sunshine rather than the powerful white heat here.

"Four months," I tell myself. "Then we'll see."

Four Months Later

. . .

Gideon

I let myself into the cottage, carrying the tray gingerly. I know anyone looking at the slightly shrivelled chocolate cake would turn their nose up, but I feel immensely proud. I made this from start to finish. I laugh because it's ridiculous. I have many acting awards which are in a cupboard somewhere, but I have never looked at them like I'm looking at this slightly charred cake. I pause. Maybe if they made the Baftas out of chocolate, I'd have been more receptive.

I look around the cottage appreciatively. It's full of sunshine and smells of furniture polish from when the cleaner came in yesterday. The Stieg Larsson book I started yesterday is lying on the table, and I shake my head. This place is hardly party central.

Nevertheless, I've enjoyed this time on my own. At first it felt strange, but as time went on, I settled into the stillness, and it became almost a triumph to be doing things for myself after all these years of employing staff to fulfil my every need. I've learnt to cook, took long walks with my brother, and read nearly everything in the cottage, and in some small way I think I'm approaching who I used to be before all the layers of anger and cynicism covered me.

Eli would be proud of me, I think, then still at the pang in my stomach. If he thought that what I felt on the ship was an illusion, he was wrong. I still miss him every day. Nothing seems quite right. It's as if the day is a painting that's missing the final hit of colour to make it a masterpiece. I shake my head. I'm not sure I fucking know myself anymore.

Thinking of him sends a shaft of worry through me. I'm as aware of the time passing as if I'd taken a pen and crossed the days off a calendar like a lovestruck schoolboy. Okay, I admit it. I totally programmed a reminder in my phone. That's how I know that the four months were up yesterday. It's also how I'm very aware that he hasn't contacted me.

Every week he's emailed me like clockwork. Long, gossipy letters full of funny details of his day, bossy instructions about my health, and occasionally blisteringly intimate glimpses into his thoughts and feelings. But he's been silent for more than a week now and I'm trying not to wonder what that means for us. Has he met someone else? Has he grown bored with the idea of a fucked-up actor and moved on to easier pastures, like that young, dark-haired man who picked him up from the boat?

I glare at the thought and put the cake down. Despite promising myself that I wouldn't do it, I grab my phone and pull up my email account. I sag. There's nothing apart from a couple of adverts for erectile disfunction and an exhortation for me to book a holiday in the Cotswolds.

For a second I stare blindly ahead, seeing his warm, open face in my mind, full of humour and kindness. Then I shake my head and move into the kitchen to deposit the cake on the counter. He knows where I am. I can't make him want me. I sigh. I wish I could.

Later that evening I sit at the table in the kitchen with the door open, letting in the scent of roses from the bush on the patio. I'm eating a mushroom risotto that I made myself and reading from a book propped against the salt and pepper grinders.

At first I try not to take any notice when my iPad chimes in the lounge, telling myself that I'm at an interesting bit in the book. But really it's because superstitiously I feel that if I look, it won't be from him. I'm therefore profoundly glad that there's no one to see me bang my shin as I race across the room towards it or the way my hand shakes as I open my email.

To: Gideon Ramsay

From: Eli Jones

Four months have gone. My job is finished.

I read the words and then read them again, my heart hammering in my chest. Then I tap out my reply.

To: Eli Jones

From: Gideon Ramsay

Come to me. I've been waiting.

CHAPTER 11

Even cranky porcupines need a cuddle

Gideon

Later that night I wake with a start, my pulse racing, and sit bolt upright in bed. "What the fuck?"

Then the banging on my front door, which has obviously woken me up, starts again. Panic settles in. *Is it Milo? Has something happened to him?*

I bound out of bed and promptly fall straight over my shoes that I'd kicked off carelessly earlier. "Shit!" I groan, rubbing my elbow which has connected painfully with the bedside table. "Shit, that hurts."

The banging begins again. "Okay," I bellow. "What the fuck? Hold on a second." I look around for some clothes helplessly, since the bedroom is covered with clothes strewn in colourful piles as if waiting for a body to come along and reanimate them.

Shaking my head, I pull on the nearest pair of shorts and a T-shirt, realising they're inside out and back to front just when the banging on the door starts again. Dismissing the state of my clothes, I race out of the bedroom and down the stairs. I fumble with the door's stiff lock, cursing under my breath until it turns, and I fling the door open.

"This had better be an emerg–" I gulp the words back as I struggle for breath. "*Eli!*"

He leans against the door post as casually as if he's calling in for a cup of sugar. Dressed in grey joggers and a burgundy hoodie, the moon sends his shaggy mess of hair white-blond and darkens his eyes, so for a second I wonder if I've conjured him up in a dream.

Then his lips quirk hesitantly. "Is it okay that I'm here?" he asks, and I break my stasis, grabbing his arm and hauling him over the threshold.

He laughs and follows willingly, his body hot under my palm. I switch the hall light on and gape at him. He's tanned a smooth golden brown from being under the Dubai sun, his hair is a sun-drenched mess, and the freckles dotted wildly over his nose make it seem like he's been dusted with cocoa powder.

"Oh my God," I say hoarsely. "You're really here. I only emailed you tonight."

He hitches his duffel bag over one wide shoulder almost nervously. "I was already back in the country when I contacted you. When you said to come to you, I set out immediately." He stares at me, the silence stretching out like spun sugar, soft and silken. "Are you pleased?" he asks abruptly.

I stare back, all my defences down for once. Right about now I'd normally be dismissive and sarcastic. Ready for sex but keeping my guards up. They're nowhere to be found now, and I swallow. It's almost like being naked in front of him, but scarier. Nevertheless, I smile at him.

"So pleased," I say hoarsely and we reach for each other at the same time, his bag thudding to the floor as I wrap my arms around him and bring him into me. The relief I feel is almost painful.

He's all slim build and hard muscles in my arms, the scent of coconut in my nostrils and a sweet smell from his shampoo. "God," I mutter. "I missed you so much."

He frames my face in his big hands, the fingers curiously gentle. "I missed you too. So much." I inhale sharply, feeling his words as a pleasure-pain in my belly. I don't think anyone has ever said that to me before. His smile turns sad as if somehow he knows what I'm thinking.

I'd normally lash out, hating to be vulnerable, but instead I stay still, touching the feelings of vulnerability and safety that run in a soft dichotomy in me when he's holding me. Then, moving slowly and savouring the moment I've been thinking about for so long, I draw his mouth to mine, running my tongue over that full bottom lip and biting gently.

He groans under his breath and opens his lips, letting my tongue slide in. He meets it with his own, rubbing it gently against mine before pulling back a slight bit and sucking softly on it. My cock pulses in my shorts, the head wet and damp at the motion, and I suck in a breath.

He pulls back, releasing my mouth. "You sure?"

I trace my hands over those high, wide cheekbones and let my fingertips run over his freckles, something I've been wanting to do for months. "So sure." I pull back and hold out my hand. "Come on."

He looks at my outstretched palm, and somehow when he joins his hand with mine the movement has a gravity to it, like it's a ritual we might be lucky enough to always perform.

We don't speak as I pull him up the winding, narrow stairs. He has to lose my hand to walk behind me, and my breath stutters as his hands grab my hips and curve down and round my arse. "So gorgeous," he mutters, his voice deep and low.

"Wait until you see it naked," I tease, my voice hoarse but happiness suddenly bubbling in me. He's here and he's about to be all mine. I still for a second at that outrageous thought, and he bangs into me.

"You okay?" he asks quickly.

I look back, the shadows over his face casting him in darkness. "I'm perfect," I say, and I mean it. This here is perfect no matter what happens because he is mine. I don't know how or why it's happened but it has, and on a twisting narrow staircase it seems oddly appropriate for me to have that epiphany. My life, after all, has been twisted and narrowed by other people's and my own expectations. Well, no more.

So, when I reach out and switch the light on it's with a sense of optimism that's completely alien to me. I grin at him and then bite my lip as he looks around the chaos of the room.

"Oh my God," he says faintly. "Were you burgled?" He pauses. "Could they find anything? Did you have to help them look?"

I laugh helplessly. "Shut the fuck up. I'm messy. Deal with it."

"I can see now where the not keeping lots of clothes comes in. The ship would have probably sunk under the weight of all this."

I shove him as I laugh and then push him against the wall, kissing him lustily. At first I can feel the laughter in him, almost like when you pet a cat and feel the purr, but then he takes my mouth in turn, forcing his tongue in and groaning in his throat.

He moves suddenly, reversing our positions so I lean into the wall. He holds my hands out to my sides and for a second I struggle against his strength which, unlike mine, isn't gym-honed but forged by moving people's bodies around so he can care for them.

The thought sends a wave of heat rushing through me, and, against my brain's urgings, I melt back against the wall, feeling the strength holding me captive in the grip of his hands and the weight of his body. "Oh God, yes," I moan and he stays still for a bright second of realisation. Then his face seems to both harden in determination and soften with tenderness, so I stare at him.

"Gideon?" he whispers, and I nod frantically.

"Yes, like that. Yes, please." The begging notes drip between us, soft and bubbling like hot jelly, red and pulsing.

He looks hard at me, a flush spreading over his tanned cheeks, and then he's stripping me, tearing my shorts off and ripping the neckline of my T-shirt until I'm naked in front of him. "God," he groans. "You're so fucking gorgeous."

I have a second of vulnerability. I'm twelve years older than him. He must be used to lovers with young bodies, not ones who are still a bit too thin. I have lines at the sides of my eyes and grey specks are starting to appear in my hair.

Then my thoughts scatter as he pushes me back into the hard surface of the wall. "Yes, you are," he says firmly. "So gorgeous, and if I say that, it's the truth. I want you so fucking much. I'm going to push you against this wall and I'm going to fuck this gorgeous arse so hard that we both come."

I should be panicking right about now because I haven't been fucked in a long time. The last time was Niall and it was many years ago. Instead, my cock pulses and I grab the base of it hard, feeling the pain chase my orgasm back a step.

His eyes sharpen. "You nearly came then?" I nod, caught in his hot gaze, the green in his eyes eclipsed by blown pupils. "God, Gid, I'm going to make you come so hard." He steps back and kicks off his Nikes, leaving him barefoot. "Strip me. Get me naked."

I stare at him, struck for a second by the reversal of the usual norms. When I'm with a man, I'm the dominant one. I give the orders. I fuck them, and I'm always in charge. I wonder when that became tiring and repetitive or whether it always has been. "Now," he says demandingly, and I feel the buzz in my blood and cock thrumming throughout my body.

"Fuck!" I groan and he grins ferally.

"I'm waiting." He seems somehow to have changed. He's firmer and more autocratic, with an arrogant tilt to his head that makes my blood run fast. But at the same time, he's still Eli of the warm eyes and soft mouth who makes me feel safe with him.

"You're bossy," I mutter, pulling off his hoodie and the T-shirt underneath and letting them fall to the carpet unheeded. "God," I mutter, tracing my fingers along the body revealed to me. His chest is wide and hairless, his nipples dark brown discs. I rub my finger roughly over one, watching it rise and pebble. I do the same to the other and he groans.

"I'm still dressed," he murmurs, and I smile slowly before reaching for the waistband of his joggers. I pull them down, the elastic catching on the heft of his cock before I lift it out and push the joggers down his legs. I gasp when I see his cock. He's erect and huge, and unable to resist, I step closer and grab it gently. My hand barely reaches around him as his cock thumps into my palm. The head is wet and slick, the smell of pre-come acrid in the air and making my mouth water.

He pushes into my palm and I tighten my fist, running my other hand down his ribs and tracing the bones while he shudders and snorts. The laughter dies as I trace the grooves of his pelvis. Then I let go of his cock and bring my hands around to cup the firm globes of his arse, feeling the soft, small hairs tickle my palms.

I mutter a protest as he pushes back. "No," I say harshly.

I want to touch him, and I watch feverishly as he kicks off his joggers, leaving him completely naked.

He looks at me, his eyes dark and his breathing rapid but the ever-present humour still there. "Gid, you're topping so much from the bottom you're practically vertical."

I snort and shake my head. "I'm used to being in charge."

"Not with me," he says somewhat arrogantly, and I feel my breathing speed up. "Let go, Gid. Let me take care of you."

"Yes," I say softly, feeling my muscles turn hot and liquid as chocolate, melting with the need to be manhandled, despite my brain's protests.

"Turn round," he says harshly. "Rest your hands on the wall and stick your arse out."

I comply, waiting for the embarrassment to hit me at being so vulnerable. Instead I cry out as a sudden red-hot flash of pain shoots across my arse.

"Did you just *spank* me?" I squeak, sounding like an eighty-year-old spinster.

He chuckles, the rich sound in my ear making me shudder. "I did. There's a nice handprint on your arse, Gid." He rubs it gently, and I moan in my throat as a wave of nerve endings spring to life. I force my arse backwards and he grabs it, palming the globes roughly.

There's a rustle, and then I cry out as he spreads my cheeks open and licks a rough swathe from the back of my balls up to my hole. "Oh fuck," I choke out, my voice garbled as he returns to the puckered opening and suckles it gently before pulling back and licking it with rapid catlike licks. "Oh," I breathe. "It's so good. I never knew."

He pulls back. "You've never been rimmed before?" His voice is soft but there's a rough demand underneath it.

"No. I never let anyone. Too close."

"Too close to the real you," he says. "Well, I'm close now, Gid, so how do you feel about that? I think I'm the closest to the real you that anyone has ever been. Am I?"

I look back and down, drowning in the heat of his gaze, and I capitulate to the demand in his voice. "You are," I whisper.

"Why?"

"Because you slipped through, and now I don't want you to go back."

"You're mine," he says deeply and something in me – some barrier that's always been there – cracks and the layers start to peel open.

"I want that," I say hoarsely.

"I look after you now," he says. "That means I'm in charge in here and you let go. You let everything go, because you're safe with me."

I send my fingers down and rub them over his square chin. His lips are full and swollen. "Yes, I want that," I say wonderingly.

He nods and kisses my fingers affectionately. "Turn around, then," he demands. "Let me have you."

The waters rush through and the barrier breaks and I shudder, turning to the wall and pressing my face into the plaster. I cry out as he returns to my arse, eating and sucking and licking at the pucker, the sound of slurping dirty and base in the quiet room.

I push my arse out to him even more and cry out again, as there's the sound of a tearing of a packet and then a slippery finger rubs over my pucker, tracing the wrinkled opening before pushing in slightly.

"Oh fuck," I choke out. "Oh *fuck*."

"Relax, Gid," he says, the command in his voice making me release my hands from the fists they've clenched into.

"God!" I shout out as the finger slowly slides in, and he makes a slight motion inside me, causing fireworks to explode across my vision as a surge of pleasure flows through my body. "God!"

"That's it," he says low. "You're doing so well, babe. Take another." And before I can say anything, I have two fingers sliding slowly in, pausing when I tense. He rests them there as I pant hard, my eyes staring blindly ahead. The pain is a sharp red but there's a pleasure there too. A throb inside me that needs to be filled. "You're so tight," he says, the marvel loud in his voice. "Have you done this before?"

"Not for a very long time." I hesitate, reason coming back a little. I feel suddenly embarrassed, but when he goes to remove his fingers I clench my passage around them. "No, don't. I like it. It feels so full. Leave your fingers in me."

"I need to have your arse, Gid. You're going to let me in, aren't you?"

"Yes," I groan as he widens the fingers in me to stretch me for his cock. His huge cock, I suddenly recall. "But lots of stretching first and I'll definitely need another finger," I say quickly and Eli grins, his teeth white and his smile wide in the moonlight.

"What did I say about topping?" he whispers, removing his fingers but pushing a third finger in before I can complain. "You're hovering above the ceiling at the moment."

"You're in charge," I pant. "Oh Christ, that feels so *fucking* good. Don't stop." *How could I have forgotten how amazing this feels?*

"My cock will be better," he murmurs. He removes his fingers and I twist my neck to watch as he opens a condom and slides it down his length, pumping more lube over it until the long length glistens in the moonlight. He looks up and strokes his cock a couple of times. "Bend over," he says deeply. "Hold onto the wall but stick your arse out." He presses the wide mushroom head against my pucker and rubs it against the sensitive opening until I cry out, begging and imploring. "You're going to take me at your own time. Breathe out and bear down and take my dick."

I do as he says, the command running like a wave of fire ants under my skin, making me shake with the desire to be owned, to be taken over, to bloody let go for what feels like the first time ever. He holds still, letting the head pop in an inch, and I pause, breathing hard. The fierce burn is there that I can remember, but already I can feel the pleasure running underneath. It makes me brave, and I bear down, taking him inside me slowly, listening to the moans and grunts he gives as he bottoms out. We rest for a second as I feel the wiriness of his pubes against the tender skin of my arse.

Then I move experimentally. His cock rubs my prostate and I give a harsh, guttural shout. "Oh shit!" I cry. "Oh, Eli."

His hands come down hard on my hips. "You feel so good, Gid. I'm going to fuck the come right out of you."

"Yes." I reach down to my cock and cry out as he slaps my hand away. It's gentle but shocking and my fingers catch my cock, the sharp sting making me even more desperate.

"You like that," he croons, beginning to move his hips, undulating against me as he forces his cock into me in tight circles. "Your greedy little hole likes my cock."

"Oh God," I gasp, feeling his words open something up in me, a hot, dark place that loves these heated words and fierce demands. "I love it. I love your cock."

"You're desperate for it."

"Yes," I gasp. "Take it. Make me come."

"I will," he promises, beginning to push into me in quick, deep strokes. I'm so tight around him that he can't move much, and he stops to pull out slightly and pump more lube on his cock before tunnelling back in, giving tight, shoving thrusts that brush repeatedly over my prostate, sending pleasure through my nerve ends and making me go hot and cold.

"Yes," he grunts. "Your hole's so greedy. It wants my come. One day we'll do this without a rubber and I'll flood this hole with spunk. Then I'll pull out and watch the jizz pulse out of you and I'll suck it up and feed it to you on my tongue."

"Oh God, Eli," I whine. "I need to come. Please make me come."

"Yes," he croons. "You need to come so bad. You're doing so well."

I open my mouth, needing something more, and as if he senses it, he reaches round and pushes two fingers into my mouth. "Suck on those," he says, and I groan and suck, feeling full. I'm stuffed at both ends as he ruts into me, dropping whispers and kisses over the skin of my shoulders as he holds on to one of my hips, his fingers bruising.

The heated words of praise and soft endearments combined with the roughness of the fuck sets something free in me that's always been closed away, and then he gives one last, lusty, battering thrust and the pleasure seizes my balls in a tight, painful grip, and before I know it my hips are jerking, and I'm coming in pulsing surges all over the wallpaper in front of me.

He pulls his fingers from my mouth, grabbing both of my hips now. "Oh fuck," he chokes out. "You came without my hand. *Fuck*, Gideon." He chokes off his words and pants in my ear as he fucks me hard, jarring my body. My prostate is almost painful now. It feels swollen as his huge cock rubs on it, but I embrace that pleasure-pain, feeling my cock pulse out another small stream of come as he pushes in, rooting deep and crying out his pleasure before sinking his teeth in my shoulder and making me cry out and come again.

He rocks slightly for a second and I hiss in a breath. "Sorry," he says breathily. "Sorry, sweetheart."

I still at the endearment and then groan at the unpleasant sensation as he pulls out of me. For a second I rest against the wall and then suddenly I feel self-conscious. I just let him do what he wanted to me, and I feel vulnerable, as if he's stripped my skin away from me as well as my walls.

Then he tugs me round to face him, ignoring my protests. "Gideon," he breathes, smiling at me tenderly, and I gasp as he steps into me and pulls me close in a long hug. His body is sweaty and hotter than a fire, his cock in the condom painting a hot, wet stripe down my leg, but his hug is warm and affectionate, and I feel the vulnerability slide slowly away.

He kisses my hair, inhaling as if taking my scent into him. "Let me look after you," he says softly. "Come on. Get into bed, sweetheart."

"I'm quite positive I can look after myself. And I'm not sure about the sweetheart business either," I try to say in my usual testy way, but he just smiles.

"Yes, you are. You just don't want to admit it."

He pushes me into the bed, ignoring my protests, and disappears. I hear a tap running and a light switch off and then he's back, sending a warm, damp towel over me, wiping away the sweat and cleaning my hole. It's still sensitive and feels horribly empty, and when I flinch he croons softly. Then I draw in a sharp breath as he swings into bed with me and pets my hole almost affectionately. I tense but he does nothing apart from hold his fingers there, rubbing gently, and I relax against them like a candle melting.

"There," he croons softly. "Does that feel better?"

"It actually does," I murmur, staring into his eyes and feeling absurdly shy. This man just stripped me, rimmed me, and fucked me so hard I can still feel it. I have never given up that much control. But as I stare into his eyes that are their usual clear olive green again and brimming with affection and what looks very much like pride, the vulnerable feeling seeps away. It's replaced by a confused mix of gratitude, pride that I pleased him, and this warm affectionate feeling that makes me want to sling my arms round him and cuddle. I wrinkle my nose. *What the fuck? I do not cuddle.* I send the men onwards with a careless thanks as soon as we're done and relish having the bed to myself.

Which is why I find myself bewildered when I allow him to nestle into me, turning me on my side rather bossily and pushing up against my back. He rubs my hole once more and then slings his arm over me.

"Are you cuddling me?" I ask tentatively.

"I am," he says sleepily, and I feel affection for him run suddenly through me like fire.

"What happened to the demon boss of the bedchamber?" There's a slight hesitation and I crane my neck. "What's wrong?"

"I've been told before that I'm too forceful in bed."

I feel a flare of jealousy at the thought of those unseen lovers of his and quash it because it makes me a gigantic hypocrite.

"I think you were just what I needed," I finally say slowly, the desire to reassure him stronger than my desire not to flay my skin open. "I've never felt like that in sex before. It's always been more of a journey from a to b." I pause. "That was more like the whole fucking alphabet."

His body eases its tension and he chuckles. "How about if the bossy me is only around during sex and then only when you need it. I can't be like that in life. When sex is over, this is what you get. A nice *cwtch*."

"Cutch?"

"There aren't any vowels in it."

"Why?"

He shrugs. "Welsh," he says in explanation.

"What does it mean?"

"It's something more than a cuddle. Something absolutely lovely. I love a good *cwtch*."

"I don't think I've ever had whatever that word is."

"Well now, that's just sad."

I shrug. "I think you have to be cuddly and loveable. I'm not that."

"No, you're pricklier than a cross porcupine. But even cranky porcupines need a cuddle."

"*Cuddling*," I say in a revolted voice that I immediately spoil by nestling closer to him.

I feel his laugh running down my spine. "Yep. Get over it, Gid. Accept what's coming to you."

"If I must." I snuggle into his body, inhaling the warm, sweet smell of him. "You smell gorgeous," I say suddenly. "Like coconut."

"It's my body lotion," he says with a yawn. "My skin gets dry. I can't remember what it's called. It's from Superdrug."

I have slept with many men in my life, and the only trace they'd left when they'd gone was the expensive designer aftershave on the sheets. I'm utterly charmed that this man wears a body lotion from Superdrug. "Don't change it," I say impulsively. "It's the smell of you in my head. I love it." I go rigid with embarrassment, but he doesn't react apart from gripping me tighter.

"I won't change it if you do the same. Your smell is so sexy and warm. Just like you."

"Okay," I say softly. I really want to query that statement because I know I'm not warm, but the quiet darkness feels so intimate and safe around us. It's enough for me to say what's really bothering me. "Was that wrong what we did?" I say softly. "Was I what you needed, never mind what I needed?"

He tenses and sits up, pulling my face gently to look at him. His expression is earnest. "You were everything I needed, Gid. I've never had sex like that either. It was right and there was absolutely nothing wrong with it." He pauses. "Do you believe me?"

"Yes," I say slowly, taking his fingers and tapping over my heart. "In here I believe you." I sigh. "It's just the rest of me that might struggle to catch up."

"We'll go slow, then," he says and lies back down, pushing up against me. I feel the warmth of his arms, the heat of his breaths, and I exhale slowly.

I've never felt so warm. I pause. I've never felt so safe. It's the last thought I have before I fall asleep.

CHAPTER 12

Why, when you want something so bad, is it always so fucking complicated?

Gideon

It's late afternoon the next day and I stand in the kitchen looking thoughtfully down at the tray on the table in front of me. A pot of strawberry jam glows a bright scarlet. Next to it is a pat of the creamy butter that is produced here on the estate. Croissants made by Maggie and stored in the freezer here have been heated up and they steam gently in a basket next to the cafetière where coffee waits to brew. I tap my lip. There's something missing, and it has to be perfect.

My mind strays upstairs to the warm body lying lax across the bed, his tanned olive skin glowing in the late afternoon sunshine. He'd been so tired, having travelled from Dubai and then straight down here, then we'd exacerbated his condition with four bouts of sex, each one even better than the first. I shift a little, smiling at the tenderness in my arse. He'd hardly stirred when I moved out of bed. Even the clandestine kiss I dropped on his shoulder blades over his dragon tattoo hadn't woken him.

I look down at the tray and exclaim, "Of course!" The backdoor is open, so, grabbing a pair of scissors, I pad outside to the small stone terrace. The garden is still a bit of wilderness, which they'll probably tame for the first guests, but I secretly like it. It's full of mature, blowsy plants that let out the most gorgeous scents that drift into the house.

One of those plants is a rose bush with beautiful flowers that are a deep purple-black and give out a heavy perfume. I look at it and painstakingly examine each bloom until I spot the perfect flower. It's lush and heavy with scent and I cut it neatly off, holding it gingerly so I don't get pricked by the thorns. Then I flinch as the front door slams, and I hear my brother shout, "Gideon!" Footsteps sound and he appears at the backdoor.

"Shush!" I say, gesturing at him furiously.

"Why?" He stares down at the flower in my hand. "Will I wake the flowers?" he enquires sympathetically as if he thinks I've finally gone off my rocker.

"What on earth are you babbling about?" I enquire acerbically, trying frantically to gather the shreds of my dignity together which are very threadbare. I am, after all, only dressed in a pair of blue and white striped pyjama shorts with a hickey dark on my neck. And I'm clutching a flower.

His eyebrows rise slowly until they almost disappear into his hairline. Then realisation dawns. "Oh my God," he says slowly. Then. "Oh my *God*," a lot louder. "You've got someone here." He looks at the rose. "Someone who deserves flowers the next day. *Gideon Patrick Ramsay!*"

"Oh, shut up," I say sourly. "I don't know what you're talking about."

My gaze involuntarily shoots to the bedroom window, which is open. I don't need Milo finding out about this. He'd have opinions. *Lots* of opinions. And I'm not in the mood for them. I'm in the mood to climb the stairs and cuddle back down against Eli's warm body that has made my sheets smell of spunk and coconut.

Milo's clever eyes have tracked me, and I see him noting the open bedroom window. "Who's up there?" he whispers.

My first instinct is a shameful and old one, and, after all these years, I almost fall into by rote. In my head I can hear Frankie say to lie. *Lie and hide and deny. They can't prove anything.* I even open my mouth to do it. Then realisation strikes me that if I lie, I will lose Eli.

We haven't discussed it yet, but I know he isn't the type to climb in my closet with me. He's too honest. Too forthright and principled. But if I have him, I'll lose my career. Everything I've worked for. For a second, the two wants fight in me, but then my reason wins.

"Eli's up there," I say.

"Eli, your *nurse?*"

"He's not my nurse," I say quickly. "He hasn't been my nurse for months."

"Oh my God, was this going on during the cruise?" His eyes are turbulent with worry.

"No," I say firmly. "No. He wouldn't do anything. Said he had to protect me and make sure I knew my own mind. The four months apart have been about making sure I'm not coming into it out of gratitude." I roll my eyes, although those protective words are still engraved on a tiny bit of my heart. "As if I don't know my own mind, and when did I ever show gratitude for anything?"

"Gideon, I don't think you've known your own mind since you were a teenager and fancied Ralph Fiennes. And you do express gratitude. You thanked Niall for getting you a sandwich the other day." He pauses. "After lecturing him on how long he took to do it." He shrugs helplessly. "It's the principle of the thing."

"Thank you," I say enthusiastically. "I wish more people recognised that."

"That a lecture is as good as a thank you? You should give etiquette classes."

"We'd have a whole new generation of coolly rude people coming up the ranks."

He shakes his head, dismissing the avenue of distraction I'm offering. My brother is resolute. Niall would totally have fallen for it.

"So he protected you?" Approval warms his eyes. "I like that. You need that."

"I don't need *protecting*," I say, revolted. "I'm not a fucking hedgehog."

"You've been enough of a prick in your day," he says smartly, expecting me to laugh, but my expression stops him. "What?"

"I was a prick," I burst out, feeling the words tumble out beyond my capacity to will them back.

"Okay," he says in an alarmed voice, sitting down at the small iron table and gesturing to a seat. "I think we need to talk about this. It's not going to be settled until we do."

I sit down, putting the rose carefully on the table, and for a few minutes we stare at each other. Finally, I sigh and scrub my hands down my face. "I'm sorry," I say. "I'm sorry for all the shit I put you through when I found out about you and Niall. It was completely out of order, and I'm ashamed of myself every time I think about it."

"Have you told Eli about Niall?"

"Not yet." I bite my lip. "I can't tell him that."

"You have to," he says sternly. "That's too big a thing to keep covered up."

"Thank you. I always try to keep my big thing covered," I say pertly, but he doesn't rise to the bait and returns to the previous topic.

"Why are you still worrying about this, Gid? You said sorry before. We had that long chat and came to an understanding."

"Yes, well, I didn't tell you the truth about everything."

"*What?*" he says, sounding unnerved. "Are you not okay with me being with Niall?"

"Of course I am," I say quickly. "Completely okay and very

happy about it. He's perfect for you. Like I said to you at the time, it was hurt pride that caused my behaviour and worry because I was losing someone I could be myself with. Or as close as I came in those days." I pause and say in a rush, "Do you remember thinking that I'd been pushing you towards him in Verbier? That I'd engineered it all?" He nods. "Yeah, I wasn't," I say quickly. "Not all the time, anyway. I was pretty fucking angry. And to be honest, that move only works in Jilly Cooper books."

Whatever I'd expected his reaction to be when I told the truth, him laughing was never it. He laughs and chuckles and when he manages to stop, his eyes are streaming. "God, that's good," he finally says.

"Milo," I say in a warning tone which nearly sets him off again. "I let you believe I'd done a good thing when in actual fact it was completely accidental."

Finally, he sobers. "I knew that," he says.

"How?"

"Because you're not a very good actor around me, Gid."

"I bloody am," I say indignantly. "Really, Milo, you're not doing a lot for my confidence. First you said I looked in my fifties."

"Your confidence shows no sign of being depleted, and I said forties," he murmurs but I continue.

"In my *fifties* and now you're saying I'm shit at acting."

"Only with me," he says, a smile brimming in his eyes. "I see through you, Gid. Not always at first, but usually when I stop to think about it." He shrugs. "I knew about ten minutes after I left you that night. I sat thinking for a bit, and I knew then."

"And you're not mad?"

"Of course I'm not," he says simply. "Because while you tend to forget every time in the past when you might have been good and focus on all your bad behaviour, I still remember. I remember how kind you are and thoughtful. How protective you are. It's a very hidden part of your character, Gid, but it's still there."

"But I haven't shown it to you. You of all people should have had that."

"But I did," he says firmly. "When you used to read me stories at night. When you came in when I had nightmares, when you stuck up for me against Jamie the next-door neighbour when he was bullying me and calling me a faggot and you pushed him in the pond. You alone believed me and sorted it out. Even though it got you sent back to school early. You sent Niall when I needed him because you knew there was something wrong." He grabs my hand. "You did everything you could for me for someone who was much older than me and who Mum and Dad pushed so far out of the family some days they didn't even remember they had another child." I flinch and his hand grabs tighter. "But I remembered, Gid. I *always* remembered. I know what they did was wrong, and I know that we don't talk about it because you're worried about hurting my feelings. But Gid, you're more my family than they are."

"What?"

"You heard," he says firmly. "Mum's love is suffocating, and Dad's so busy at work he lets her get away with it. But the problem with her love is that she doesn't see me apart from an extension of herself. You, however, have always seen me. You might have been impatient and cross and you might have behaved badly. But at the end you corrected yourself, and you made me see what was in front of me that I might have lost otherwise, because I was too in my head to see Niall clearly. Whether it started off with good intentions or not, the result was the same. I got Niall, and you let me have him." He stares at me curiously. "Would you behave the same way again?"

I bite my lip. "In the interest of complete honesty, I probably would. I was a shithead then."

Milo laughs, and I stare at him. "Gideon, you might have been a shithead then, but you're a brutally honest one now." He lifts my fingers and drops a kiss on them. "At the end of the day, I took someone from you. Probably the only person you really had who you could be *you* with, and you were hurt."

"Please," I scoff. "Niall and I were fucking on and off for years. It wasn't Scarlett O'Hara and Rhett Butler."

"What a disturbing image," he says faintly, and then we gasp as a rough voice still hoarse from sleep speaks from the door.

"You were sleeping with Niall? *Niall*, your brother's boyfriend?" Eli says incredulously.

"Oh lovely," I sigh. "Well, at least I can cross off telling Eli from my itinerary today."

~

Milo mumbles a greeting and scarpers away quicker than a nun in a brothel, leaving me standing in an uneasy silence on the patio.

I shift from one foot to the other, wishing I had shoes on and a T-shirt, and maybe a suit of armour. Eli is dressed only in a pair of loose tobacco-brown shorts that hang from the sharp bones of his hips, but he looks as composed as if he were in a dinner suit.

He stares at me, his eyes narrowed, his gaze flitting from the faint marks of his fingers on my hips to the dark mark on my neck. He can't help the gleam of satisfaction, and I feel a surge of hope.

"Did you sleep well?" I ask brightly.

"You were sleeping with your brother's boyfriend?"

"Not at the same time," I say indignantly. "That would have been tacky."

"*Tacky?* Out of every word in the dictionary, that's the one you come up with?"

"I don't think you should lecture me with your constant mangling of the English language, Eli," I say primly.

He laughs but then scrubs his hand down his face. "*This* is what you were hiding. I knew there was something." He shakes his head. "It's like an episode of fucking *Dynasty*."

"Well, as long as you and Niall aren't wrestling in the fountain, we should all be fine."

"I could totally take him," he says meditatively.

"That should not be as hot as it is." I walk towards him, loving the way his hands come up to bracket my hips, the way his fingers twitch as if he's stopping himself from grabbing me. "It was off and on, and it meant *nothing*. Just an itch to be scratched."

He shakes his head. "Why, when you want something so bad, is it always so fucking complicated?"

"Is that me? You want *me* badly?"

"*Cariad*, of course it's you."

"What does that mean?"

"It's Welsh for sweetheart." I blush with pleasure and his eyes sharpen. "Oh, you liked that," he says softly, his voice almost purring. "Look at your face, Gideon. You like endearments."

I try to shrug. It's the worst acting job I've ever done. "Eh, it's okay."

"Oh really, let's see. How about *enaid* which means soul, or *annwyl* which is beloved?" He draws me close. "Or how about *calon bach* which means little heart?"

That low, hoarse voice whispering endearments against my skin makes me flush hot all over. I slide my arms around him, feeling him grab me tight and the thrust of his cock against mine.

"Eli," I whisper, and he takes my mouth, forcing his tongue in and twining it with mine. All my thoughts fly away, and I open my mouth wider, groaning under my breath and letting him push me against the wall because his cock can rub against mine perfectly in that position. He kisses me for a long time, pulling back only to whisper heated words that would make me red-cheeked if he said them in normal conversation. But out here as the sky darkens ominously and the first few promised drops of rain start to fall, it feels right. Like we're animals and wild and free. No cares, no obligations. Just me and him and his bloody stupid fucking soft words.

He pulls back and I stare at him. At that freckled nose, the clear olive eyes dark as seaweed now, the full lips swollen from my kisses. "God, you're gorgeous," I whisper, and his face twists.

"No, that's you, Gid. What you see in me is beyond me, but I'm not complaining."

I open my mouth to dispute this. *Doesn't he know what he is to me?* I still inside. *What is he to me?* But before I can complete the thought, he reaches out and pushes my shorts down, leaving me stark naked on a small cottage patio.

"What are you *doing*?" I whisper furiously.

"Ssh," he says, smiling at me wickedly. "There's no one around, and the hedge is hiding us."

I cast a glance around, and he's right. When I look back, he's smiling. "There's my Gid," he says deeply. Then he pushes me into the chair I'd been sitting on.

"What are you doing?"

"Ah now, it must be fairly obvious."

"Out here?" My voice is slightly squeaky, and he smiles.

"Where else?" Then he leans in and nuzzles my balls, and all my thoughts fly away. I should be scoping the area for press, the way I look for them before I do anything. Frankie would shoot me for sure if he knew about this risk. But all I can feel are the drops of rain starting to patter onto my skin, the coldness of the drops almost stinging against the heat of my flesh.

I cry out as he licks and sucks gently on my balls, his hands rubbing soothingly up and down my thighs, a juxtaposition to the fierceness with which he pulls back and sucks bites into my inner thighs. I spread them and he murmurs approvingly.

He mouths up the crease of my thigh, stopping to inhale deeply. When he looks up, his eyes are dark as gooseberries and his eyelashes spangled with rain. "Smells so lush here, love, eh?" he says deeply, bending to nibble at the thin skin of my hipbones and ignoring my cock as it jerks and thumps against my stomach.

"Eli, please," I groan.

"What, love?"

"I need you."

"Where?"

Unable to articulate my need, I grab his head and push him towards my cock. Instead of laughing, he gives a low groan and takes me into his mouth, the heat inside shocking after the cool air. Pulling back, he licks the veins, pausing at the root where he nudges his nose in, inhaling again. I groan and shove my hips forward. He holds my cock firmly and I can feel the raindrops on it, the cold startling after the heat of his mouth, like tiny stinging pinches.

"Oh fuck," I choke out, and he bends to take it in his mouth again, licking off the rain before taking me to the back of his throat and swallowing around me. "Oh, Eli," I whisper. "Fuck, that feels good."

He pulls off. "Pinch your nipples, Gid. Go on and do it." Then he bends back to suckling, and I reach up and twist my nipples, crying out at the arc of pleasure that runs from the nubs to my cock. My hips move and push against him, and I can feel his nose in my pubes as he swallows again before pulling back and sucking the head while jacking the base.

"You too," I say, staring at the image of him, hair and chest wet in the dim light. "Get naked, Eli."

I grab the base of my cock with a protesting moan as he levers up and strips his shorts off, kicking them to one side. I eye him appreciatively. His wide shoulders, the sleek chest narrowing down to slim hips and long legs, and the ruddy length of his cock standing up proudly between his legs from a thatch of blond curls. He's uncut and the head is a dark angry purple colour where the hood has pulled back.

He lowers himself to his knees between my spread legs, and I stay him. "You too," I say hoarsely. "Touch yourself while you suck me off."

He groans and, lifting my cock to his mouth, he deep-throats me effortlessly while lowering his hand to his cock and starting to masturbate fiercely.

"Oh yes," I croon. "It feels so fucking good, Eli."

I spread my legs and when he pushes his hand at my face, I take his fingers into my mouth and fellate them furiously, making them messy with lots of spit. Then I lean back and groan as he rubs one wet fingertip across my puckered rim. "Yes," I hiss. "Fuck me with it."

Then I cry out as he inserts the finger slowly, the rough calluses catching my sensitive rim. "Oh God, it feels amazing," I say through gritted teeth as I look down at him, at the erotic image of the length of my cock between those full lips, the absorption on his face as he fingers me, and suddenly lightning fizzes in my groin. "Going to come," I grunt, and he dips his head, and I shout out into the evening sky as I pour come down his throat in thick spurts.

For a second I stay there panting, his finger still in my arse, his mouth constricting around me as he swallows my come, incredibly wringing out another spurt of fluid. Then he leaps to his feet, holding his cock. "Yes," I say throatily, looking at him. "Come on me, Eli. Mark me with it. Come on my fucking face."

The slippery thwacking echoes around the still garden, and then he gives a deep groan. His cock jerks and I close my eyes as hot come lands on my face mingling with the rain, its acrid, sharp smell a counterpoint to the sweetness of the flowers nearby.

For a few minutes there's only the sound of our choked pants as we struggle to get air in. Then he moves and I feel fabric rub over my face, removing the fluid. I open my eyes in time for him to climb into my lap. My arms come up automatically, and it's strange because although I've never held a man like this before, something about it feels as if I've done this with him a thousand times. Somehow in another time I must have cuddled him on my lap, his balls damp and hot on my thigh and his arms around my neck. It's the only way to account for this shocking sense of familiarity.

"Jesus," he says, burying his head in my neck. "Jesus, Gid, why is it like this with you?"

"I don't know," I whisper, pushing my hand into his mass of dirty-blond waves that are damp now with rain. "I wish I did."

He looks up. "Did you love him?"

It takes me a second to work out what he's talking about. "Niall?" He nods, his expression worried. I stroke my fingers down his face.

"*No,*" I say clearly, watching his shoulders sag slightly. "No, I love him as a friend and that's all. It's all it should ever have been if we hadn't been stupid. He doesn't love me either."

"Really?" He huffs and something warms in my chest.

"Yes," I say. "Contrary to popular belief, I'm not very loveable."

He stares at me, emotions running over his face. "Well, I'm not sure about that, Gideon Ramsay." For a long second we stare at each other until I reach out and grab the rose from the table and hand it to him. "For me?" he asks, astonished.

I nod and sigh. "It's like you. Warm and open and the dew's still fresh. You're so young, Eli."

He shakes his head. "Not that young. You make me sound like Macaulay Culkin in his heyday. Don't use my age against me as well."

"As well as what?"

"As well as everything else that stands in our way." He stands up, carefully holding the flower. "Come on," he says cheerfully, holding his hand out to me with all traces of seriousness suddenly gone.

I reel at the abrupt change of subject and mood. "Where?"

"Inside." He shudders. "It's fucking freezing out here, and my hair doesn't react well when it gets wet."

"I remember," I say tartly. "You had more curls than Leo Sayer when we went swimming on the ship."

His laughter follows me into the house as does the swat he gives me on my backside.

Inside, he bounds upstairs while I pull on a T-shirt and gather the late breakfast together. He appears next to me a few minutes later as I pour boiling water into the cafetière. He's barefoot and has flung on jean shorts and a stripy T-shirt, his other shorts sacrificed to clean up jizz. His hair is a wavy mess, and he glows with something that looks very much like contentment. I hope it is because that's my predominant emotion too.

"The croissants are cold," I tell him abruptly, unable to articulate what I'm feeling at the moment and hating it. He's given me so much, the least he deserves are my words, but for the first time in my life they've deserted me, leaving me an incoherent mess.

"Doesn't matter," he says happily, recalling me to the food. "Let's have some cheese, and I noticed some deli bits. Let's have a picnic in the lounge."

I shake my head. "How old are you?"

"You're only as old as the man you feel," he whispers, goosing my arse and making me jump.

"Ancient then?"

"Oh yes," he says smugly. "Probably older than Simon Cowell."

I try to be indignant but can't summon it up. "Help me with the stuff," I say instead and, grinning, he complies.

We throw the blanket down and while I arrange the food, I nod at the old record player. "Put something on. There's quite an eclectic choice as long as you don't want anything made after the fifties. Although I think there's some Bowie in there and other bits."

He rummages through the old crate, exclaiming in pleasure as he pulls out records and stares at their sleeves. "I hate CDs and downloads," he says. "I love vinyl."

"You're not old enough for vinyl," I scoff, and he shakes his head.

"Not the first time round, no, but who is?" He laughs. "Oh, that would be you." I raise my middle finger at him, and he laughs before exclaiming and pulling out an album. "I *love* this one. Used to listen to it in my bedroom at home while I was wallowing in teenage angst."

I peer at the record in his hands and try to dismiss the fact that I was probably falling out of pubs and having threesomes when this album came out. "'Abattoir Blues.' That's got to be Silas's. He went through a Nick Cave period a few years ago, and he's always loved vinyl."

"It's that crackle," he muses, taking the record out carefully and placing it on the deck. He lowers the needle carefully, and we both smile at the crackle as "Babe, You Turn Me On" begins to play. "Appropriate," he muses, and I smile almost shyly at him before shaking it off.

"Come and eat," I command, and he wriggles around to sit next to me cross-legged. We eat, and drink a bottle of red I found in the wine rack. Its dry, earthy taste complements the food, and I sip it slowly, watching him as he talks with his hands flying around like normal, his deep voice with that wonderful Welsh accent making even the mundane words sound like poetry. He's tactile too, constantly touching my leg and arm and smiling at me as if this is the best time he's ever had. Ever since I met him, I've envied him this ability to stay in the moment.

"Are you okay with the Niall thing now?" I ask abruptly, and immediately want to punch myself in the throat for spoiling the moment.

For a second he looks startled but then settles back against the chair. "Yes," he says slowly. "Not being funny, it is a bit strange, but your past is your past, Gid. I haven't got any control over what you did and who you did, just as you don't have any control over my past."

"So? What's the problem? I know there is one."

"It's just that you have such a tie with him. I saw that at the hospital and I overheard some of your conversation with Milo, and a year ago you seemed to be singing a very different tune."

"A year ago I hadn't met you," I say softly, reaching over and brushing back his hair so I can look into his eyes that are turbulent tonight. "Niall knew me." I shrug. "Actually, he knew the bits of me I showed him. But we're still friends. Good friends. And I felt like I was losing my chance to be me if he stopped the thing we were doing. Totally selfish and not based on anything more than hurt pride and muddled emotions that I confused with real feelings."

"It's not just Niall. It's the future too," he says slowly. He smiles deprecatingly. "Listen to me. I'm about to ask your intentions. Jesus Christ, I'm one badly behaved rake short of a Georgette Heyer novel."

I run my fingers through the waves of his hair. "I want a future," I say slowly. "I never *ever* thought I'd say those words, but I can't help it with you."

"But? I sense a but?"

"There's always one of those." I frown. "I don't know what's going to happen, Eli. I've been closeted for so long. I want to be with you, and I don't want to shut you in there with me. You're open and honest and it would kill me to make you hide a part of yourself. But equally, I don't know what will happen when I'm confronted with this. My first reaction has always been to lie, to smooth things over with clever words. What happens if I do that again and you leave me?"

He reaches over and grabs my face, his hands smelling of the rose I gave him that he proudly put in a mug in the lounge. "Easy," he says slowly. "Gideon, everyone comes out in their own time. I would never *ever* pressure you to do something you're not ready for."

"What if I'm never ready?" I ask, my breath catching in my throat.

He cocks his head to one side and examines my face, his own clouded with uncertainty. At that point the record changes and "Oh Children" comes on, the slow song filling the silent air.

He stands up and extends his hand. "Come on."

"Come on where?"

"Dance with me."

"*Here?*"

He smiles. "Yes, here. Why? Would you rather I'd booked the *Strictly Come Dancing* stage?"

"I've never danced with a man before," I say slowly.

He smiles so wide my hand shoots out and slides into his before I can think about it. He pulls me to my feet and into his arms. "Then dance with me," he says. "Let me lead."

I snort. "When are you *not* doing that?"

He pulls me close, his arms sliding around my shoulder blades, their heat startling against the thin material of my T-shirt. "I'm not sure of that," he whispers into my ear, making me shudder. "You've led me to some places I've never been before."

I want to ask what those places are, but he shushes me and pulls me tighter against him. I slide my hands around his slim waist and lower my head into his shoulder as he starts to move, slowly shuffling. I follow him as if he's the lord of the dance, and somehow it feels magic in this dim room lit by the murky twilight and the glow of a lamp and with the scent of the rain drifting through the open window. It's like I've been bespelled.

I have dined in the fanciest restaurants, seen the wonders of the world, and lived with riches that few ever attain, but here in this small room, in this man's arms, shuffling to a beautiful song, I'm happier than I've ever been.

Happier than I probably ever will be again. At some point he's going to leave me. Everyone does. I want to grab the memories and greedily drink them in, but he pulls me closer, and I'm blind once again to everything but this man. This poetic, perennially cheerful Welsh man who makes me feel safe.

CHAPTER 13

I have never in my life felt as connected with anyone as you

Eli

For the next few days we don't stray far from the cottage. Or, in fact, the bed. In the future I'll only have to catch the scent of lilac and I'll be transported back to this bed: sweating, knackered, but so intensely satisfied I can feel it down to my bones.

On the fourth day I pull out of Gideon gently with a groan. "Fuck, I think my dick fell off."

He snorts, his face buried in the mattress, his hair wet with sweat. "Has it fallen off in me? Oh, if only we had a medical professional on the premises."

"Don't worry, sir," I say in an officious voice. "Mr Jones is in the building and will cater to all your needs."

He groans. "Any more catering and I'll be dead."

I whip off the condom and, tying a knot in it, I make a stab at throwing it towards the bin. It probably doesn't make it because I'm definitely not LeBron James.

I snuggle next to him, running a hand down the sleek tanned skin of his back and cupping his arse before pushing my finger into his hole and gently massaging the stretched entrance. He gives a sigh of happiness and we lie for a while in a comfortable silence broken only by birdsong and eventually the rumble of my stomach.

"Was that you?" he says, coming up on his elbows, his face alight with mirth. I look my fill at that patrician face – so stern when I first met him, but now relaxed and open in a way I'd be willing to bet it's never been before – and then I grin.

"It might have been because you talked about catering."

"Sex and food," he groans, turning on his back and putting his hand over his eyes. "If it's not one it's the other. You're insatiable."

Only for you, I think, able to look my fill at him with his eyes covered. I rake my eyes over that lean body with the wide shoulders, flat stomach, narrow hips, and long legs. Even his high arched feet are attractive. His cock lies spent in its nest of black curls. Instead of saying the words, I nudge him. "Come on. Don't lapse into a coma, Grandad. I'm starving. You can't treat a boy from Cardiff like this."

He removes his hand and the frown on his face can't conceal the twitch of his lips. This man loves backchat like no one I've ever met. It's an eternal mystery to me why so many people are so polite to him. He's crying out for sarcasm and snark.

"I can think of many ways to treat this boy from Cardiff, but none that they'd put on the tourist leaflets."

I wink and sit up, slapping him on the hip. "Come on. Feed me."

"You're like a fucking gremlin but one that's already badly behaved."

"Shall I order a takeaway?" I say brightly, reaching out to the bedside drawer. "Didn't you put the menu from last night in here?"

"Other drawer," he says quickly, reaching out a hand, but I've already opened the drawer and I'm gaping at the contents. I reach in and draw out the sheaf of papers.

"Gid, these are my–"

"Emails, I know," he says, looking steadily at me but with a flush over his sharp cheekbones.

"You kept them?"

"Obviously, oh master of the blindingly obvious."

I shake my head and reach out and pinch him before he can move.

"Ow," he says indignantly. "What was that for?"

"Sarcasm," I return briefly. "I can't believe you kept them," I say softly.

"Yes, well, don't read too much into it, Eli," he says grumpily. "My eyes get tired looking at a screen. That's all."

"Oh, okay, Pinocchio." I smack a kiss on his lips and bound out of bed.

"Wait. Where are you going?"

"To get this," I say, pacing over to my laptop bag where it's lain on one side for days, abandoned and forgotten. I pull out an identical sheaf of papers and brandish them at him.

"Oh," he says softly. "Are those mine?"

"They are." I come to stand by the side of the bed. "And I'm not going to use the excuse of bad eyesight. Mainly because my eyes are young and still full of vitality. Ouch!" I leap away and then climb onto Gideon's supine figure and bend to kiss him. "But mainly because I wanted them close to me because I missed you so much while we were apart."

"You did?" he asks almost shyly, which he'd be utterly horrified to know makes him look adorable.

I raise an eyebrow. "Well?"

He sighs. "Okay, I might have missed you a bit." He shakes his head. "Who am I kidding? I missed you so much it was like losing my arm." He pulls me down to him and takes my lips in a soft kiss.

I pull back eventually, feeling my breath picking up and the pulse in my body. "That was lush, that was," I whisper. He smiles at me, looking slightly vulnerable, so I cock my head on one side. "Snog, marry, or kill Charlie Hunnam, Luke Evans, and Daniel Craig?"

"Pardon?"

"If you had to choose one, which would you go for?"

"No," he says, pinching me so I roll off him, laughing. He stands up. "I refuse to answer that because, while it sounds perfectly innocuous, I just know that you'll find a way to turn it into an examination of my deepest feelings."

"Spoilsport," I say with a pout.

"Yep, and a hungry one. Come on. Let's shower and get dressed."

"For takeaway? Can't we be naked like normal?"

Gideon stares at me, thoughts running over his clever eyes. "No. Let's have a walk up to the main house. The chef at the tea rooms makes wonderful food. I had some while you were away. Plus, they have wonderful homemade cakes." My stomach rumbles and he grins. "There's that sweet tooth. Come on. Let's go and grab some food."

"In public together?" My breath catches but I make my expression calm. "You sure?" I hesitate. "I'm not sure I can be next to you without letting it be known how I feel."

He stills. "How do you feel?" he asks and the air turns thick between us. I inhale and open my mouth but he holds up his hand quickly. "No. Not like this, Eli. Not as part of a fucking awful negotiation where we have to set limits on how much we can touch each other without the shit hitting the fan."

I stare at him. "Okay," I say slowly.

"But just know," he says, talking quickly, the words almost running into one another, "that I probably want to say the words back to you. In fact I'm fucking desperate to. And when it's the right time you'll make me so happy."

I swallow hard, the gravity of the moment containing a sweetness that stabs me in my heart and throat. Searching for something to rescue him because he looks like he's considering making a run for it, I widen my eyes. "I never knew you felt so strongly about milk."

"What?" he says abruptly.

"Milk. You asked me what I felt like. That's it."

He stares at me and a slow, sweet smile crosses that thin face, making it incredibly beautiful. He says huskily, "Well, I do. I love milk. More than *anything*." We stare at each other and I swallow hard before yelping as he smacks my arse. "Shower. Now."

"So bossy," I say wonderingly. "Does the press know about this?"

"Not at all. I'm renowned for my sweetness of manner and my perennial good nature when faced with obstacles."

I laugh and follow him to the shower, letting him fuss over me and wash my hair and enjoying the feel of that lean, wet body next to me and the scent of spicy vanilla shower gel all over me.

An hour later, dressed in a denim shirt, khaki shorts, and battered navy Converse, I wait as Gideon locks the front door of the cottage and then jump as he grabs my hand. "What are you doing?"

"Holding your hand," he says softly and firmly as he steers me down the path.

"You can't. We could be seen."

"Not yet." He pulls us to a stop and jerks me round to face him. "I will drop it when people are around, but I don't want you to think it means nothing. It means everything, and I need to sort it out in my head."

"It's okay," I say softly, tugging him close with my unoccupied hand and inhaling the warm smell of him. "In your own time, remember."

"Well, my own time isn't at the expense of you," he says, pulling back and starting to walk forward, drawing me after him.

"What do you mean?"

"That it won't be for long. I promise you. I just need to sort out the way forward in my head before I force anything."

He holds my hand up the path, only dropping it when we turn

onto the main drive, but even then he walks close to me, letting his hand brush against mine. It's oddly sweet. Like being courted.

I gape up at the huge house in front of us, rising golden out of the late afternoon sunshine and glowing as if painted by sunbeams. Thousands of lights twinkle in the windows as the mullioned glass catches the sun. "So beautiful," I breathe.

He looks up. "It's better now. When we visited as kids, the estate was run down by his father. Silas and Oz have done a good job."

"Were you friends with him like you were with Niall?"

He laughs. "That's the most tactful question I've ever heard."

I shove him lightly. "Answer the tactful question, then."

"No," he says lightly. "Silas was just my friend. It was only Niall that I fucked on and off." He stares ahead at the gravelled path contemplatively. "I always felt slightly left out, to be honest. Silas and Niall roomed together, and they've always had this close bond. I felt a bit isolated from that." He shrugs. "I've felt isolated from everything in my life. Always have." He frowns. "Maybe, thinking about it, that's why I slept with Niall. Maybe I wanted something that they didn't share. Hmm." He laughs. "Shit, that's deep."

"Do you feel isolated from me?" I ask in a low voice, and he stops walking and turns to face me. His eyes are hidden as the sun shines brightly behind him.

"Never," he says, and his rich voice is full of a conviction that reassures me instantly. "I have never in my life felt as connected with anyone as I do with you."

I follow him into the tea rooms, trying to discreetly ogle his tight arse. He looks as calm and cool as ever in navy shorts, a navy gingham shirt, and white Vans. His distinctive face is made slightly less so by the new beard he's grown and the Ray-Bans that conceal those clever eyes.

The tea rooms are apparently the converted stables, and his friends have done a good job of renovating them. The ceiling is high, the beams have been sandblasted, and the place has a laid-back, rustic feel. Huge old pine tables dot the room with mismatched chairs drawn up to them.

The big room is full of people and noise, which comes as a bit of a shock after the last few days of it being just me and Gid in that small bedroom filled with the sound of just our laughter and groans as a breeze blows over our bodies and ruffles the curtains.

Waitresses zip about between tables, and the room rings with the sound of crockery and loud chatter. We wait at the entrance to be seated, and I lean against the waiter's station, eying Gideon contemplatively as he looks around the room.

I know I said I was okay with keeping us secret, but I never realised how fucking difficult it would be to stand near him and not touch him. Especially after the last few days when we've been joined by my cock more times than I've had hot dinners. It isn't that, though. I don't want to maul him. I just want to hold his hand, to touch him and have him look at me the way he does in private when there are no secrets. But I can't, and even though that makes me sad, I'm still going to wait this out, because he's worth more to me than anyone I've ever met. Maybe in the end I'll leave if he forces me into a small, private box, but not yet. For now I'm happy to be with him.

I feel a stroke on my hand and look down to see his finger twine with mine. It's a small gesture hidden by our clothes and he isn't looking at me at all, but it's somehow more intimate than anything we've done so far.

The next second I jump as a small dark-haired man with sharp features comes up next to us. He's dressed in tight jeans and a *Chi an Mor* navy T-shirt with tattoos gleaming black on his arms.

"Well, if it isn't our resident Oscar winner," he says.

"I never won an Oscar," Gideon says with a gleam of amusement alight in his eyes.

"Didn't you? Oh no, Christian Bale beat you. Silly me. What a scatterbrain I am."

"Yes, that's just the word I was looking for to describe you," Gideon drawls.

The small man laughs and says something else that makes Gideon snort, and I hear the Irish in his voice and realise that this is Oz, his friend's husband. He's not at all what I expected. He grins at me, and I'm helpless not to smile back. His face is fierce and beautiful, but what stands out most is the amusement lurking there and the kindness. Not at all what I was expecting, and I'm glad of it.

He reaches out to shake my hand. "Oz Ashworth," he says. "I'm married to Silas, Gideon's friend."

"Have you got a title too?" I ask and Gideon laughs.

"Many, but none that are listed in Debretts."

Oz laughs, but at that second a few things happen simultaneously. A woman shrieks. There's a gasp and a thud and the shattering of crockery. I spin round just in time to see an older man topple off his chair like a doll.

I'm in movement before my brain realises what's happening, striding over and kneeling next to the man.

"Sweetheart," the older woman cries, racing round the table to the man's side.

I bend over him, examining him intently. "What happened?" I ask, and she must hear the calmness and command in my voice because she stops the tears that are threatening.

"He said his chest hurt and his arm. Then he went a funny colour and collapsed."

"Does he suffer from angina?" I ask.

"No," she says, and I can hear the fear in her voice.

"It's okay," I say. "I'm a nurse. I need to help him."

She breathes in to control herself. "No, he doesn't have angina."

"Okay, Mrs ...?"

"Andrews."

"Okay, Mrs Andrews. What's your husband's name?"

"Jack."

"Jack, can you hear me?" I say to the man who is groaning under his breath and clutching his chest. His eyes flutter. "I know you're hurting," I say clearly, moving him onto his back. "Is it just your chest?"

"Jaw," he mutters before groaning again.

Oz and Gideon race up next to me. "Have you got a defibrillator?" I ask Oz, pulling the man's shirt apart. Sweat lies clammily on his chest.

"In the kitchen."

"Get it for me." He races off immediately. "Gideon, ring for an ambulance. Tell them suspected heart attack."

"Okay," he says, obeying instantly, pulling out his phone and tapping one hand on my shoulder in support.

The woman starts to cry, but to my relief her friend comes round and pulls her back.

"Okay, Jack," I say calmly as Oz falls down next to me with the green box containing the defibrillator. "I think you might be having a heart attack. I know it hurts, but try to breathe. I'm going to attach some pads to you, but try not to worry. You just concentrate on breathing."

He groans pitifully, and I look around for something to clean the sweat off him. Not spying anything obvious, I grab the tablecloth and give it a sharp tug. Crockery falls to the floor on the other side of the table, but the cloth does the job of cleaning his chest so I can attach the pads. I place them on him quickly with the long ease of practice, continuing to talk soothingly as I take his wrist and count his pulse. It's thready and uneven, and as I reach over and switch the defibrillator on and attach the wires, his eyes roll back and he stops breathing.

"Shit," I mutter, bending over him.

"What's happened?" Oz mutters.

"He's stopped breathing." I lean over him and start chest compressions. "Count them, please." He obediently starts to count.

Gideon slides back next to me. "Ambulance is on the way. Estimated time is five minutes."

"Shit." I keep the chest compressions even, feeling the sweat starting under my arms. "Take over," I snap at Gideon. "While I start manual breathing."

He comes down next to me and, like the well-trained actor he is, he immediately starts the movements which are perfectly timed.

"Okay, stand back and don't touch him," I say to Gideon, pushing him free so the machine next to me can analyse the patient. When it announces that shock is advised I press the red shock button, and a few people gasp audibly as his body flails on the ground. The defibrillator announces that compressions can be resumed, so I start the process again, breaking off to shock the man.

Then it's back to more chest compressions and mouth respirations before shocking him again, but this time, to my relief, he moans and his eyes flutter. "Welcome back, Jack," I say, smiling while I feel the muscles in my arms burn. "It's okay. You're safe."

The next second the thunder of footsteps announce the arrival of the paramedics, and I sit back. They crowd around, and Oz moves the onlookers back while I give the paramedics a brief summary of my qualifications and the treatment I administered as the man receives oxygen.

A few minutes later they strap him onto a stretcher and start to move off. His wife comes round to me, exclaiming and muttering thanks, and I smile and accept them before they whip after the paramedics and silence falls, broken only by the mutters of the crowd as they leave.

I move to rise from the crouch but my muscles lock and tremble after kneeling on the hard floor. I falter but then Gideon is there, grabbing hold of my arms and pulling me up so I lean against him. I stay there for a second before realising that he's hugging me in full view of an entire tea room. I go to pull back, but he says, "No," sharply, so I subside, secretly glad to feel him touching me.

"Fuck me," Oz says as he comes back, his eyes bright. "That was fucking scary. Will he be okay, do you think?"

"He's got a good fighting chance," I say, feeling the sweat on me and longing suddenly for a cold shower. "We kept him breathing during the critical point when there wasn't anything moving the oxygen around his body."

"You were so impressive," he says. "Thank you so much."

"It was nothing." I say, but Gideon murmurs and, to my amazement, he presses a kiss to my temple.

"It was everything," he says softly. "Well done, you." I can hear the praise in his voice and the pride, and it warms and amazes me at the same time.

"Thank you, but I have to say anyone could have done it."

"Not me, not Oz, and I didn't see anyone else queuing up to help. You're wrong," he says quietly. "You're not your mum and dad. You're *far better*." The conviction in his voice stills me, and I stare at him. He smiles. "You may not be conducting surgery, but at the end of the day that man would have died without you. That may not rank in numbers against your mum and dad, but it certainly ranks in fucking importance to his wife and family. He can't be replaced and neither can you. I'm so proud of you."

"Thank you," I say softly. It feels like he's reached inside me and soothed a bruise that's always lain there, that every conversation with my mother and father makes worse and more painful. I doubt it'll ever go, but his words have soothed the sting.

"What was that cracking noise?" Oz asks, leaning against the table, his eyes as bright and curious as a sparrow.

"A couple of his ribs," I say casually.

"You broke his *ribs?*" Gideon says incredulously.

I shrug. "Better ribs than death."

"I'm sure there must be other options in life than those two things," he says. "You must be terrible at birthday parties. I'm certainly never letting you give me the bumps."

We end up going back to the cottage without food, and as we get through the door, Gid pushes me towards the stairs. "Go and have a shower."

"Is this a less than tactful way of telling me that I smell?"

"When have I *ever* been tactful?"

I laugh. "Point taken." He shrugs, looking uneasy, and my focus intensifies. "What's going on?"

"I want you to take a shower while I cook something."

"*You* cook something?"

"I have taken cookery lessons here."

"So I read in your emails, Gid. But I have seen no sign whatsoever of this culinary expertise. Unless we're counting toast or croissants, and I'm pretty sure they're not on the menu at Le Gavroche."

"Well, now I'm cooking, smart arse. Have a shower and don't put any clothes on when you get out."

I stare at him and rub my hands. "This is already shaping up to being a tidy afternoon. I like your thinking." Gideon smiles but it fades, and he almost looks bashful. "What is it?" I ask softly. "You can tell me anything."

"I know *that*," he says in a slightly aggrieved manner that says it's incomprehensible that I have to point it out. It warms my heart, as do his next words. "I just want to look after you," he says softly.

I step into him, drawing him into my arms and hugging him tight. "You do look after me."

"Not like I want to," he says stubbornly. "You take such good care of me, Eli. I want to do the same."

"Okay then," I whisper. I step back and smile at him. "I'm going for a shower." He kisses me, his lips soft against mine.

I take my time in the shower, enjoying the cool water. I pinch his body wash, relishing having the scent of spicy vanilla on me. A little piece of him. I close my eyes and shake my head. *What the hell?*

I wander into the bedroom when I get out, rubbing my hair dry, and come to a halt when I see Gideon waiting by the bed wearing only a pair of black sports shorts. "What's going on?" I then inhale at the scent of food coming from the table by the window. "That smells lush. What is it?"

"Bit of everything that we had left in the fridge," he says gloomily. "Turns out you actually need ingredients to cook."

I laugh. "Who knew." I hug him and wander over to the plate.

"I'd rather have this anyway," I say, looking at the food. "Hummus, pitta breads. Stuffed peppers. All my favourites."

"I think I got that when you practically had an orgasm in the deli. We really will have to do a food order at some point this week."

I slap his arse. "Man cannot live on sex." I pause. "Although we've really given it a bloody good go this week, Gid." He laughs as I grin at him. "I don't mind takeaways, but they're not very good for us. I'd like to eat some proper meals too, and it would be good for you." I tear off a piece of pitta bread that's steaming softly and dip it into the golden-brown hummus. I gobble it down, only realising how hungry I am when I practically inhale the first piece.

"Good?" he asks, laying a towel down on the bed.

"So good," I groan. I watch him for a second as I eat. "Are you intending to murder me?"

He blinks. "Not right this minute. Why?"

"The towel."

"Oh no, that's for a massage." He pauses. "But I'll put it to one side with the saw just in case I need them later."

"There's good thinking." I laugh and eat another pitta bread, watching him potter about the bedroom. I pop a stuffed pepper into my mouth.

"You finished?" he says, standing by the bed with a brown glass bottle in his hand. "It's probably best that you don't eat too much right now. You can eat afterwards."

"After what? This all sounds interestingly seedy."

He chuckles, the lines at the sides of his eyes lengthening in a way that always makes me want to kiss him. So I do. I step into him, holding his hip and kissing him deeply and thoroughly. When I pull back, we're both breathing heavily.

He steps back. "Lie on your stomach on the bed and make sure you lose the towel."

I raise my eyebrow. "Gid, this is all so sudden. I'm not that sort of boy."

"You are definitely that sort of boy," he says affectionately. He shoves me down onto the bed. "I'm going to give you a massage," he says, unscrewing the top on the bottle which lets out a sharp lemony scent.

"Massage. Have you done that before?" I ask doubtfully.

He shakes his head and smiles. "I may not have massaged anyone for pleasure before, but I do know how to do it. I had to take a course in it for a film I did a few years ago."

"Which film?"

"Something that hopefully sank deep into the ether and never rears its head again," he says fervently.

My interest sparks. "Porn?" I ask and he shakes his head.

"Of fucking course not. *Porn*. What part of hiding my sexuality for years and being a selfish lover makes me a candidate for porn?"

"You are most definitely not a selfish lover with me," I say throatily.

"Yes, well, that's just between us," he says as I settle on my front.

"It bloody well is," I say, and the fervency sounds loud in my voice. For a second there's a startled silence and then his hands touch my shoulders. He starts to rub them firmly, working those long, thin fingers into knots I didn't know were there. I squirm.

"Shit, that's so good," I mumble, burying my head in my arms and melting into his hands. "Hurts and is good at the same time."

"It's because you carry your stress and tiredness in your shoulders. I've noticed before how tight they get."

"I need you to do this for forever," I say blissfully, and then still. *Fuck, what did I just say?* I cringe and wait for the sound of him belting down the stairs and making a Gideon-sized hole in the door.

Instead, to my amazement, he chuckles, and his voice is light and full of laughter. "I think I could actually make you say or do anything when I'm doing this."

"I think you could."

"Even that I was good in the *Oliver* remake?"

I snort. "You're not that good a massager, Gid. Nothing could make me say that."

He pinches me, and I moan as his fingers move to the base of my back, digging in and pushing upwards. "You *could* make me say anything," I finally say softly.

He pauses, and his hands still on my back. "I don't want to make you," he eventually says in a low voice. "I want you to always do what makes you happy."

"That's why I'm here," I say and smile when he leans down, and I feel a kiss soft on my shoulder. "Oh *God*," I moan as he starts to massage again. "That's so fucking good."

"Your muscles are very tight. That's probably this afternoon." He pauses. "It must take a lot of brute strength to break some poor fucker's ribs."

I snort, feeling my body melt into the mattress. "I'm alarmed by the relish in your voice. Perhaps I should go out tonight and break ribs left and right in St Austell." He snorts. "In the interest of honesty, anyone could have done what I did today. Anyone with a rudimentary first-aid knowledge could have been talked through that procedure."

"But not as good as you," he says stubbornly. "You didn't hesitate. Just got straight in there. I'm not interested in anyone else anyway. It was you I was very proud of. Nobody else."

"Thank you." I grab his hand as he touches my shoulder and kiss the fingers. "You look after me so well," I whisper. "Thank you."

"You should be looked after," he says gruffly. "Always."

I try to think of something to say that won't freak him out but can't find anything and settle for lowering my face into the mattress. As if agreeing with me he steps up the massage, digging into knots.

The massage turns slow after a bit when the knots and tight spots have eased, and his strokes seem more languid, as if he's relishing the feel of my skin. I feel my cock rub against the rough towel as my body senses the change in mood.

"Gid," I moan as his fingers lower to my arse, and he squeezes the cheeks, his fingers warm with the oil. "Oh fuck," I choke out as he spreads the cheeks, and I feel the first touch of his tongue. "Gid!"

"Let me," he says low. "I've never done this before for anyone."

"You don't have to," I whisper.

"I know," he says, his voice expressing his utter incredulity that anyone could make the great Gideon Ramsay do anything he doesn't want to. Incredibly I smile, but it dies as he licks a path from the back of my balls to my hole. "I want to," he whispers.

Then all I can do is moan and rub my cock against the towel as he sends catlike licks around the sensitive rim before suckling the hole. *Shit!* I groan and rut harder against the mattress. "That's so good," I hiss. "Keep going."

He moans and steps up the pace, coming down on the bed behind me and spreading my cheeks with his big hands. He suckles and kisses me, sending the tip of his tongue inside once the hole slackens a little. I can hear the slurping noises and groans he gives loud in the silent room. A spurt of pre-come dampens the towel. "Oh God, I need …" I stop. "I can't think," I finally admit.

"You don't need to." He rolls me over and, before I can say anything, he takes the head of my cock into his mouth and starts to suck.

"Oh shit!" I cry out and arch up. "Sorry, sorry," I whisper frantically as he gags. "I'm so sorry."

Gideon lifts his head, his face red-cheeked and intent and his eyes dark. "Don't be," he says in a low voice. "I like it." He licks a stripe down my cock before sucking at the base, his hand jacking my length, the way eased by the moisture from his mouth and the oil on his hand. "I'm not very good at this," he mutters, looking slightly embarrassed. "It's always been done to me. I didn't reciprocate very often."

I stroke his hair back, feeling the dark strands slip through my fingers like rough silk. "You're doing so well," I whisper fiercely. "Do anything you like, and I promise I'll love it."

He nods, his face intent and focused on me, and I stretch languidly under him, feeling his gaze hot as warm honey on my body. Then my thoughts vanish as he takes me into his mouth farther this time and sucks hard. "Oh shit, like that," I hiss and then there's no more talk as he sucks my brains out through my cock, jacking it in his warm fist and sucking and licking.

I'd be embarrassed at what a short time I last for, but I've got no brainpower left as I feel my balls draw up. "Gid," I groan. "Coming."

I intend it to be a warning, but he seems to take it for encouragement, and then I can't think anymore as I shoot into his mouth, feeling his throat work greedily as he swallows my jizz.

He pulls back when I've finished. "Oh God," I say weakly, raising a feeble hand and feeling it flop back down onto the bed. "I'll do you when I get back my muscle coordination."

"What a charming offer," he says dryly. "Eli, you silver-tongued charmer."

I laugh. "No, seriously," I slur. "Give me your cock."

"No need," he says, drawing the cover up over me.

I force my eyes open. "What?"

I'm stunned when he leans down and kisses my forehead. "This was about you, not about me. I don't want to come now. I'm going to make you a plate of food and bring it back to bed so we can have a *cwtch*." He pronounces the word perfectly. "I want to look after you at the moment."

"You do that so well," I say, grabbing his hand and kissing the fingers. "Thank you."

"No, thank you," he says solemnly, and I'm quite sure he isn't expressing gratitude for me coming down his throat. There's too much emotion in the words.

I know he won't say any more, so I reach up pleadingly and we kiss softly, emotion underplaying everything as the afternoon fades into a golden evening and we lie on the bed gilded by the sunlight, cuddled close and talking softly.

This is what a cwtch really means, I think as I look at his happy face and feel his arms around me.

CHAPTER 14

You're like a thirty-nine-year-old toddler. You'll need a nap soon and a short stay on the naughty step

Gideon

The next morning I wake up and stretch. The sun is beaming through the low window and dancing on the sheets. I turn my head and smile. Eli is sleeping like the dead and, just like normal, he's spread out over more than half the bed, his arms and legs stretched out like he's preparing to land on Earth. His head is shoved under the pillow and I know that when he emerges he'll have a head of hair that's wilder than Robert Smith's from The Cure.

I stretch again, feeling the ache in my arse with a smile. After the massage we'd lain cuddled together for a long while, and he'd slipped into sleep easily. However, he'd woken up energised in the middle of the night, and I'd reaped the benefits.

I think back to that moment in the café. He'd been truly impressive: focused and strong and the calm centre of the storm. I associate Eli with sunshine and snark, kindness and a wild strength. Seeing him like that was like seeing a lion in its natural habitat when you'd thought he was a house cat. He was effortlessly in charge.

I'd watched him as he worked and felt a surge of pride. I wanted to shout out that he was mine. My man, my person. But I couldn't, and the reason for that is starting to loom larger the more important he grows to me. I know a reckoning is coming, but whether I force it is another matter. I've always been strangely apathetic about my career, drifting in whatever direction Frankie steered me. Niall and Silas could never understand why I did as I was told when I seemed to be allergic to authority in every other area. They never understood the hold that Frankie has over me.

Had, I should say, because it's been fading for a while as my dissatisfaction grows. It's hard to admit that someone you've trusted implicitly could be wrong. Makes you call everything into question.

I think of the firm of accountants I hired a few weeks ago to examine my accounts. I have a feeling that they'll yield a poisoned crop because I'm pretty sure that Frankie has been skimming money for years. I've just been too drunk or stoned to notice.

Sighing, I scrub my hands down my face. Yep, a reckoning is coming. I can feel it in the air.

As if sensing the turbulence of my thoughts, Eli stirs. He stretches out his legs, giving a contemplative *hmm*. I smile. That sleepiness won't last long. Within minutes he'll be up and raring to go. My Eli is not one for sleeping in. I still. *Is he my Eli?* I shake my head and smile. Of course he is. And I'm his. It seems as natural as breathing to be with him. We've slotted together as if we'd been intended for each other. All of my sharp angles meeting his smooth lines and making an interesting and quirky whole.

He pushes the pillow away and lifts his head, his eyes searching for me. When he finds me, he gives a wide, wonderful smile that fills his face, wrinkling that freckled nose and lighting up those olive eyes so they gleam.

"Morning," he says huskily, the Welsh lilt strong in his voice like it always is first thing in the morning. It's as if his brain defaults to its natural setting overnight. As he moves through the day, his voice will ever so slightly lose that obvious tell.

"Morning," I murmur, turning on my side to face him and grinning as he hugs me, burrowing into me so I feel all his body, the sleek planes and hairy surfaces melding into mine. His face nestles into my neck and he inhales deeply. We lie there for a second listening to the birdsong outside the window.

Finally, he emerges and reaches up. "First kiss of the day," he says happily.

I bend and fit my mouth to his, smiling at the same time and feeling it meet his own grin until he groans and takes the kiss deeper, rubbing his tongue over mine. He rears up, pushing me onto my back and coming down over the top of me.

He's just started an eye-crossing rubbing of my cock when the most hideous noise rumbles through the house and we break apart as if someone has thrown cold water over us.

"What the fuck?" he breathes.

"I know."

"What is it?"

"It sounded like someone clearing their throat over a loudspeaker," I mutter. The noise happens again and my eyes narrow. "Because it *is* someone clearing their throat over a loudspeaker. What the fuck?"

I slip out of the bed and pace over to the open window, aware of Eli following me. I open the curtains feeling him mould his body against mine as he curls around me to look out of the window. "Fuck," he mutters and starts to laugh.

I lean out of the window. "What the fuck are you two doing?"

Silas and Niall are standing under the window on the patio, wearing identical grins. "Attention," Niall says through the megaphone, leaning back slightly as it screeches. "Attention," he says again in a very posh voice. "You are hereby ordered to evacuate the bed and each other's bodies."

Silas shakes his head, his body quivering with laughter.

"You are a fucking arsehole," I inform him, leaning slightly out of the window.

"An arsehole with a loudspeaker," Niall says triumphantly. "That makes me the boss, Grumpy Boy. Now, put Eli down before he dies of either starvation or sexual exhaustion."

"Is this discreet behaviour?" I demand.

"No, and do you know what else isn't discreet or polite, Gideon? Sexing your guest to death and not coming to a barbeque at my house. That is neither discreet nor polite."

"Those are the parameters for politeness? You should write a column."

"I'm too avant-garde for columns," he says loftily. "Come on." He pauses. "But shower first. I haven't got any spare hazmat suits, and Milo will be cross if you get bodily fluids on our new patio furniture."

I groan and look at Eli, who's smiling but looking slightly nervous. "Do you want to go?" I ask. "If you don't, don't worry about it. I'll make an excuse." I pause. "Or just tell them to fuck off."

"We can actually hear you, you know," Niall shouts through the loudspeaker.

Eli hesitates and then nods. "No, let's go. I haven't really met everyone properly yet."

"You sure?" He nods and I lean out of the window again. "We'll be over in an hour. You may start the party then. I like my steak rare, but Eli likes his medium. Make sure that there's a good selection of salads."

"Why did we want to invite him?" Niall asks and Silas laughs, taking the loudspeaker from him and waving farewell.

I turn back to Eli. "Are you sure?"

He nods. "I am…"

"But?"

"The last time they met me, I was your nurse. It doesn't look good."

"Eli, you haven't been my nurse for fucking months. How long is acceptable? Should I be drawing my pension?"

He laughs and steps into me, my arms coming up automatically to pull him close. "That's not long to wait." I pinch him and he jerks and laughs but then sobers quickly and nestles closer. "I know. I just don't want anyone to think I've manipulated you."

"I don't think that's likely," I say dryly. "They tried to hypnotise me for a movie role once and gave up."

"Which movie role?" he asks, pulling away slightly.

"The magician thriller."

"I saw that. You were brilliant in it."

"Yes, well not so much with the actual magicianing. I nearly decapitated the actress playing my assistant and my card dealing was absolutely atrocious." Eli laughs and I brush his hair back. "I like to see you smile," I say softly.

His eyes leap to mine and hold. "Really?"

"Yes, you should always be happy."

"That's not possible."

"If I had anything to do with it, I'd make it so."

"That's lovely." He pauses. "And also somewhat worryingly godlike."

I shrug and smile at him. "Don't worry. They're lovely people. You'll have a good time and they'll love you," I finish confidently.

"Will they?"

"How could they not?" The simple statement rings with certainty as we stare at each other. Then he coughs and moves back slightly.

"I'll take your word for it. Come on, let's shower."

An hour later we walk up the drive towards Milo and Niall's house. Eli looks at my outfit and smiles. "What?" I ask, looking down at my navy shorts and sky-blue shirt. "What's the matter?"

"Your shoes match," he says, affection and amusement running through his voice.

I look down at my sky-blue Vans. "And your point is?"

"Well, look at me. I'm wearing denim shorts and an old T-shirt, and I have holes in my shoes, and you look like you've stepped off the catwalk."

I pull him to a stop. "And yet I can't take my eyes off you. You don't need expensive clothes or designer labels. All I can see is you, and you're fucking gorgeous."

His expression softens, and after a quick look around he pulls me to him for a soft kiss. "Then I'm happy." He nudges me. "You make me happy."

I try not to let my smile take over my face, but I can't manage it. "You make me happy too," I say gruffly and feel him squeeze my hand.

The house appears ahead of us and Eli looks up at it curiously. "This is lovely," he says, and I smile at him affectionately.

"This was a wreck too. Niall restored it and then let Milo run amok with the décor."

"What do you mean?"

"You'll see," I say in a doom-laden voice. "You'll approve if you like paint colours that let you imagine you're living in a circus tent."

He starts to laugh and looks around. "Could you live somewhere like this?"

I consider it. "I've never really lived anywhere apart from hotels," I say slowly. "I've owned lots of houses." I pause. "In fact I think I still own houses." He gives me a despairing look, and I flush slightly. "But I never lived in them. They were investments. I just stopped at hotels because it was easier."

"That sounds rather rootless."

"I have less roots than moss," I say. I pause to consider the tranquil setting, the smell of barbeque smoke in the air, and the sound of voices and laughter coming from the back of the house. "I have enjoyed being in Cornwall, though." I turn to him. "Do you like it here?"

"Cornwall?" I nod. "Oh yeah, I love Cornwall. I've surfed here on lad's holidays before. It's a gorgeous coastline."

"Could you live here, Eli?"

He hesitates, staring at me. "What are you saying?"

I scuff my foot slightly in the gravel. "I'm just saying that if I hypothetically bought a house down here, could you hypothetically see yourself living in it? Not here, obviously." I look around. "I do actually require a few shops and pubs and people."

He reaches up and cups my cheek in his big hand and smiles. It's a tender smile that warms his eyes, and I see it a lot when he looks at me. It always makes me feel humbled, and also slightly wary because there's obviously a history of mental instability in his family if he's looking at me like that.

"*Cariad*, I'd live anywhere that you were," he says slowly.

"Anywhere?" I ask flippantly, stopping to clear my throat.

"*Anywhere*," he promises me. He pauses. "But only if this hypothetical house was bought together with shared money after we'd hypothetically dated for a while beforehand."

"That hypothetically makes me very happy," I say gruffly.

"I'm hypothetically glad," he says solemnly, twisting away, laughing as I pinch his nipples. "Nah, not those, Gid. I need them."

"What could you possibly need your nipples for?" I say loftily, reaching up to press the doorbell. "Unless you're considering breast-feeding in the near future."

He shakes his head. "It isn't on my ten-year plan, I have to say."

"You have a ten-year plan?"

"Of course." He looks at me warily. "Doesn't everyone?"

"Not me." I turn at the sound of footsteps on the other side of the door. "I have a ten-minute plan. Anything after that smacks of too much structure."

"You're like a thirty-nine-year-old toddler," he says wonderingly. "You'll need a nap soon and a short stay on the naughty step."

The door swings open before I can reply, and Oz peers out. "Afternoon, sex addicts."

Eli groans, and I shake my head. "Do you live here now too? This place gets more like a commune every day."

"If I lived here I'd be forced to murder Niall," he says smartly. "And Milo wouldn't talk to me for a while."

"How long?" Eli asks.

Oz stops to consider it. "Probably a couple of days, I'd say. Or just until he realised how peaceful and tidy it is without him."

He stands back. "Welcome to not my home," he says, throwing his arm out like an estate agent. "We're in the back."

"Where's your daughter?" Eli asks.

"She's with my mum," Oz says happily. "She met a bloke on a cruise a few months ago and he's brought her down here for the weekend. They've taken Cora to Newquay."

"Well, I suppose someone has to." I shudder slightly at the thought.

He laughs. "Cora will love it. Tacky shops, sand and sea and endless 'e' numbers." He pauses. "We do need to move this along, though. Silas and I are here to drink and eat loads and then it's back to the house for us so we can have incredibly noisy sex without our daughter shouting for a new nappy."

Eli laughs. We wander down the hall, and I smile and shake my head. "Purple."

Eli looks up at the walls which are a rich aubergine colour. "What's wrong with that? It's a lush colour, that is."

Oz laughs. "Niall didn't do colour in this house when he was on his own. The boldest he got was painting the lounge grey, and I think he had to have a sit down after that. Now, he has red on the walls in the kitchen, bronze in the bedroom, and the downstairs loo is yellow. This is all Milo, and because it's him, Niall is of course adamant that he likes it."

Eli looks at me as if expecting me to wince at the mention of Niall's devotion, and I shake my head at him. "I keep expecting him to grow a handlebar moustache and crack a whip," I muse.

Oz grins. "He's definitely bossy enough to run a circus."

"From what I've heard of the men he employs, he's already achieved that dream."

"Is one of them called Phil?" Eli asks. "Because Niall sent him to prune the rose bushes in the back garden yesterday. It was while you were up at the big house."

"Did he do it?" I ask.

He shakes his head. "No, he dug up a big bush in the field and then chased the sheep for a bit." He pauses. "He didn't catch any, though, so that's okay."

"Of course he didn't," Oz says, pushing the back door open. "Because the sheep are far too wily for Phil. They'll have told him they were tourists."

"Probably better behaved than the tourists on this estate," I say, blinking as we move out into the garden. It's changed since I was here last. The patio of York stone has been extended, and on it they've set a long patio table with eight chairs around it. The rest of the garden is a riot of colour with a big silver birch tree bending elegantly over everything.

"This is nice," I say as Milo comes towards us, smiling happily.

"Thank you," he says, hugging me and then letting me go to hug Eli too. Eli blinks but tentatively returns it, and I smile as I look at the two men who mean the most to me.

"Welcome," Milo says to Eli. "You've been locked up in that house with Gideon for *so* long."

"He wasn't locked up," I say indignantly. "He could leave at any time."

"Not until the Stockholm Syndrome had passed," Niall offers from his position next to the barbeque.

I raise a middle finger, and Milo laughs before turning back to Eli. "Still, do you need anything after the last few days? A drink, some Valium, a psychiatrist?"

I shake my head as everyone including Eli bursts into laughter. "Wankers," I say calmly and make my way over to where Silas is sitting in a patio chair, his long legs stretched out in front of him. His hair is wild, his beard even wilder, but he looks contented and slightly sleepy.

"I'll sit with you," I say decisively. "At least I'll get some relief from the constant piss-taking."

He grins at me. "You seem happy."

"I'm surprised you haven't been round to see me," I say, taking a bottle of Bud from Milo with a nod of thanks.

"Oh, I called round." I look at him and he winks. "The window was open and there was a lot of very loud groaning and shouting. I presumed you were rearranging the furniture."

Milo laughs loudly, and I shake my head. "Why did I think you'd be a bastion of mental stability?"

"It's beyond me," Niall offers. "Have you met his husband?"

Oz settles down into the chair next to Silas and raises a lazy middle finger at Niall, who laughs and turns back to the food.

"I was thinking today that it's been a bit like having Errol Flynn on the property," Silas muses. "We were just missing the sword fighting. I bet you could do a cracking Australian accent, though."

Oz snorts and I shake my head. "How old are you? I know you're nearly forty, but inside you must beat the heart of an eighty-year-old."

"While you have Jim Morrison's."

"I'll take that." I kick out a chair for Eli as he comes over to the table. "Come and sit down." I smile at him. "Although I'm apologizing in advance for this lot."

"How rude," Oz sniffs and spoils the impression of indignation by winking at Eli. "How are you enjoying Cornwall, Eli?"

He hesitates and then gives his wide, lazy smile. "Well, I haven't seen much of it, to be honest. What with Gid chaining me to his bed and all. But it's been a nice holiday and a bit of a rest for me."

Everyone bursts into laughter, and I lean into him and smile because I can't help it.

Niall starts to dish up the food, and Milo moves around setting out platters of salads and bread on the table and replenishing drinks.

As he puts a plate of steaks down on the table, Oz looks around.

"I think we've actually got enough numbers now to form a group like the Spice Girls."

"What would your nickname be?" Milo immediately asks.

"Snarky Spice," Niall shouts.

Oz shakes his head. "While yours would be He Thinks He's Funny but He's Actually Not, so He Needs to Stop Talking Spice."

Niall blinks as he comes over with a plate of burgers. "That's a bit of a mouthful. Can't I have something short and snappy? That's not you, by the way, Oz."

Oz raises his middle finger. "Yes, you can have something short and snappy. How about Twatty Spice?"

"What would his outfit be?" Eli asks, settling back in his chair and taking the hand I offer him. I smile at him, aware of Silas watching us.

"Something slutty," Milo offers.

I laugh, and Niall shakes his head. "Milo, you actually *wound* me."

"I'd wound you more if it wasn't the truth."

"Not anymore," Niall says and kisses the smile on my brother's face.

We fall on the food, making appreciative noises and occasionally pausing to take the piss out of Niall.

Finally, Oz settles back. "So, Niall is Twatty Spice."

"I am not," Niall says crossly.

"So Niall is Twatty Spice," Oz continues undeterred. "I'm obviously Super Spice and Eli is I'm Just Taking a Mental Health Break Spice." Eli laughs loudly, and Oz grins at him. It's obvious he's taken to him. "What about Silas, though?"

"Daddy Spice," Milo says with a wicked gleam in his eyes. Silas chokes on his beer, and Niall pats him on the back helpfully.

"Silas is definitely not a Daddy," Oz says. "He's irredeemably democratic."

"Why does that sound like a complaint?" Silas bemoans.

"Because the bossiest you get in bed is telling me to turn the light out." Oz winks at Silas, who shakes his head.

"There's only room for one bossy person in our family and let's face it, Oz, that's you."

"I'll second that," Niall offers and grins when Oz glares at him. "I'll even third, fourth, fifth and sixth it. In fact I'd infinity it."

"What about Gideon?" Eli asks, sitting back in his chair, looking relaxed and amused. I knew they'd all get on. He fits like we've been saving his place all these years.

"Got to be Perfection Personified Spice," I say as they groan. "But I somehow know it's going to be Grumpy Spice."

"Only if Badly Behaved Spice is taken," Oz says.

"Don't mock Princess Sparkles," Niall warns him, and Milo laughs loudly as I stick two fingers up at them.

Silas shakes his head. "I don't think you're Grumpy Spice, Gideon."

"What's my name, then?" I ask, startled.

Silas smiles. "That's going to take a bit of thought. You're a whole new classification now." He pauses. "Maybe Happy Spice." He looks at Eli. "Thank you."

Eli looks startled. "What for?"

"For giving us Gideon. The new and improved version."

"I'm not a MacBook," I say crossly.

Eli smiles at me. "If you were a MacBook, I'd definitely be asking for an instruction manual."

The others laugh and start talking loudly about something to do with the estate, but I lean closer to Eli. "I think, out of everyone in the world, you are the only person who will never need that."

"Really?" His lips are close and his eyes are so merry and warm that my heart hurts.

I nod and he smiles. "Maybe I need one because making you happy is something I want to work at," he whispers.

"You don't need to work at it," I say gruffly. "You manage it effortlessly."

He stares at me and I nod abruptly. Unable to speak for a second,

I sit back quietly, eating my steak and drifting while listening to the lively piss-taking banter around the table. A hand comes down on top of mine which is resting on the table.

"You alright?" Eli asks.

I smile at him, turning my palm over and taking the hand he offers and squeezing it. "I can honestly say I've never been better."

He grins but whatever he was going to say dies away as the back gate clicks and, like a villain appearing on a stage set, Frankie appears minus the bang and smoke. However, he looks like he's got smoke coming out of his ears at the moment. Dressed in a black suit even in this hot weather, his hair is slicked back, and he'd look suave if his face weren't red and his hands weren't clenched into fists.

I feel Eli's hand tighten on mine as Frankie walks towards us, and the conversation dies away.

"Good afternoon, Frankie," Niall says. "I'm so sorry we started the party without you. We'd quite given up on you appearing completely uninvited."

Frankie shakes his head impatiently. "I haven't got time to banter with you, Niall. This is serious."

"What's happened?" I say slowly, feeling the blood starting to pound in my temples. Eli squeezes my hand, but I can't return the gesture. All my attention is on my manager and the sick feeling that's growing in my stomach.

Frankie throws me a look that seems to combine extreme stress with some sort of dark satisfaction. "Seems like your secret's out, Gideon," he says loudly, his flair for dramatics showing for a second until he battens it back down again.

My stomach sinks so quickly I feel a surge of nausea. "What do you mean?"

He shrugs, taking out his phone from his inside pocket and palming it. "I mean that someone sold some photos of you and nursie here. They'll hit the papers tomorrow." He looks at me, and, for an incredible second, I could swear a smile is hovering on his lips. "Game's up, Gideon."

CHAPTER 15

The bastion of havoc and bad behavior

Eli

Gideon stiffens all over like he has rigor mortis, and I tighten my grip on his hand.

"You alright?" I ask in a low voice.

To my amazement he doesn't show any sign of hearing me. Instead, he stands up, and I feel my hand fall away unnoticed and unneeded. I lift my fingers and massage my chest as I watch him stride over to Frankie.

"Show me," he demands, his voice tight and very, *very* controlled.

Frankie fumbles with his phone and holds it out to Gideon. He takes it and looks intently at the picture before sinking suddenly into a chair. Milo exclaims and hugs Gideon's shoulders as Niall takes away the phone and stares at it. He shakes his head. "Wankers," he says in a low, angry voice, and then, to my amazement, he hands the phone to me.

I take it tentatively, feeling like it might turn around and bite me. It's as if it's a sentient being. I look down and gasp. It's Gideon and me, and the first gasp is one of relief because out of every photo someone could have taken of us, the one of us hugging in the coffee shop is probably the least harmful to Gid's career. I think of the blowjob in the garden and shudder.

However, when I look again, I realise how very incriminating this photo actually is. Gideon is holding me close, one hand clutching low on my hip and the other cradling my face. He's talking intently and the fondness in his eyes is unmistakable even in this grainy image. It's an incredibly intimate pose, something no straight man would entertain, but it's my face that really gives the game away because I look like I'm drowning in him, all my attention on him and the love I feel visible in my eyes. I hope that it's just visible to me. I shudder, and Niall takes the phone away.

"Gideon," I say in a low voice, willing him to look at me, to smile, to wink, even to say something typically acerbic that will bring a smile to my lips. But he does nothing. Literally nothing. Instead he ignores me, staring ahead into the distance as if he's far away.

"*Gideon*," Frankie snaps and my heart feels sick at the way Gideon immediately responds to his agent as if conditioned to do it. Like a dog.

"What?" he says hoarsely.

"Gideon," I try again, and Frankie shoots me a glare full of intense dislike mingled with pleasure that Gideon is again ignoring me.

"It'll be alright, Gid," he says quickly. "I'll fix it. Yeah?"

"Fix it by lying some more," Milo says acidly, and Gideon stirs.

"Not now," he whispers.

Milo hugs him but it must be like hugging a rag doll because Gideon just flops against him, his gaze still far away and turned inward.

"Yes, lying," Frankie says angrily. "What else do you suggest we do, Milo? Fess up that he's fucking his bloody nurse?" Milo opens his mouth, but Frankie shakes his head, his eyes alive with disgust. "No," he says sharply. "You've had your way, Milo, and look what's happened. Gid's career is over." Gideon stirs, and Frankie grabs his shoulders. "We can fix this, though," he says, talking low.

The man's charisma even now is unmistakable, his voice taking on a commanding take-no-prisoner turn. I can see how he captivated a lonely young boy. How he's maintained a hold on him for so many years. I swallow hard.

"Look at me," Frankie says insistently, and Gideon raises his eyes to him immediately. Niall swears and moves away, scrubbing his hand through his hair in a short stabbing motion. "I've got you an interview with Steven Hawksworth," Frankie says, holding on to Gideon's neck and forcing him to keep looking at him. "He owes me a favour, and I've called it in. He's waiting at the studio in St Austell. You'll go in now and deny everything. *Everything*," he says with a heavy emphasis. "Eli is just a friend of yours. Nobody special." I flinch, waiting for Gideon to deny it, but he doesn't. Instead he watches Frankie as if hypnotised as the man carries on talking. "Eli had just rescued that man and nearly fell over. You propped him up. Nothing else." He nods his head firmly. "Drop Jacinta in. *No*," he says sharply as Gideon looks at him. "The time for doing it your way is gone, Gid. You need to listen to me. Steven won't ask you anything difficult."

"But he's known for asking bitchy questions and going full pelt at celebrities," Silas says slowly.

"Not this time," Frankie says smugly. "Put it this way, I have something on him that he doesn't want known. If he wants it to stay unknown, then he'll do as I ask. So, Gideon, you are going to put on the suit I have for you in the car. Then you're going to get in the car and you are going to lie your fucking arse off. And when you've finished and your career is saved again, you will remember to thank me." He claps Gideon on the shoulder. "Come on, son, shake a leg."

Gideon gets to his feet stiffly as if he's a marionette, and Milo steps back, his hand falling away and finding Niall's outstretched one.

"Sorry," Gideon says hoarsely to him. "Sorry for breaking up the party."

"Don't do this," Milo says softly. "Think about what you're doing. You're selling your soul. It'll destroy you." His eyes flicker to me. "It'll destroy *everything*."

Gideon hesitates for a second but then shakes his head and steps back stiffly. "Sorry," he says again, his voice clearing a little bit but still wooden.

"I'll come with you," Frankie says decisively, but Gideon shakes his head immediately.

"I don't want that, thank you. I need to be on my own for this."

"Well, if you're sure?"

For the first time Frankie seems unsure, but Gideon ignores him, moving away and towards the gate. His way forward takes him past me and without my brain telling it, my hand shoots out and stays him.

"Gideon," I say softly, and a shudder runs over his body like a small wave breaking on the beach. He looks down at me, and I stare helplessly back. "Do you need me?" I ask.

He immediately shakes his head. "I have to do this on my own," he says and, stung, I go to pull my hand back, but he holds on to it as if he can't let go. In that moment, I really look at him. His eyes are dark and distant, but somewhere underneath that, I can see my Gideon there. He's hidden under layers of blind panic and rage, but he's there and it gives me the strength to smile at him.

"Well, I'm here if you need me," I say softly.

"Will you still be here when I get back?"

I flinch because he just seems to be accepting that I'll be leaving him at some point. It breaks my heart. Instead of hugging him like I want to, I nod my head fiercely. "I'll be here," I say steadily and firmly. I squeeze his hand, heartened when he squeezes back. "Be true to yourself," I whisper. "Whether that's staying hidden or coming out. But make sure that it's what *you* want and not what others tell you is best."

He stares at me for a long moment, and his hand tightens almost painfully on mine. He opens his mouth to say something, but at that second Frankie stirs.

"Let him go, Eli," he says angrily. "This is mainly your fucking fault. If he knows anything, Gid will bin you when this is all over."

I stiffen, but for the first time since Frankie has arrived, Gideon's face displays some emotion. "Don't you fucking talk to him like that," he hisses at his manager, and Frankie steps back in surprise. "He is *nothing* to do with you," Gideon shouts. "Fuck all. He's mine, and you are not interfering in that."

For a second I think that Frankie is going to explode but then he visibly calms. "But you are still going to lie your arse off about him, aren't you?" he says coldly.

Gideon stares at him, an emotion I can't identify crossing his face. "You're the boss," he says slowly. Frankie smiles, and Gideon turns back to me. He lifts up my hand and kisses it. "I'll see you when I get back?" he whispers, a pleading tone in his voice, and I nod.

"You will."

And then he's gone, disappearing round the corner and leaving a heavy silence.

Frankie hesitates and then mumbles something about getting the suit for him and disappears after him. I jump as a hand comes down on my shoulder. I look around to find Silas watching me with a concerned look on his face.

"Don't worry," he says in a low voice. "It'll be alright."

"Will it?" I ask in a hollow tone.

"Yes," he says with a firm nod. He looks at Oz for his opinion. It's a totally natural reaction, as if the pair speak as a longstanding team. Oz has sat throughout this whole exchange without speaking, his eyes as intent as a cat watching mice. Now he smiles at his husband and then at me. It's sharp with an edge, but still kind and encompassing.

"It'll be alright," he says clearly, the Irish in his voice thick. "I've been watching Gideon for a while. It'll be fine."

"But w-what if he lies and goes back to his very t-tiring version of normal?" Milo says, his stutter noticeable.

"Then he does," I say sadly. "It's up to him and not any of us. He has to do this himself."

"And if he l-lies? And denies knowing you?"

I shrug. "Then he does that. It's not like I've been lied to. He's been honest from the word go with me about who he is and what he can do."

"That's why I'm sure it'll be alright," Oz says, getting up and leaning against Silas, sure of his welcome. As Silas wraps his arms around him, Oz looks hard at me. "You're the only person Gideon hasn't lied to. Ask yourself why."

I stand up. "I'm sorry, but I'm going to go back to the cottage just in case he needs anything."

"Don't worry," Milo says, squeezing my arm. "Do what you've got to do."

"And then come up to the house," Oz says. "We can watch the interview, and you should be with us when you do that."

"Why?" I ask, wincing because it comes out rudely, but none of them look the slightest bit offended.

"Because you should be with friends," Oz says, slapping me on the back and starting to walk towards the gate. "And family."

I walk back to the house, pacing quickly along the gravelled path. The sun is low now and the smell of hawthorn is strong on the air. I remember Gid's email about the scent and marvel at the fact that it was only a few months ago. So much has happened between us, and I feel as close to him as if I've known him forever.

I pick up speed so that I'm almost running, but I know as soon as I let myself into the house that he's gone. It has the empty feeling of a stage set. Nevertheless, I walk from room to room checking for him. The bedroom is empty, his clothes from today slung onto the bed and the covers still tangled from when they'd wrapped around our bodies.

I sink onto the mattress, lifting his T-shirt to my nose and inhaling deeply. The scent of vanilla and a trace of clean sweat fills my nostrils, and I close my eyes and lie down amongst the sheets that still smell of sex. I lie still for a while, listening to myself breathe in the stillness and feeling my heart beat fast.

I know I said he has to do what he must, and I truly believe that, but it doesn't stop the desperate hope that he won't lie and the knowledge that it will fucking devastate me when he does. When he looks into the camera and denies everything we are becoming to each other, I know he will break my heart, just as I know that I will still be here when he comes back because I promised, and I won't break my promises to him. He's had too much of that in his life and seen far too many people walk away from him easily.

After a few minutes, I sigh and open my eyes. I go still, because lying on my bedside table is a rose. It's freshly cut, the petals starting to open. Darkly lush with a sweet, sensual smell, it's the same as the ones he cuts for me every morning and leaves on my bedside table, waiting for me to wake up and see them. I have a vase full of them now.

I know it wasn't there this morning, and hope stirs in my belly. He must have cut this for me before he left. What does it mean? I sag slightly. Fuck, I hope this isn't a bloody goodbye gesture. I reach for it and see a yellow Post-it note underneath, and my hearts pounds so hard it's like it wants to leave my body. In Gideon's scrawling handwriting is written four words. *Please don't leave me.*

"Never," I whisper, but my fingers curl around the stem, and I hiss as a thorn cuts me. Blood wells out as I watch. Fuck, I hope that's not a bad omen.

∼

An hour later, showered and dressed in khaki shorts and a grey and white striped shirt, I'm as ready as I'll ever be for this TV ordeal. I make my way up the steps and into the huge old house. Inside it's shady, the flagstones cool and the air smelling of beeswax and furniture polish.

"Hello," I call out, my ratty Converse squeaking on the floor.

Oz pops his head around a huge wooden door. "Hey," he says, smiling at me. "We're in the study." He looks around. "Frankie is somewhere around," he says, shuddering. "Talking very loudly into his mobile phone so we all know how important he is."

"Gross," I mutter, following him through a huge room with tall mullioned windows through which the sun dances lazily and shines on suits of armor. We march down some steps and into a large room filled with floor-to-ceiling bookcases. I stand back to let a stern-looking middle-aged woman out.

Oz smiles at her. "Are all the tours done now, June?"

"Just one left, Oz."

"Would it be possible for you to keep them away from the study?"

For some reason a smile crosses her face, and she winks at him. "I always approach the study with a certain amount of trepidation now, Oz."

To my amazement he flushes and then rallies. "Sassy woman," he says smilingly, and she laughs.

"You know it." To my amazement she squeezes my arm as she walks past. "Please make sure you tell Gideon that he has the staff's loyalties and all of our support." She nods firmly to emphasize the point and walks off, her back ramrod straight.

Oz stares after her and shakes his head. "If women like that were in charge of the world it would be a very calm and orderly place. And for some reason she's very fond of Gideon."

"The bastion of havoc and bad behavior," I say disbelievingly and he laughs.

"Go figure."

I walk into the room and look around. At one end of the room is a pair of French windows letting in the pungent scent of lavender, and in front of a high fireplace are a long sofa and chairs. Silas is standing in front of a huge oak cupboard opened to reveal a TV, and I jerk when he moves, and I catch sight of Gideon on the screen.

Dressed in a navy suit with white shirt and red tie, he looks pale under his tan and his lips are drawn thin.

I wander over, exchanging weak smiles with the others. "How does he seem?" I ask, my eyes glued to my lover. "Has he said anything yet?"

Silas shakes his head. "No. It's just the usual preliminaries."

Steven Hawksworth is rather pretentious and likes to let the audience watch the stars being set up for interviewing. They can watch them being made up, going through questions, talking to Steven and chatting and laughing.

Gideon isn't laughing or even smiling. We watch silently as he sits looking sleek and expensive in his designer suit, his foot crossed over his knee. His expression is spare and under tight control, the only sign of agitation the tic in his jaw and the way his foot is jiggling. Steven tries to speak to him a couple of times and both times Gideon doesn't appear to be listening to him, making the interviewer look slightly petulant.

Oz stirs. "Why does the camera keep cutting to Steven laughing and shaking his hair? It's like a *Eurovision Song Contest* segment."

"He likes the camera the way my old dog liked bacon," I say meditatively, and Niall laughs. I turn my head and look at him in surprise as he and Silas sink into the sofa next to me. Niall smiles innocently, and my eyes narrow.

"What are you doing?"

Oz laughs. "Only known you a few days and already he knows you're up to something. I rest my case. I said you could never be a secret agent."

"And you could?" Niall asks crossly. "You've got a mouth bigger than the Channel Tunnel."

"All the better to eat Silas with," Oz says, winking and laughing as Silas groans and covers his face.

Niall turns to me. "Gideon rang me and Silas on the way to the studio."

"He rang *you*," I whisper, feeling the betrayal slam into me.

He immediately holds up his hands in a panicked fashion. "No. No. Not like that. He only spoke for a few minutes. Just long enough to ask us to look out for you."

"To look out for *me*? Why?"

"Because Frankie is on the war path. Gideon wanted us to have your back."

"It might have been nice for Gideon to share those concerns with me personally," I say acidly.

He winks. "Nah, you know him. You know that's not his way."

"Do I know him?" I ask helplessly.

"Yes," he says, looking intently at me. "You do. You're probably the only one in this room who really does. And you'll know immediately that I was stunned because Gideon is not and has never been very sensitive to people's feelings."

"No!" I gasp. "*Really?*"

He grins suddenly, white and wide and somehow approving. Then he nudges me. "Only yours."

"What?"

"You don't need to be bothered about what Gideon and I did in the past."

"I'm not," I say defensively.

"Oh, okay," he says, patently not believing me. "But if you had been, you shouldn't have bothered because I was never the right person for him, and he wasn't for me." I stare at him, and he shrugs. "He never *ever* considered coming out for me in all the years we were fucking around. There's nothing there but friendship between us. Good friendship, though. For all his faults, Gid makes a good friend. He's loyal and cares deeply, whatever he says to the contrary. He just has to be practically clubbed over the head to notice a problem and then he's all in. Ask Jacinta." He pauses. "He's just very difficult to know."

"Not really," I say hesitantly, because he isn't. Gideon is an open book most of the time.

Niall smiles kindly. "Not for you. To be honest, there probably shouldn't ever have been anything between Gid and me because the potential for fouling up the good relationships we've found later in life could have been high."

I stare at him. He's one of the most attractive men I've ever met, and I don't mind admitting that I've felt threatened by him since I first found out. But now, not so much, because I see how he is with Milo and I see how Gid is with him. It's very different from the way he is with me. He never looks at Niall the way he does me.

"Actually, I'm sort of glad there was," I say, my words surprising me, but I realise that it's true. "I'm glad he had someone he could be himself with."

"I don't think he's ever been that," he says thoughtfully. "Until you. Silas and I got different bits of him, but you, you get everything. It's like he's dropped all his guards with you." He pauses as Milo wanders over and perches on the side of the sofa and leans into him. Niall smiles at his boyfriend and then looks back at me earnestly. "Please look after Gid. He's a wonderful man. He just never realises it. He needs someone to remind him of the fact."

"I'll do that every day," I promise. *If I'm given the chance,* I think sadly.

We smile at each other, and I know with an inner certainty that we'll be fine now.

At that point, Frankie walks in just to really top the shit cake off with an even shittier icing. "Great," I mutter, and Frankie glares at me.

"Come to see what you've done to his career?" he says venomously.

My mouth falls open as the normally mild-mannered Silas turns on him.

"I'd like you to remember that you are a guest in this house, Frankie," he says sharply, his posh accent frigid with politeness. "And as such you will be held to the same standard of behavior as the other guests. If you persist in being rude, you can sod off and find somewhere else to watch this."

"Are you not going to tell *him* that?" Frankie demands, pointing at me. "He's a guest too."

"No, he isn't," Silas says coldly, turning away. "He's family."

There's a truncated silence in the room. When I look up, Oz is fluttering his eyelashes at Silas, who is trying not to laugh. I feel a sense of warmth run through me that I've been accepted by Gideon's friends. I hope it's not for nothing.

The standoff between Frankie and Silas is broken when Niall leans forwards. "He's on."

Everyone clusters around the sofa as he turns the volume up. I notice a few ladies led by the redoubtable June coming into the room just as the introductory music comes on and the slides start of Steven interviewing seemingly everyone who is notable in the world. When the music stops and the screen shows Gideon, we all lean forward as if synchronized.

I stare at my lover. His face is set and resolute, but there's a subtle change. "Does he look different to you?" I say to Niall, who stares at the screen.

"Not really," he says doubtfully. "He just looks like Gid."

But he doesn't. Not to me, anyway. The sick shock seems to have faded and there's something else playing on his face and a strange gleam in his eyes. I wonder what it is, but the thought flies away as Steven starts his introduction, showing Gideon in stills from his many films and plays.

I smile a little when he shows photos of him in school performances. He looks truculent and sulky and just so him that it makes my heart hurt and my brain wonder if I've gone completely mad handing this man my heart.

Normally, at this point the camera will cut to the guest who will look incredibly modest and express their delight at Steven actually deigning to interview them. This time, however, the camera cuts to

Gideon who just looks incredibly bored. It obviously slightly discomposes Steven, who fumbles his words before managing to welcome his guest.

"Well, I'm delighted to welcome one of Britain's most talented actors to the sofa tonight. Gideon Ramsay, star of stage and screen and one of Britain's most popular exports."

"That makes me sound like a crate of raspberries," Gideon says coolly.

Steven laughs somewhat nervously. "Ah, I've heard many things about you, but humour wasn't ever particularly mentioned."

"I wonder why that was," Gideon says, leaning back in his chair and actually looking like he's starting to enjoy himself.

"Could it be that you're always so focused on your roles that you inhabit them twenty-four hours a day in your pursuit of true excellence? I've seen your face before in pictures taken on the set. You always look like you're totally in character."

"Or I'm just a bit bored and ready to go down the pub," Gideon offers, and someone in the audience gasps and smothers a laugh.

Steven hesitates barely perceptibly before firming his lips and shooting straight into the reason for this interview.

"Now, Gideon, despite being pictured with many very beautiful women over the years, the rumours have never actually been put to bed that you're gay. They persist out there with people saying that you're living a lie, covering your true self in an attempt to cling onto your fame."

"Rather dramatic," Gideon says, slouching slightly in his seat. "The last thing I clung onto was the wall, and I was desperately hungover then."

Oz laughs but I stare at Gid. His face is almost expressionless, but there's a slight light in his eyes that has never, in all the time I've known him, *ever* presaged anything good.

I sit forward slightly, as do Niall and Silas who obviously recognise the look too.

"You're right," Niall says, turning to me and offering me an approving look. "He's up to something."

Steven nods thoughtfully at Gideon. "And yet there have been photographs published in the papers today showing you embracing another man. They're very intimate photos that suggest strongly that you're not exactly straight."

Gideon smiles blandly at him. "Well, I'm not. I'm gay," he says clearly and very casually.

There's a huge gasp from the audience and Steven sits back looking utterly astonished, his mouth opening and shutting like a fish taking in food.

In the study, I sit up, feeling like my heart is about to come up my throat as Silas and Niall jump to their feet, and Frankie curses loudly and creatively.

"What the *fuck*?" he breathes, looking panicked. "What the fuck is he doing?"

"Being truthful," Milo says, and Frankie glares malevolently at him.

"Milo–"

"Shush!" I say crossly to him.

"But you've said that you're straight on many occasions," Steven says, leaning forwards now, his expression aiming at intent and settling for somewhere between glee and panic.

"Have I?" Gideon looks patently amazed. "I don't actually believe I've ever said anything of the sort." He waves his hand in a very cavalier fashion. "I don't bother reading the labels on my clothes, Steven. Why on earth would I put one on myself?"

"I find that a bit rich," I mutter. "He's never done his own laundry. Up until a month ago he didn't even know that clothes could be worn more than once."

"But you've been seen many times with women," Steven says. "Jacinta Foxton, for one."

Gideon smiles coldly. "I've also been seen walking her dog. I've never been accused of shagging it."

Someone off camera laughs, and Steven gets the look of a man whose simple interview is getting away from him. "Apologies for that use of language," he says primly. He looks at Gideon for a second as if expecting some show of remorse. There isn't any. "Moving on," he says hurriedly. "So, you're really gay?"

"That's not moving on. That's actually just moving back to the previous question," Gideon says in a helpful sort of way. Then he relents and all traces of sardonic amusement fade. "I haven't exactly been honest," he says slowly. "Even if I haven't directly lied."

"It's like Bill Clinton all over again," Niall murmurs, and Milo shoves him.

"Shush!"

Gideon's expression becomes stark. "I let my fans assume something about me for years because I was always told that they would hate my sexuality, and me for it. I'm sorry for that, because I think I was putting my own murky feelings about everything onto them. I actually believe that they're a lot more intelligent than I've ever been, but at the time I wasn't comfortable and couldn't believe they would be either. And for a long time they were all I had."

"Aww," June says from behind me. "Poor man."

Steven looks suddenly infinitely friendlier. The interview is obviously turning into the scoop of the year in front of his eyes.

"So, what changed? Is it the man in the photos with you? Is he your boyfriend?"

My heart skips a beat. This is it. This is the moment when he'll either acknowledge it or hide me.

Gideon makes a moue of distaste. *"Boyfriend!"*

My heart sinks, and Frankie gives a humourless laugh. "I knew it. Did you really think he'd claim you in front of millions of people, Eli? Get real. Gideon's gay, not desperate."

I open my mouth, but I'm not sure what to say because it looks like he's right, but then Steven leans forward. "Is that part of your conflicted feelings about your sexuality raising its head?" he says sympathetically. "You can't even say the word boyfriend?"

Gideon looks slightly revolted. "No, I just hate that word. Makes me sound like I'm thirteen and going to Roller World." Oz laughs, ignoring Frankie pacing and sweating.

Gideon shoves his hand through his hair. "Let's just say that he's my person." I gasp loudly and Milo squeezes my arm with a huge smile on his face. "And yes, he is responsible for the change in me," Gideon carries on. "Mainly because he's a wonderful person and if he sees something in me that's worthwhile, then maybe it's really there."

"Aww," one of the ladies says from behind me. "That's so sweet."

Steven starts to wind the interview down, his expression friendly and engaged as he and Gideon laugh at something. I'm dimly aware of the women leaving as I stare hard at Gideon. He looks so vulnerable all of a sudden, and I want to grab him and hug him and I actually want to cry. He's done it. He's bloody done it. And in his own inimitable way. I start to laugh.

My laughter stops as Frankie rounds on me. "*You*," he hisses. "This is all your fucking fault."

"How?"

"Turning his head. Making him think he can have a relationship."

"Well, he can," I say simply and coldly. "He can have any relationship with me he wants."

"Because of his money," he sneers. "I see you, Mr Jones, and what you're after."

"Not for the money," I say steadily. "But because he's clever and funny and he needs me like no one has ever needed me before. Because he's gentle and kind and needs to be shown it's alright to be like that rather than a cutthroat shark like you."

He grunts and comes round the sofa at a fast pace towards me. Niall stands up but I wave him back.

"I would really suggest that you don't hit me, Frankie," I say sharply, coming to my feet. "Because I don't want to hit you back."

"Oh really? Why? Does it go against your nursing code?"

"No, it's because I'm a nurse and I know in detail where to hit you back so it really fucking hurts."

"Oh, you're a nurse now. You weren't one when you turned my fucking client gay."

"Has he got a magic penis then?" Oz enquires, laughter rich in his voice. "Does it do tricks too? Maybe it can do my bookwork."

Frankie ignores him, pacing to get into my face. His breath is sour, and I can smell the sweat on him. "I'm going to have you struck off," he hisses.

"How?" I say tersely.

"For fucking your patient."

"I have *never* fucked a patient," I say angrily. "He wasn't my patient when we got together."

"So you say."

"It's the truth," I say loudly, feeling my fists clench and anxiety flood me.

His eyes sharpen and I know he's reading me. "Well, your truth probably won't be believed when I make this public." He drills one long finger into my chest. "And I will. I'm going to let the press know that Gideon's nurse took advantage of him when he was at his lowest and weakest point and is taking advantage of him now by living off him. When I'm finished with you there won't be anything left to whore out."

A deep, rich voice comes from behind us. "Goodness, how extraordinarily quaint. Now I suggest you take your hands off my boyfriend."

We both gasp and turn to the door to find Gideon standing there with a man dressed in a very expensive-looking suit next to him. The man is extremely good-looking with jet-black hair and very blue eyes behind black-framed glasses. He's also staring at Frankie with a frown on his face.

Milo looks at the TV where Gideon is shaking hands with Steven and then back at his brother. "How are you here?

He smiles. "It was recorded a couple of hours ago when I first got to the studio."

"Gideon," I say stupidly. "Are you okay?" I inhale as he turns to look at me, his eyes fairly eating me up. He has spots of colour on his cheeks, but he looks resolute and even calm now.

"I'm fine, love," he says. I gasp at the endearment, and he makes to take a step towards me, but the man next to him says something, and he pulls back, turning to Frankie. "Follow me please, Frankie," he says quietly. He looks at me intently. "I'll be back," he says. "Please don't go."

I swallow, feeling my eyes sting at the vulnerability in those simple words. "I'll be here," I promise. He stares at me for a long second and then as one, he and the man turn and leave the room with Frankie trailing behind.

I turn back to the other men. "What the fuck just happened?"

"I've got a feeling that Frankie's reign is coming to an end. That's John Harrington, Gideon's lawyer," Milo says gleefully.

Niall stirs and looks admiringly at him. "You have such a ruthless streak," he says happily.

"Thank you," Milo says demurely. Then he smiles at me. "Come on. Let's go and get something to drink."

"I should wait here for him," I say hesitantly. "Just in case he needs me."

"He does need you," he says simply. "Probably more than you'll ever realise. But he needs to do this on his own. You'll be there waiting for him at the end, won't you?"

I stare at him, aware of the others looking at me. "Of course," I say simply. "Always."

CHAPTER 16

You're my form of coming home, and you always will be

Gideon

I move into the room Oz uses as an office. Its windows are wide open, letting in the scent from the lavender. It's a curious juxtaposition of a workmanlike environment with a sturdy desk and filing cabinets, and a family room with a brightly coloured playpen in the corner filled with toys and, along one old cupboard, pictures of him and Silas and Cora.

I turn as John, my lawyer, and Frankie enter the room.

"What the fuck is this?" Frankie demands immediately. "Why is John here?" He looks belligerent and nervous, and it's the nerves that finally convince me that what I've been told is true.

"You've been stealing from me," I breathe, and he jerks.

"What the fuck? No, I haven't."

John settles himself down on one of the chairs, crossing his legs and flicking a thread from his trousers. "Be careful, Frankie," he says calmly.

"Careful," he explodes. "Careful when this ungrateful wanker accuses me of stealing money and forging signatures."

"I never said anything about forging," I say, and it cuts through his bluster like a knife through butter. "You said that." I settle back. "Your mind went straight to the contracts."

"Rubbish," he scoffs. "What are you? Fucking Hercule Poirot now? Really? What a load of bollocks."

"But it's not," I say, feeling the sadness suddenly run through me. "I employed Carter, French, and Santer a few weeks ago." He pales at the name of the famous forensic accounting firm. I shrug. "They're very thorough, Frankie. They went through everything."

He sags suddenly, all the bluster running away as he sinks into a chair, looking pale and sweaty.

"*Why?*" I say, the words bursting out of me, and John stirs, giving me a warning look not to let go of my temper. "Why?" I say in a more measured tone. "I gave you anything you asked for, Frankie. Was it not enough?"

"I don't know what you're talking about," he says woodenly, casting a glance at John.

"How about the money you skimmed off my contracts? Bit here, bit there. The shit you bought on my credit cards. The three houses you bought in my name." I shake my head. "I've got to say, Frankie, it came as a surprise to me that I'd signed those deeds over to you. I know I was stoned a lot, but even I'd remember giving away hundreds of thousands of pounds in property."

"Thousands," he scoffs. "You've got millions more."

"I have," I say mildly, feeling a wave of sickness run over me. I trusted this man above everyone else. "But that's sort of the point. It's mine. My money. I earned it and you had no right to steal it from me."

"Please," he scoffs. I shoot a glance at John as Frankie explodes into motion, levering out of his seat and starting to pace. John makes a gesture as if to say *keep him talking*, but I can't stop him now. "I fucking made you, Gid. You were a pimply-faced teenager when I got hold of you. I dressed you right, got you to meet the right people, got you the roles. I created you, you ungrateful bastard, and what did I get? Carping and whining about wanting to be honest. Wanting to be the *authentic you*. What a load of old horseshit." He glares at me. "The real you is pathetic, Gideon. Fucking gay. What a fucking joke. You could have been anything you wanted." He smiles suddenly and humourlessly. "You've done it now, though, Gid. They'll ruin you. You've shit on everything I ever did for you."

"You didn't do it for me," I say sadly. "You did it for you. Let me think you cared. Let me think you wanted the best for me."

"I did."

"Well, your best wasn't and isn't good for me."

"That's fucking obvious," he scoffs. "It never was. So, why shouldn't I take what I wanted? I fucking earned it. All those years of pulling you out of random twinks' beds, covering up and creating the perfect image. I did fucking everything for you, you ungrateful little twat."

"I know," I say slowly. "And I'd have given you everything you chose to take if you'd just asked me."

"What?" he says, looking shocked.

I nod. "I'd have given you anything you wanted, Frankie, because for a very long time I was certain you were my only friend. The only one who supported me." I shake my head. "I was wrong."

"So, what are you going to do?" he snaps, and I almost want to admire him. Even now he's cocksure. It's no wonder I believed everything he told me. No one disbelieves someone so determinedly certain as Frankie. "Going to send me to fucking prison, Gideon? Because it'll be a noisy day in the press when I start talking."

"You won't talk, actually," John says coldly. "Because you signed a nondisclosure just the same as the other men you made sign them in the past." He smiles slightly. "But the difference is that you signed one of mine, and they're so watertight Houdini couldn't have got out of them."

"You can't stop me," he says loudly, the bluster showing he knows it's true.

"I can," I say, idly clicking the top of a pen on and off. "You owe me a lot of money, Frankie. There is a very clear and indisputable paper trail following you around detailing the thefts and the forging of my signature on various documents. That's a prison sentence all on its own."

He seems to deflate suddenly. "So, what now?" he says, sitting back down. "What do you want? I don't have that money and you know it. You'll fucking ruin me."

"I don't want that," I say slowly. He looks up, hope rich in his face. I stare at him coldly, watching the flinch he can't help. "I trusted you," I say in a low voice. "I even loved you. Saw you as my de facto father for some fucked-up reason. It's for that reason alone, because I cared a lot for you, that I'm going to let the crime go."

"Against my advice," John says coldly. "I don't find theft and fraud charming, Mr Grantham."

I shrug. "Here's what's going to happen," I say, standing up and shoving my hands in my pockets. "You are going to leave here with John and go back to London where you will box up all my data from your office as I am no longer your client." Incredibly, he looks like he wants to argue. "I am going to move management and will release a statement saying it's a mutual decision and that you are retiring immediately. You can sell your business, which should fetch a pretty penny, and John will then set up a repayment schedule for you to pay everything back. The time for that is not infinite. And that is it. You will keep your reputation, clouded as it is. In return, you will not talk about me or my family." My face hardens. "You will most certainly never utter a word about Eli. Make no mistake, he is the most important thing in the world to me. Hell, he *is* my world. If at any point you get greedy or vengeful and talk shit about him or about anything I consider to be my private business, I will unleash hell.

Because all of the proof of what you've done will be sitting with John, and make no mistake, Frankie, he's dying to hobble you for this."

I shake my head and turn to face the window. "Goodbye," I say quietly.

There's a long silence and then I hear him say faintly, "I'm sorry, Gid." For a second, my memory floods with all the times we laughed together, the huge plans we had, our victories and extravagant celebrations, and I squeeze my eyes shut as the door closes silently behind me and a part of my life comes to an end.

Eventually, I slump into a chair. I feel hollowed out. I don't know whether I've done the right thing for my career, but I'm sure I've done the right thing for my sanity and my life. However, what I do know is that I feel free. Free and able to be with the man I love, and I have a sudden powerful yearning to feel his arms around me and hear that beloved warm voice calm me.

Suddenly the room fills with the scent of pipe tobacco and leather. I look around, startled, as a breeze that doesn't come from the window ruffles my hair, and I feel a sense of almost paternal approval and watch the room lighten as if the sun has flooded through it.

"What the fuck?" I breathe out as the room seems alive with a presence even though there's only me here. Then my phone rings and the light vanishes, as does the smell.

"What the fuck?" I say again disbelievingly. The phone rings again, and I pull it out and click to answer. Not recognising the number, I say hello tentatively.

"Is that Gideon Ramsay?" a voice with a strong Yorkshire accent says.

"It might be," I say slowly. "Although if you're selling something, then it most certainly isn't Gideon Ramsay."

There's a startled silence for a second and then a deep chuckle sounds. "You're exactly as I pictured you."

"Is this a pervy phone call? Because I don't know if you've seen my latest interview, but I'm most definitely taken now," I say quickly.

"I did," the voice says. "It's the reason for me ringing you. I'm Asa Jacobs."

I blink. Asa Jacobs is a hugely popular actor. A big bloke with wild hair who's famously bisexual. He got married to a male model last year, and I'm always seeing pictures of the two of them looking extremely happy together. I'd long held him up as an example to Frankie, only to be dismissed as it not being possible for me.

"We were talking about me doing the series with you," I say slowly. "But then you backed out. Said I wasn't what you were looking for." That had fucking hurt at the time.

"Not actually the case," he says mildly. "Your manager put the kibosh on it. Didn't want you associating with us sexual delinquents." He pauses. "Only in light of your current relationship status, I'd like to offer you a place with us sexual rogues. It looks like you'll fit right in."

I start to laugh incredulously. "Really?" I'd wanted desperately to do the show. It's a fantasy series based on a set of incredibly well-written books, and there isn't a taboo they haven't covered. The part they'd offered me had been as a baddie, and it was incredibly juicy. I had been so looking forward to doing it, having grown tired of the perfect-looking characters Frankie kept putting me up for. Boring heroes.

"Well, I don't know whether you're aware, but I actually haven't got a manager anymore."

"Mate, that's very good news," he says warmly. "I don't like Frankie. Never did." He pauses. "So what are you going to do?"

I shrug. "Interview new ones."

"Well, if I might make a suggestion, my manager, Max, is the best. He's old school, though, so don't expect any smoke blowing up your arse."

"How disappointing," I murmur, and he laughs. It's contagious, making me smile.

"How about you meet him?"

"I'd like that," I say, suddenly feeling like I've had a road appear under my feet that's never been there before. It might end up leading me off a cliff, but it's a path I'm choosing to tread myself rather than being forced to follow.

"I know, how about seeing as you're in Cornwall, you come for a couple of days and stay with me and Jude in Devon? We'd love to have you."

"Would I be okay to bring my partner?" I ask, the words sounding awkward but good at the same time.

"Mate, we'd love to meet him. What's his name?"

"Eli," I say, and I can't even say his name without smiling. "Eli Jones."

Five minutes later, with a weekend invitation secured and the offer of a plum role extended, I come back into the study to find Niall and Silas standing alone talking.

"Where's Eli?" I ask immediately. Panic fills me. "Has he gone?"

"No," Silas says quickly. "Of course he's still here. He's not going anywhere far from you." I relax, and he pats my arm. "He's gone with Oz and Milo to make something to eat." He smiles at me. "You did well, son."

I feel warm inside at that. Silas's good opinion has always been something I've yearned for and never quite had the feeling that I'd got. "It had to be done. I had to be honest."

"I'm incredibly proud of you," he says calmly, and we smile at each other. "You did well with finding Eli too. I couldn't have picked someone better than him for you." My smile widens. Somehow, praise for Eli means more to me than praise for myself.

"Probably good that you didn't try," Niall says tartly, slinging his arm around my neck and hugging me tight for a second. "Given Silas's taste in men runs to impossibly bossy Irishmen, I'd count yourself lucky, Gid. You'd have spent your time being told what to do by a very loud person."

"Ah, Eli has his moments," I say slowly. Silas smiles and looks at me contemplatively. "What?" I ask, slightly worried. "Why are you looking like that at me?"

"Do you want a house on the grounds?"

"What?"

"You can have the cottage you're in now or any of the free ones if you want something bigger."

"Why?"

"Because I like my family around me," he says calmly.

Niall grins. "Come on, Gid, you know you want to live with us forever and ever."

"No, I bloody don't," I say in a revolted tone. "It's like you're setting up a gay commune. We'll be wearing robes and chanting next."

"Well, I'll leave that to you with your extensive knowledge of meditation," Silas says smoothly.

I sigh. "Eli told you, didn't he?"

He breaks into peals of laughter, joined by Niall.

I smile at them affectionately. "I don't want a house here, but I am intending to buy nearby if Eli wants to." Silas smiles and I grin at him. "You twats are the closest thing I have to family."

"Gideon, you're virtually a poet," Niall says.

"I know. Don't try and copy me," I say loftily. "There's only one of me."

"I wouldn't dare," he says calmly. "I'd be belted one within the first twenty minutes."

I laugh and suddenly Eli is at the door, followed by Milo and Oz carrying a tray of food. They're laughing together. I clear my throat. Eli jumps, and when he turns and sees me his smile widens and heats, making me swallow.

"Can you leave us?" I say abruptly, and everyone turns and stares at me. I shift slightly awkwardly. "I mean can I be alone with Eli, please." They don't move and I wrinkle my brow. "Now," I suggest.

Oz laughs loudly. "How is it that Milo has trouble asking for anything that he wants and Gideon never stops?"

Silas snorts and they pass me, Oz smiling at me with a light of what looks like approval in his eyes.

Milo and Niall come towards me. "Well done," Niall says, and I grin at my oldest friend. His approval has always meant a great deal to me.

"Thank you," I say hoarsely.

Milo hugs me, and I hug him back, inhaling his sweet, herby scent and feeling most of his hair attempt to insert itself up my left nostril. He pulls back and cups my face. "I am so very proud of you," he says carefully but very clearly, and I feel tears in my eyes.

"That matters a great deal to me," I say hoarsely. "You'll never know how much."

"I do," he says serenely. "I love you very much, Gideon, and I'm proud to be your brother."

Then he and Niall are gone, and I stare after them, feeling like I've been punched in the face. "Did you hear that?" I say, slowly turning to look at Eli.

He's right in front of me and all I can see are his clear olive-green eyes, the open and freckled face, his steady smile and warm eyes, and suddenly I need him so badly I could cry.

"Oh God, can you hold me? I need you so fucking much," I whisper. I have never in my life begged anyone for anything since I was seven. Only him. Because he's safe, and I know he's all mine.

Instantly he opens his arms, and when I step into them and his scent enfolds me, I feel like a tortoise must feel who's stepped back into his shell. Safe and warm and calm for the first time on this hellish day.

The words spin out of me like I've been whirled around and had them shaken free. "I love you," I say into his throat. "I know it's quick but I love you so fucking much. You're everything to me. Please don't ever leave me." His arms tighten hard around me, banding almost painfully as he sucks in a breath. "Too tight," I gasp and instantly he pushes me back slightly.

I utter a faint sound of protest, and he pulls me closer. Unable to look into his eyes, I look down at the battered old Converse he wears everywhere and run my fingers over the cotton of his shirt. I feel almost flayed open. I have never been as honest with another person as I have him.

"Gideon," he says, his voice hoarse. "Look at me, *cariad*." My eyes instantly shoot to his and I relax immediately because no one could mistake the love shining back at me. "I love you too," he says, his Welsh voice soft, devotion running through it. For me. I feel humbled.

"You do?"

He nods. "I do. I have for a while now." He cups my cheekbones, his big hands warm on my face, and I realise how cold I've felt being away from him today.

"I'm sorry," I say quickly. "I'm so sorry that I didn't respond well in Milo's garden. I was just so shocked and–"

"Ssh," he says, stroking my hair back. "I know, Gid. You didn't upset me."

"Really?" I say doubtfully. His look in that garden has been in my head since I left him there looking like I'd punched him.

He shrugs. "Maybe from now on, though, we work as a team. You don't have to talk to me immediately, but you do have to tell me that there's a problem and you want to talk at some point. As long as I know that I can help you, I'm okay with doing it at your pace." He pauses. "Although maybe not as slow as this time. That was glacier slow."

I nod quickly. "I promise," I say. "And, Eli, you have to tell me too." I fidget with his collar after sneaking a quick look at his calm and merry eyes. "I just want you to be happy and stay with me. That's all I really want, and I'm not very good at being with people," I say in a sudden rush. "I don't spot hurt feelings well, and I know I'm a bastard. I'm opinionated, bossy, and rather cavalier with people's feelings. I don't play well with other people. I'm messy, can't cook properly, and it turns out I'm also rather careless with my money."

"Hush," he says, looking like he's trying not to laugh. "Gid, I know you inside out and I have to say, sweetheart, that's how you've been with other people. Not with us. In all the time I've known you, you have never discounted my feelings."

"Maybe that's a fluke," I say, trying for total honesty.

He laughs almost helplessly. "I don't think it is, but to make really sure, how about we try to help each other?" He sobers. "I have to tell you that I'm incredibly proud of you. You did a very big thing today."

"Maybe it was only a big thing in my head." I sigh. "I should have done it fucking years ago."

"How do you feel?"

I lean my forehead down on his shoulder, feeling myself rest against him and how he holds me up. I have to do the same for him, I remind myself. I can't always take. I have to give him this support too.

"I feel free," I say slowly. "And scared out of my wits because my career is probably finished. While I was in the car coming back, Hal Finchley rang and said he couldn't use me in the film. Said I wasn't the right fit."

"Bastard," he says, his Welsh accent sounding loudly in his agitation. "Wanker. He's a complete cockwomble. Wait, are you smiling? Have you gone *loony*?"

"I'm smiling because I never wanted to play that role anyway. It was so fucking *boring*. I'm also smiling because Asa Jacobs rang me ten minutes ago and offered me a job I've had my eye on for years. It's a baddie."

"Well, you'll be good at that."

"I'm not sure what that means," I say slowly.

"No," he says cheerfully. "That's good, then."

I shake my head and he smiles, looking at me curiously. "You could have lied and gone on with pretending. I'd have stayed. You know that, don't you?"

"Not like that," I say quickly. "It was because of you, Eli. You're too important to me. I did consider it," I add hastily, trying to get the honesty out, to tell him my sins. "I have to tell you that. I could have stayed in the closet. I had my career to think of and all the money."

"Why didn't you?"

"Because I discovered something I want more than money and fame." He looks at me, and I smile and pull him close. "I want to hold your hand walking down the street. I want to kiss you when I feel like it. I want us to live together and have a future, and I can do none of that if I'm not honest with myself and society and, most importantly, with you. You're everything to me. You're kind and funny and clever and wise and just being with you makes me want to be a better person. Makes me feel like I *am* a better person because you love me."

"I do," he says clearly. "I love you very much, and I'm so very fucking proud of you. Whatever happens, that will never change."

"Hope not. Because I'm probably going to be walking in the ruins of my career for a long time, and you'll more than likely be supporting me."

"That's fine," he says loftily. "I'll buy you all the Pot Noodles you can ask for, pretty baby."

I flutter my eyelashes. "I've always fancied being a kept man. Pot Noodles sound a lot better than diamonds and pearls."

"You can do that, then," he says airily. "I'll dress you in silk and you can eat chocolate and watch *This Morning* whenever you like."

I snort. "My hero."

He smiles at me, the laughter fading to something soft and sweet. "How about we just support each other with the knowledge that none of that fucking matters at all? Only this thing here – this love between us – matters, and it's the only thing that ever will."

We kiss as the late evening sun dances in my hair, and I feel alive right down to my fingertips for the first time in years. Alive but contrarily...

"I feel peaceful, Eli," I say wonderingly as we pull back for breath. "I've never felt that before. It's nice."

"That's because you're settling into yourself," he says as wisely as ever. "There's peace in the knowledge that you like yourself enough to show yourself to the world. It's a form of coming home."

"No, *you're* my form of coming home, and you always will be."

I hug him close, inhaling the scent of coconut and laundry detergent. All my life I've had glib words on my tongue for every situation. I've talked myself out of and into more trouble than I could ever count. But with him, my glibness falters under the beauty and simplicity of his own words spoken in those low Celt tones. Maybe I've lost the facility now because I don't need them anymore. Because with him I'm finally myself, and I'm easy and content in that knowledge.

EPILOGUE

Thank God for pneumonia and dissolute living

Seven Years Later

Gideon

I come awake when the shower in the en suite goes on. Ten minutes later he slides carefully into bed beside me, bringing the scent of freshly washed skin and coconut.

"I'm awake," I say sleepily.

"Shit, *cariad*. Did I wake you up?"

I open my eyes. The room is full of moonlight, letting me see his face as if it were daylight. His hair is damp and curling in waves around his face. I smile at the sight of him. I always have. I probably always will.

Then I frown at the lines of strain around his eyes. "Tough night?"

He nods and I raise my arm so he can cuddle into me, throwing his leg over mine and nestling his head into the gap between my neck and my shoulder. "Car accident," he mumbles, the Welsh still strong in his voice after all these years. "Two people didn't make it."

"You did your best," I say with absolute certainty.

Eli is a paramedic now and although nights like these happen, he loves the job passionately. I've always thought that there are places, people, and jobs that feel right straightaway, which is why I'd pushed Eli to do this. He's fantastic at it, bringing all the calmness and quick wits to the job that he honed in lands far away from here.

"It wasn't good enough tonight," he mumbles, and I tighten my grip around him, loving the way he nestles closer. This is all I can do for him on nights like these, but somehow, blessedly, it's enough for him.

"Tell me about it," I whisper and he does, the words floating around the moonlit room. I hope they float out of the open windows and far away from him.

Finally, he falls asleep, and I lay there holding him and drifting until I hear the patter of footsteps. The next second the covers rise and a little body slides in next to me. I raise the arm that isn't wrapped around Eli and another part of my heart cuddles close, nestling her head into me.

"Bad dream?" I whisper. Our four-year-old daughter, Hetty, nods her head furiously, her skull digging into my shoulder blade.

I let her be silent for a bit as nothing comes of trying to drag things out of her. She's as stubborn as a donkey. I'm not sure where she gets that from. She's a funny little thing with mad-looking hair and knees that seem permanently scraped, but she's immensely kind and fiercely intelligent. I find her endlessly fascinating, the way her mind lights from one subject to the next like a ratty-haired hummingbird.

When Eli had first brought up the subject of children, I'd been bewildered. I'd never in my life dreamt of having them. Why would I when I'd made a career out of being congenitally selfish? Being with Eli was also so amazing I couldn't comprehend adding anybody to our lives who would demand so much of his time and attention and maybe take some of his love away from me. I told you – congenitally selfish.

But after I got over the shock and that instinctive reaction, I'd known that I actually wanted those babies and I needed them to be Eli's. The idea that there would be more of his kindness and joy in the world made me instantly happy. I'm so glad we did, because the kids are him all over. Wild hair, happy natures, and calmness personified. Even the seven-month-old Gus is calmer than me. He seems to permanently chivvy me along like he's an old soul.

When we knew Hetty was on the way, my terror had intensified. I am not the person who most people would associate with being a good parent. I'd managed conclusively to screw myself up. What the fuck would I do with small people?

Then, as always, Eli had been steadfast in his belief in me. It's one of his strangest characteristics that I'm most grateful for. Other people look at me and think "total fuck-up," but he sees someone worthwhile. I'm still not a paragon of virtue, but for him I try when I won't for others because his good opinion is worth more than gold to me. If he's happy with me, then I can shrug and think "fuck off" to the rest of the world. I always try to live up to that because the last thing I ever want to see in his eyes is disappointment.

Fatherhood was therefore rather traumatic for me before the babies came along, filled with worries and fears. But conversely, as soon as Hetty arrived, I seemed to settle into it instantly. Maybe it's because I'd expended all my worries beforehand.

And I've learnt so many lessons, predominantly that true love makes us unselfish and that real love is infinite and perfectly capable of expanding without diluting anything. My love for Eli has grown as I watch him navigating fatherhood with all of that loving calmness and joy that I've always seen in him. Equally, I'll often find him watching me with the children, whether it's when I'm reading to Hetty or sitting in the kitchen feeding Gus, and in his eyes is something precious and raw that warms me all the way through. I'll never completely know why I make him happy, but I don't question it anymore.

That security had allowed me to find it slightly gratifying that Eli was the one to panic when Hetty had come along. It had been nice and rather novel to be the one coaching him for a change and calming him down. I enjoyed it while it lasted. It obviously hasn't happened since, as he's once again always two steps ahead of me.

"What was it about this time?" I finally whisper, cuddling her close.

"Monster," she says in a small voice. "It came and eats me and Gus."

I smile. When Hetty realised that Gus wasn't going to do anything interesting for a while, she lost interest. She's slightly jealous of him and at the same time startlingly protective.

"I think if a monster got past all that hair you children have without choking, it would consider itself lucky," I mutter under my breath.

"What?" she says suspiciously.

"You and Gus are always safe here," I say in a slightly louder voice, and Eli stirs. I wait but he doesn't wake, which should tell me something about how tired he is because he has ears like a fucking bat where the children are concerned. "As if we'd let a monster in this house, Hetty Ramsay. Monsters can't *ever* come in a house where daddies live."

"Is Dadi asleep?" she whispers, using the old Welsh name for father for Eli. I wince because her whispers are at a decibel level that most people would consider shouting.

"He is, poppet, so we have to be as quiet as mice."

"I don't think they're very quiet, really. They squeak a lot. I saw it on *CBeebies*."

"Well, it must be true, then," I say wryly. Her body is losing its scared rigidity and melting into me. "It's still nighttime," I whisper. "Why don't you have a little bit more sleep and then we'll get up?"

"And you and me can get icy biscuits," she bargains, her eyebrow raised in a way that's so like Eli it makes my heart clench.

"Absolutely."

"Just you and me and *definitely* not Gus. He's too little," she says slightly scornfully.

"He's too little at the moment," I say firmly. "But when he's older he'll come too because families do things together."

"Like you and Uncle Milo?" she asks.

"Of course," I say with absolute certainty, and I want to smile at the thought of me ever saying that and meaning it, but I do. Eli and the children have taught me a new version of family, and it's one I treasure and cling to.

"And you'll watch over me while I'm asleep?" she whispers.

I nod and kiss her forehead, inhaling the scent of bubble gum from her shampoo. It's supposed to cure tangles, but I'm afraid the manufacturers have never come up against anything like my children's hair.

"Hetty, I will watch over you for the rest of your life," I say very firmly. It's a promise I intend to keep for as long as I have breath in my body.

Eli

I wake in a tangle of sheets and sunshine. Stretching, I feel the breeze from the open window wash over me and listen to the melodic clanking and tinkle of the rigging from the boats moored on the river outside.

I turn on my side, pulling the sheets around me, and look out through the French doors that lead out onto a small balcony which looks over the River Fowey. It's summer, so the river is busy. Large yachts jostle for space between small boats, and little dinghies zip across the river, hanging around the big destroyer that moored yesterday like small children bugging their older siblings at parties.

I sigh contentedly because I fucking love this house. We lived for a while in the cottage at *Chi an Mor* when we first got together, enjoying the respite from the cameras that seemed to follow us everywhere at that point. I'd initially made moves to find a flat so we could date at a slight distance but Gid had put his foot down, and really I didn't want to do that either. I loved being with him – chatting, laughing at our own private jokes, and just being us together. Anything else would have been conforming to what society might expect, and it has to be said that this is not and never has been one of Gid's strong points.

He'd refused to hide me from sight until the furore had blown away. Instead, he'd determinedly taken my hand whenever we were out and doggedly told every interviewer how good I was for him. I'm not sure of that because he's done the same for me. In his utter refusal to see any limits for me, he'd encouraged me to go back to college so I could become a paramedic, and four years later that's what I'm doing, and I'm loving it. I love the adrenaline rush of being first on the scene.

Carol, my partner on the bus, is a spiky, very sarcastic Cornish woman with jet-black hair and a huge family. We'd taken to each other instantly, which had been enhanced by the fact that she and Gideon took one look at each other and recognised a kindred spirit. As such, she's often at our house, sparring with him in the kitchen.

After a few months at the cottage, Gideon declared his intention to buy a house locally. It was the start of a turbulent time for us, as I was determined to play an equal role in buying a place. The only problem was that my money would never have bought even a room in the size of the house that Gideon could afford. Gid went along with me for a while, displaying a patience that would amaze anyone who didn't really know him.

He viewed tiny house after tiny house, giving each one a chance before we had to dismiss them, mainly because the press would practically be in our front room if we moved in. The turning point came when we found this place. It's an old, five-bedroom house right on the banks of the River Fowey, and we'd fallen in love with it at first glance, loving the large sun-filled rooms that seemed to move with the lights from the water speckling the ceilings and walls.

I still remember when Gid had turned to me and said that this was the one, and I had to get over my pride. The row that followed had been loud, as had the sex afterwards, and looking back probably neither should have taken place in the prospective house, but luckily our estate agent had scarpered when the raised voices started.

Afterwards we lay together under the window of what is now our bedroom and he hugged me close, whispering about what I gave him. Things that he could never say thank you enough for. And I realised what a twat I was being.

So we bought it. I insist on my wages being put towards the bills, and he humours me, even though those bills are a tiny blip in what he earns. That's true even now. Yes, he lost work and jobs in the ensuing months of his coming out, but he gained so much more. He branched back into the theatre and had a two-year stint on Asa Jacobs's show that led on to so many other diverse and interesting roles.

Lately, though, he's scaled even those back, preferring to narrate audiobooks. He installed a studio at the bottom of the garden and most days find him pottering around in there. He's happy and it fairly shines out of him these days.

As if reminding me of one of the reasons for this joy, the monitor on the bedside table warbles into action, and I lie for a few minutes listening to the sound of the baby cooing and babbling away to himself happily. When the noise becomes louder I take my cue and slide out of bed. Paying a quick visit to the bathroom, I clean my teeth, run a cursory hand through my hair, and pull on shorts and a T-shirt.

When I round the nursery door, Gus is there, sitting up and prodding a stuffed bear rather dubiously. When he sees me, his smile explodes across his face, and he wiggles, putting his hands up. "Up," he demands, which is actually the only word he knows apart from "no." He's definitely been brought up in a house filled with Gideon's personality.

I lift him up, feeling his little weight settle against me. I press a kiss into his blond curls, inhaling the scent of baby powder and shampoo.

"Alright, *cariad*?" I say. "Good sleep?"

My son gives me a gummy smile, his olive-green eyes creased in happiness.

I change his nappy and dress him in shorts and a t-shirt, nibbling on toes and making him give his little chuckle. I stroke my fingers down his soft cheek, marvelling once again at the gift we've been given.

When we'd first discussed surrogacy, I'd been very dubious. The surrogate laws in the UK give parental rights to the mother and her partner if she changes her mind, which had spelt disaster to me. I'd therefore been very wary. However, Gid had no doubts whatsoever, and as I got to know our surrogate I realised how right he was. She was lovely, and we intend to tell the children all about her when the time comes. She gave us a great gift and I'll never stop being grateful to her. The handover of parental rights had been smooth with each child, and I think it was only then that I took a full breath.

Once Gus is dressed, we wander down to the kitchen which lies in a pool of sunny stillness. Knowing where Gid's gone without him even having to leave me a note, I amble down the garden with Gus to where a wooden jetty lies. The water sparkles today like it's been fractured into a thousand shiny pieces, and Gus and I settle ourselves down on the lawn so he can have a look around.

He won't crawl and for some reason travels everywhere on his arse which Niall says he definitely inherited from Gideon, given that he tends to look at life through his arse.

I smile at the thought and look up as I hear the *phut phut* of the outboard motor approaching. The bright yellow dinghy zips across the river coming toward us. Gideon sits at the back steering, while at the front our terrier dog stands dressed in his orange life jacket, barking shrilly as if instructing Gid on how to moor the boat. My husband steers one-handed, his other hand moored firmly around the waist of Hetty.

I grin at the sight of father and daughter as the boat comes to a neat stop. With Gus on my hip, I take the rope he flings me and hold on as the dog jumps neatly out and starts to jump around me, his little tail coiled scorpion-like along his back. We got him from a local farm as a puppy, and this tendency to jump to great heights had led to him being named Tigger.

The firm bond he has with Hetty and the fact that she frequently looks like she's been dragged through a hedge backwards has inevitably led to them being nicknamed Stig and Tig.

Gus coos, reaching for Tig, and I watch as Gid hands out Hetty and vaults out of the boat himself, clutching paper bags that smell of gorgeous things.

"Dadi," Hetty shouts, darting at me and hugging me tightly round the leg. Gus chuckles and reaches for her, tangling his hand in her blonde waves. I remove it quickly, knowing from experience that he'll get it caught again and we'll end up having to cut bits of her hair to get his hand out.

"I had icy biscuits with Paula," she announces. "And Daddy bought lots and lots of wossants."

"Croissants," I say as I take off her life jacket.

She gives me her wide, gap-toothed grin. "Then we came back across the river and Daddy said 'shit' really loudly at some boys in a boat when they got too close."

"Oh look," Gideon says quickly as I turn to stare at him. "What *is* Tig doing?"

"Not swearing at tourists so that our daughter can go to school and teach the children that word, the same way that she taught them pillock the other week."

"She knows they're naughty words," he says, holding her upside down while she shrieks. "Don't you, Stiggy?"

I look down at my daughter. "Oh my God, who dressed her?" I say faintly.

"She did," Gid says, grinning as he lets Hetty down to the ground. He hands me the bags, which I know will contain a selection of pastries still warm from the oven at the bakery in the town. I also know that Gideon will have stopped for a coffee and a gossip with the owner Paula, while Hetty and Tig will have sat with him nibbling on the fresh iced biscuits that Paula saves for them.

It's a scene I've seen so many times, as Gideon has taken to Fowey like it was meant to be. He's often to be found zipping across the river in the boat, calling in at cafes or the pub to see the locals who've formed part of his set here. For a man who said he hardly had any friends, he certainly seems to have been gifted with them now. The locals, who can be insular, have taken to him like he's one of their own, so now we're invited to endless house parties, meals, and nights at the pub. I love it for him that he can potter about dressed like a tramp and with contentment oozing from him.

"Why do you allow this?" I mutter, looking at our daughter as she dances about on the grass wearing bright orange shorts and a shocking pink T-shirt that badly needs an iron. Her blonde wavy hair is sticking up in all directions, and she's wearing green heart-shaped sunglasses and ratty old yellow Converse with a hole in the toe. Her arms are also loaded with more plastic bracelets than Madonna wore in her heyday.

"It's good for her to dress herself," he says, bending to kiss Gus, who grins and kicks wildly when he sees his daddy.

"That's lovely, and when we're reported to social services for the holes in her clothes you can enlighten them as to the benefits of our daughter looking like a tramp."

"I shall," he says grandly. "And they will listen because I am the Man with the Golden Voice."

"I knew I shouldn't have let you know about that award," I say ruefully. "You'll be wanting a superhero costume next."

"I very well might," he muses. Then he comes close and whispers, "But I definitely won't wear pants."

He laughs, and I eye him. Dressed in jeans and a faded purple Ralph Lauren polo shirt, he looks a world away from that thin, stressed man I first met. Now, his hair is longer and touched at the sides with grey flecks that make him look even more gorgeous. His eyes are creased at the sides with laugh lines and his wide, mobile mouth is stretched into a big smile. He's tanned from the sun and looks wonderful. Warm and rumpled and all mine. I savour the feeling for a second, putting out a hand and catching my fingers in his shirt when he kisses me and goes to move away.

"You okay after last night?" he asks immediately. My happiness is always top of his list, and he will move heaven and earth to stop me from ever being sad. I smile because his efforts often backfire on him but just make me love him more.

I nod. "I'm fine, and I got a lie in." I shrug, then whisper, "Just happy, I suppose. Love you, Golden Voiced Man."

"Love you more," he says deeply, and in his eyes is everything that we are to each other. Warmth and home and safety and laughter. Lots and lots of lovely laughter.

Gideon

Giving me Gus and taking Hetty with the stated intention of making breakfast and combing her hair with a garden rake, Eli wanders back up the garden. I watch him go, enjoying the sight of his arse in those shorts and his wide shoulders and messy hair. He can say what he likes, but our daughter has inherited his hair and there's no getting around it.

My phone rings and I reach into my pocket, smiling as I see the number for Russ, my old driver.

"You on the way?" I ask.

He chuckles. "I'm at the airport now, Gid. I'm ready to leave Ireland for a few days and show you how to fish properly."

"You talk big, old man," I say loftily, smiling at the sound of his laughter.

"I'm looking forward to seeing you and Eli and the babies," he says, suddenly serious. "Makes me so happy to see you like this now."

"Alright, Maeve Binchy." I laugh at his curse. "I'm looking forward to seeing you too," I say softly. "We'll pick you up from the airport as normal."

"You certainly will. You drove me round the bend for years. It's time you did it in a car."

"It'll be infinitely more pleasurable than your crap driving. I'm quite positive that I'm a much better driver than you."

I grin at the sound of his laughter and we exchange goodbyes. I'm looking forward to the weekend. He comes every couple of months, sometimes with his wife and sometimes on his own, but I'm always happy to see him, as well as Constance when she and her new husband visit us. Both Russ and Constance adore Eli. With all of them and Jacinta and Alex visiting often, our spare rooms are always full.

I look at Fowey sparkling in the sun. The air is full of the scent of brine and the calls of the gulls overhead, and my son babbles in his soft baby language enlivened by the usual interjections of "up" and "no." It sometimes amazes me that I've been given all of these riches in life. A family who I love madly and an actual home. I'd bought so many properties over the years, and none of them ever had this air of permanency and solidity. Come to think of it, I lacked those attributes as well. Now, I don't. I feel as rooted here with Eli and the babies as the oak tree from which Hetty's swing sways in the breeze.

As soon as I saw this house I knew it was for us. I had to use a lot of words to get Eli to agree, but I was right. This was our home and it was waiting for us. I always credit it fancifully with helping us too. We went through a slightly rough patch after I came out. It was like Eli lost sight of the fact that I loved him and in return I froze, too scared of losing him to address the problem. Looking around this house had precipitated the worst fight we've ever had, but it was also the backdrop for us understanding each other and forging the blueprint we've lived by ever since.

At first we intended to knock it down and build a modern house with every amenity, but Eli insisted on living in it for a bit and the old place wove its spell. It was built in the Victorian era and, as such, it's full of period features like the bay windows with their stunning views of the river, the wooden floors, and the high ceilings. All it seemed to be waiting for was to be filled with laughter and loud voices.

Well, it definitely got that, and with some love and care and a fuckton of money, it's now a warm, sunny space full of life. The rooms flow from one to another, enlivened by shelves of books, colourful rugs, and comfy furniture. Our friends visit and sit on the patio outside or around the huge table in the white oak kitchen. The children's rooms are bright and filled with toys and books, and Hetty's friends from school visit and run about the house filling the air with shouts and laughter. Then at night our bedroom is our haven, filled with moonlight and silence, the big bed with its soft covers sheltering us as we make love and talk over the day, wrapped around each other like bindweed.

It seems to me that I've been very lucky in my life because I haven't only gained a family with Eli, I've found my original one again.

I'm not talking about my parents here, even though Eli still persists in inviting them to stay. They'll come for a few days and during that time we'll orbit each other, unsure of anything apart from a desire to please Eli. Then the time will be up and with sighs of relief we'll retreat to our own corners of the world again.

No, my real family, besides Eli and the children, is my brother and our friends. I see Milo all the time. We meet for lunch or dinner and talk on the phone every day. I've also grown closer to Niall and Silas, conversely finding the friendship I'd always wanted with them when I'd stopped expecting it. Eli and Oz have also formed an unholy sort of bond. They're always on the phone to each other, usually accompanied by a lot of laughter.

Sometimes I look back on that illness so long ago as being my saviour. Through it, I gained Eli and my babies and the men I call my family. I smile. Thank God for pneumonia and dissolute living. Then I make a mental note to *never* pass that bit of advice on to my children.

I smile and shake my head, leaning down to tie up the dinghy properly while Gus shouts "no" loudly at a passing boat. I pet Tig, who's still doing his impression of a canine trampoline, and Eli appears in the kitchen door and waves to me, shouting about breakfast.

"Come *on*, Daddy," Hetty shouts, and Eli grins.

"Yes, come on, Daddy," he says deeply, the smile reflected in his eyes.

I shake my head at the twat I chose for a life partner and walk towards him like I'll do for the rest of my life. It's like he's my North Star and I follow him, not because he'll guide me home from my travels, but because quite simply he *is* my home.

We could be in the worst place and I'd still settle down happily if he and the children were with me. I don't need anything more than him and this family we've built together. The years stretch ahead of me, and if they're as filled with life and laughter as the ones gone by, I know I'll die a very happy old man. And as long as it's with him by my side, I really don't need anything else. For a man who once grasped for every possession my money could buy, it's a humbling realisation and a blessing I'll never be sure I deserve, but one I know I'll work for and protect for the rest of my life.

THANK YOU

My husband. He's always first because I couldn't do this without him. This is for all the laughs and the way you let me talk your ear off on our walks.

LesCourt Author Services. I can't imagine releasing a book without them. Thanks to Leslie and Courtney and everyone there for the beta reading, the editing, the ARC management, the promo, the funny messages and the great advice. It's a full and brilliant service offered by people I consider to be my friends.

Hailey Turner for all the long chats in different time zones and for being an amazing friend.

Edie Danford who is a great friend and does a wonderful last proofread. I still say I wouldn't hesitate if David Gandy blocked my way to free chocolate!

Mary Grzesik. For all those last little details.

The members of my Facebook group, Lily's Snark Squad. You're funny and you make me laugh every day. I love my time spent with everyone in the group.

To all the bloggers who spend their valuable time reading, reviewing and promoting the books. Also, the readers who liven up my day with their messages and photos and book recommendations. I love being a part of this community, so thank you.

Lastly, thanks to you for taking a chance on this book. I hope you enjoyed reading it as much as I enjoyed writing it.

I never knew until I wrote my first book how important reviews are. So, if you have time, please consider leaving a review on Amazon or Goodreads or any other review sites. I can promise you that I read every one, good or bad, and value all of them. When I've been struggling with writing, sometimes going back and reading the reviews makes it better.

NEWSLETTER

If you'd like to be the first to know about my book releases and have access to extra content, you can sign up for my newsletter here

CONTACT LILY

Website: www.lilymortonauthor.com
This has lots of information and fun features, including some extra short stories.

If you fancy hearing the latest news and interacting with other readers do head over and join my Facebook group. It's a fun group and I share all the latest news about my books there as well as some exclusive short stories.
www.faccbook.com/groups/SnarkSquad/

I'd love to hear from you, so if you want to say hello or have any questions, please contact me and I'll get back to you:
Email: lilymorton1@outlook.com

ALSO BY LILY MORTON

Mixed Messages Series

Rule Breaker

Deal Maker

Risk Taker

Finding Home Series

Oz

Milo

Gideon

Other Novels

The Summer of Us

Short Stories

Best Love

3 Dates

Printed in Great
Britain
by Amazon